TOUCH OF TERROR

Recent Titles by Patricia Matthews from Severn House

THE DEATH OF LOVE
MIST OF EVIL
NIGHT VISITOR
OASIS
SAPPHIRE
THE SCENT OF FEAR
THE SOUND OF MURDER
TASTE OF EVIL
THE UNQUIET
VISION OF DEATH

TOUCH OF TERROR

Patricia Matthews

with

Clayton Matthews

This first world edition published in Great Britain 1995 by
SEVERN HOUSE PUBLISHERS LTD of
9–15 High Street, Sutton, Surrey SM1 1DF.
This first world edition published in the U.S.A. 1995 by
SEVERN HOUSE PUBLISHERS INC of
425 Park Avenue, New York, NY 10022.

Copyright © Patricia and Clayton Matthews 1995
All rights reserved. The moral rights of the authors have been asserted.

British Library Cataloguing in Publication Data
Matthews, Patricia
  Touch of Terror
  I. Title II. Matthews, Clayton
  813.54 [F]

ISBN 0-7278-4746-5

Typeset by Hewer Text Composition Services, Edinburgh.
Printed and bound in Great Britain by
Hartnolls Ltd, Bodmin, Cornwall.

Prologue

It was a half-hour before midnight, and in the clear night sky the moon cast a wash of reflected light across the top of the mesa.

In the distance, the wailing cry of a single coyote sounded, followed by an an eerie silence into which not even the sound of night insects intruded.

A moment later a faint glow appeared at the head of the trail that ended at the edge of the clearing – a flaming torch borne high. As the light grew nearer, its glow exposed the figure of the person carrying it, first the head, then the torso; a figure robed and cowled in black. As the figure attained the clearing it lifted its head, and a flash of polished silver gleamed from beneath the cowl. Other similar figures filed up behind it, until there were thirteen in all. They gave the appearance of faceless shadows, brightened now and then by the glow of their silver masks. As the thirteen formed a small circle, it could be seen that other figures followed them, forming a sizeable group to one side. These figures were also disguised by robes and cowls, but the robes were brown, and the masks they wore were those of animals, and demons. No one spoke; the only sounds were the soft scuffle of footsteps and the hiss of the torches.

The thirteen robed figures now set their torches into metal holders that had been set into the ground in a rough circle. The light now revealed a smaller circle surrounding a five-pointed star, the outlines of which had been constructed of small stones. In the very centre of the pentagram sat a large, flat, rectangular boulder, clearly a crude altar. Dark splotches stained the surface of the stone and ran down the sides.

When the last torch had been placed, the thirteen robed figures moved into the circle, standing with their backs to the altar, facing north.

Now, one of the robed figures stepped forward. In a strange, mechanical voice, the figure spoke. "The hour of midnight is upon us. Bring the offering forward."

The people who had followed the thirteen up the mountain, some fifty in number, had all gathered on the north side of the circle of torches. For the first time a sound came from them, almost a low chant. "Ye–es, Master."

They parted in the centre, and a huge man stepped forward. Cradled in his arms was the inert figure of a woman. She was dressed in a long, white, flowing garment. She appeared to be either unconscious or heavily drugged.

The man carrying her stopped at the edge of the circle of light, his fleshy face showing apprehension.

"Have no fear," the Master said in his strange voice. "No harm will come to you, so long as you obey my commands."

Without further hesitation the man stepped into the circle.

"Place her on the altar," the Master commanded.

The man glanced fearfully at the pentagram, then, stepping gingerly over the stone lines he moved forward, placing the somnolent figure gently, almost reverently, on the altar. Before standing up, the man carefully pulled down the white garment from where it had risen on her thigh. Now, straightening, he stood looking down at her. The woman appeared to be in her early thirties and she was very beautiful. The motion hidden from the watchers, the man crossed himself, his broad face set in sorrowful lines.

"That will be all!" the Master said sharply. "You may step back outside the circle."

The man turned obediently and joined the others. All eyes were on the man called Master, and an expectant hush fell.

In the silence, the Master raised his arms to the night sky, and turned his masked face toward his congregation. "I, Master of Masters, call on thee, by all the names given to thee down the ages, to witness and give thy blessing to what we are about to do here tonight. This offering to thee may be unworthy to sacrifice in thy name, but we beg of thee to look with favour upon thy faithful children as we offer up to thee she who now lies on the altar."

An awed murmur swept through the watchers, like a hot wind sighing through a field of dead grass.

"Father of all Evil, we beseech thee to grant the wishes of thy children, to see that they enjoy great prosperity from this night henceforth, and that no human retribution fall upon them because of what transpires here on this night. It is all done in thy name, O Great Lord of Darkness. This female unbeliever has brought great harm to some of thy children here tonight. For that she must pay in blood, and in so doing we dispatch her soul into your keeping. And for that offering we ask only that you grant thy favours upon our endeavours here upon earth!"

The Master stood silent for a few moments, the upraised hands now clenched into fists.

"We now perform the sacrifice in thy name!"

Lowering his hands, the Master turned toward the altar. From the folds of his robe he drew a curved dagger. In the light of the flickering torches the dagger glinted evilly. Holding the dagger in both hands, the Master raised it high. Another murmuring sigh swept through the watchers.

The Master held the dagger above his head for the count of ten. Then he brought it down with all his strength, plunging it to the hilt in the woman's breast. Her body arched off the altar, twitching as her blood fountained high. A cloud, seemingly out of nowhere, crossed the moon; and when it had passed, the woman's form lay still and unmoving.

Chapter One

The minute Casey Farrel entered her office and crossed behind her desk she saw the yellow memo sheet.

"Farrel: In my office. Pronto."

No signature was necessary. Casey knew that the summons came from her boss, Bob Wilson, the supervisor of the Governor's Task Force on Crime. She sighed, checked her message basket, picked up her purse, and prepared to go down the hall to Wilson's office. She knew that any undue delay on her part would only get his temper up. He always seemed to know the instant she entered the building; he either had extrasensory radar or some spy in the building who called him the minute she came in.

She well knew that her irregular hours scalded Wilson's butt, but that didn't bother her overmuch. Since in her job as investigator for the task force, she kept no regular hours, often working far into the night, she could pretty much choose the time she came in in the mornings, unless she was in the middle of an important case. Wilson would dearly love an excuse to fire her, but he didn't dare over something as petty as keeping her own hours; she had the best record of any investigator on the task force, a well-known fact even to Bob Wilson. To get rid of her, he had to have a very good excuse if he was to escape censure from the media, as well as other law enforcement people in Phoenix and the state of Arizona.

On the way to his office she stopped at the rest room to check her hair and face. She had learned from experience that it was best to appear calm and cool when facing the dragon. Casey had never minded the sight of her own face – it was her, and she had always accepted it. Now, looking at her reflection in the mirror, she was reassured by what she saw: a heart-shaped face with high cheekbones – legacy of her Hopi mother – honey-coloured skin, surrounded by a mass of soft, black curls. Slightly slanted dark eyes, a straight nose, high cheekbones and rather full but well-shaped lips. No lines yet. Not bad for a thirty-two-year-old broad. And the old bod wasn't bad either. Smallish, but well put together and strong. Feeling cheered, she left the rest room and continued down the hall to Wilson's office, knocked on the door, and heard his reedy voice bark: "Come in!"

Wilson had a corner office with a wall of glass behind his desk. He could spin around and look out on the capital building across the way, the focal point of his burning ambition. An ardent supporter of the current governor, Wilson had laboured long and hard for his election; as his reward he had been appointed head of the task force after the first supervisor had resigned. That had been two years ago; Wilson had higher ambitions, but so far those ambitions had not been realized.

Although Casey knew that Wilson knew she was there, he didn't look up immediately, his head bent over some papers on his desk as though the fate of the nation totally depended on his intense study of them. Casey recognized it for the slight it was, but it was something she was accustomed to. Wilson was a good administrator, with a keen intelligence, yet he was small-minded, sometimes to the point of viciousness. The two years stuck in this job he considered beneath his dignity had soured his already rotten disposition even more.

Now he leaned back, running a hand over the thinning hair atop his narrow skull. His small mouth scrunched like a miser's purse, he said, "Well, Farrel, it's about time you were getting in. That cop boyfriend of yours keep you up to all hours?"

She didn't think the remark was worthy of an answer. Composed, she waited.

When he realized that he wasn't going to get a rise out of her, Wilson bent his rail-thin body over the desk and shuffled though the clutter on his desk, muttering to himself. "Ah!" he said in triumph and held up the front section of a newspaper. "Seen this morning's *Republic*?"

"I didn't have time to read the morning paper."

"Didn't watch the TV news, either?"

"Afraid not, Bob."

He scowled at her. Casey knew that he disapproved of her calling him Bob instead of Mr Wilson, but when he was in this kind of mood, she liked to slip the needle to him.

"Here, read the front page, right hand column." He thrust the paper at her.

The column was datelined "Sedona, AZ":

The nude body of a woman was found early last evening on Oak Creek, about a mile north of downtown, just off Highway 89. The victim was identified as Barbara Stratton, 36, Vice President of Camden Industries, located in Beverly Hills Ca. The means of death has not been released, but, according to a spokesman for the Yavapai County Sheriff's Department, it is likely Ms Stratton was killed somewhere else, and the body moved to Oak Creek. No other details about the crime are available at this time.

Wilson said: "This is the third murder victim discovered within the past month in and around Sedona. No substantial progress has been reported in solving the two previous murders. Speculation has been that they are random killings, possibly the work of a serial killer."

Casey stopped reading, glancing up. "And so?"

Wilson gestured impatiently. "Did you know about the two prior murders?"

"Only what I read in the paper and on the TV news."

"The Governor called me this morning, first thing." Wilson's skinny chest puffed out as he mentioned the Governor's name.

"Again, and so?" Of course, she already knew what this was all about, but she wanted him to spell it out.

"He thinks the three murders are connected."

"Does he have hard information that they are, something the press doesn't know?"

Wilson hesitated, and Casey nodded. "It appears that he does. What is it?"

Wilson frowned. "Keep this to yourself, okay? The local law inforcement agencies have kept it quiet for the obvious reasons. All three bodies were killed by the same means, one knife wound direct to the heart."

Casey whistled. "That's a tie-in all right; and it could mean a serial killer. That still doesn't explain why you called me in here, Bob."

"He wants the task force to become involved. And he wants you on the case." He smirked. "He asked for you specifically."

"Okay, I have nothing pressing right now. But the Sheriff's Department up there may not be too happy."

"To hell with them. Besides, they probably won't even know."

"And why is that?"

"Because this one, Farrel, you're going to work undercover."

Casey blinked. "Whose idea is that, yours or the Governor's?"

Wilson grinned unpleasantly. "Mine, of course. It's the only way I can see to make it work."

"Why?"

"What do you know about cults?"

"Again, only what I've read and that's precious little."

"Well, they seem to be pretty active in the Sedona area."

"You think some cult is behind these killings?" She stared. "From what little I know, most of the action in Sedona is from New Age groups, and they don't normally go in for violence. Some people think they're kooks, but they seem pretty harmless."

"Well, the cops who have been investigating the killings seem to feel that some kind of cult is involved, the one stab in the heart business, for instance."

"Cult killings? I suppose it's possible. I've heard that there are some satanic cults in the area, but I thought it was mostly rumour. Some of the fundamentalist Christian groups have gotten all neurotic about anything that they think smacks of anti-Christianity; and that includes just about anything that doesn't fit in with their hard line."

"Well, whoever *is* involved, they have to be found. The governor is afraid that is going to turn into a disaster, like all those foreign tourists being killed in Florida."

"Were any of the three foreign? I don't recall that . . ."

Wilson waved an impatient hand. "No, no. You're missing the point. If it gets out that tourists are being murdered in Sedona, it'll dampen the tourist and convention trade, and that's the lifeblood of Sedona."

"I still don't grasp this undercover business."

"You should figure that out easily enough. Best way to learn about a cult is to join. To do that you have to assume another identity." The unpleasant smile again. "Being the media star that you are, Farrel, you'd be spotted the minute you entered the city limits."

"Since, as you say, I've had some media exposure, it's going to be difficult to go undercover."

"Come on, Farrel! Think about it. Take another name, maybe go in as just another tourist. Change your hair colour, dress differently, maybe even change the colour of your eyes. They can do that with contact lenses."

Casey was silent a few moments in thought. Since the case of the Honky-Tonk Killer, she hadn't handled an important, challenging case. And it was midsummer in Phoenix now, with the temperature in the hundreds every day; Sedona was always at least ten degrees cooler. Her son, Donnie, was on summer vacation and had been bugging her to take him to Prescott to spend some time at the ranch of her uncle, Dan Farrel. She could leave him off there while she worked the case in Sedona. And then she thought of something else.

She said, "From what I recall of the other two killings, the victims were either well-to-do, or at least important business people, in Sedona on business. The same with this third victim. Am I right?"

"Insofar as I know," Wilson said warily. "So what?"

Casey was smiling broadly. "That means they were staying in the best accommodation available. If I'm going up there in disguise, with a new identity, if I'm going to make myself a target, that means I'm going to stay at the same type of place. Right?"

"I hadn't given that part much thought, but I suppose you're right."

"Is the expense account strong enough for that?"

"Not exactly sure what you mean, Farrel."

Casey grinned. "Sure, you do. I figured I'd stay at the Enchantment, which is by no means cheap." Unlike you, you bastard, she thought gleefully; most times when she ran up an unusual expense he squawked like a wounded chicken.

This time he fooled her. He leaned forward, grinning up at her. "This time spend whatever your greedy little heart desires, Farrel. If there are any complaints from upstairs, I'll tell them that the Governor authorized it. That'll back them off in a hurry!"

*   *   *

During the more than two years that Casey had been an investigator for the Governor's Task Force on Crime, the task force had been repeatedly assured of an upgrading of their quarters; better offices, better equipment, et cetera. Except for one thing these promises hadn't materialized. The exception had been a sophisticated computer system that contained all of the state's newspapers, going back years, on file. That was where Casey headed when she left Wilson's office. Her own desk computer was hooked into the system, but she figured she'd have more privacy in the computer room, not to mention fewer interruptions.

Settling herself, she called up all the information available on the two earlier murders.

Both prior victims were male. Clyde Waters, chief executive for an oil company in Texas. Waters had been sixty, quite well off, married to a prominent Dallas socialite, with three grown children, and he had been in Sedona for the annual stockholder's meeting of the oil company employing him. No mention of why the meeting had been held in Arizona instead of Texas. But then who could fathom the reasoning of Texas oil companies? Of course, Arizona was well known as a retirement reserve for the wealthy, so perhaps a large number of the company's stockholders resided there.

The second victim had been Riley Masterson, vice president of a prominent grocery chain; 48, also married with three children, residing in Utah, the headquarters of the company. He had also been in Sedona attending a convention.

Both men had been found dead and nude at two different locations along Oak Creek. Both had been well-to-do, near the top of the ladder in their profession, and in Sedona on business conventions. Also, both, like the current victim, had apparently been murdered somewhere else, then moved to Oak Creek.

Well, it was a start, but she would have to collect a lot

more information before she could even begin to get a fix on things. Of course, it was always her practice to begin speculating at the very beginning of a new case, despite the words of her mentor, Josh Whitney: "It's not a good idea, babe, to leap to conclusions until most of the facts are in. Tends to set your thought processes in concrete."

But much as she loved Josh and admired him as a homicide detective, he had his ways and she had hers.

Having garnered all she could from the news stories, Casey gathered up her notes and went along the hall to her office. Deciding that there was no need to delay, she placed a phone call to the Enchantment Resort in Sedona and made a reservation under a false name: Rena Rainier. That should be exotic. Of course there was going to be the problem of papers for her false identity. For instance, she wouldn't be able to use her Cherokee name in Sedona; anyone with reason to check on her would blow her cover with ease. Well, Josh would be able to help her with that. She knew that he had operated undercover a number of times early on in his police career.

Next, she called home, a condo she had recently purchased in North Phoenix. Donnie was at home today. At least he'd better be! At twelve her adopted son insisted that he was too old for a baby-sitter. Since he was pretty responsible for a boy his age, Casey had reluctantly agreed to a trade-off: he would be without a sitter in the daytime, as long as he would faithfully inform her if he went out of the condo, and he would consent to a sitter when she had to be out at night.

Donnie answered on the second ring. "The Farrel residence."

Casey smiled softly; he sounded so grown up of late. "Hi, kiddo. How you doing?"

"Casey! I was playing a computer game."

"Winning?"

"Naw, I can't get this knight out of the castle."

"Keep working at it, you'll manage." She cleared her throat.

"How'd you like to go spend a few days up at Uncle Dan's ranch?"

"Wow, that would be great, Casey!" he said eagerly. "When we going?"

"Depends. I have a couple of things to do. Either later this afternoon or first thing in the morning. Just to be on the safe side, why don't you pack, so you'll be ready?" She laughed lightly. "After you've rescued your knight, of course."

Next, she called Josh at the station; luckily he was in.

"Hi, babe," he said in his deep voice. "What's up?"

"You too busy to have lunch? I'm buying."

"It's a slow day. I'm never too busy to have lunch with my woman. What's the occasion?"

"*My* woman? Watch it, Detective. I have a thing or two to tell you, plus I need a little help."

She hung up before he could interrogate her.

She gathered her things together and left the office quickly. On her way to meet Josh she made a quick stop at a bookstore and bought several books about cults.

Chapter Two

"What!" Josh said explosively, rearing back, hamburger halfway to his mouth. "You're going to do *what*?"

"I'm going undercover to investigate these murders in Sedona. What's so hard to understand?"

Josh returned the half-eaten burger to his plate. "Whose bright idea was this?"

"Bob Wilson's, but I agree with him. For once. I think it's the first bright idea he's had in years."

"It's stupid, is what it is," Josh said in a growling voice.

Casey looked quickly around. They were having an early lunch in Denny's, and the place wasn't too crowded yet. The booths on either side of them were unoccupied, and Josh's rising voice seemed to have aroused no attention. "Keep your voice down, Detective. I don't want my undercover assignment blown before I ever get out of Phoenix."

He glowered, but spoke in a softer voice. "That might not be such a bad thing."

She stared at him, smiling faintly. Joshua Whitney was a big man in his early forties, six feet four, with broad, sloping shoulders. His weathered face was craggy, with a prominent nose, and harsh planes. His eyes were grey, usually warm with good nature, but in moments of anger they could be cold as slate. Right now, they were somewhere in between; they held much affection, but he was close to being furious with her.

"What are you staring at?" he snapped.

"At you, what else? Sometimes you can be stubborn as a donkey, always totally convinced you're right."

"That may well be, but in this case I am. Depend on it!"

Yet he had to smile at her; even though she could be infuriating as hell, he could never stay mad at her for long. How could he, when he loved her so goddamned much?

Now she said composedly, "I think it might be fun. Certainly it'll be different, a change of pace."

He gave a snort. "Fun? It'll be dangerous. Any time a cop goes undercover, his, or her, life is at risk every minute."

"But you've worked undercover a number of times. You told me."

He nodded. "That's true. And that's why I know the risks, babe."

"Yet you did it. Were you ordered to, or did you volunteer?"

He had the grace to look sheepish. "I volunteered. It's rare that a cop is ordered to work undercover. You have to really want to do it to be very effective."

"But I was ordered to. Wilson is just looking for an excuse to dump me, you know that, Josh." She finished off her Coke. "Why did you volunteer?"

"I was young, gung-ho. I wanted to do it all, know it all."

"What were you working on?"

"One stint with Narcotics, which is really mixing it with the scumbags. The other was undercover with Bunko. That wasn't so bad. In fact, it was rather fun." He looked at her across the table. "What exactly are you supposed to accomplish with this undercover?"

"Well, as I said, there's the possibility that some cult is behind the killings. I hope to be able to find the cult and join it." She didn't tell him that, in her disguise as an affluent business person, she might also be making herself a target.

He stared at her, grey eyes shrewd. He shook his head,

as though he could see behind her half-lie. "Fooling around with cults can be dangerous as hell. Look at James Jones, that mess down in Waco. I can think of dozens of other instances. Any time a bunch of fanatics, of any stripe, band together, they can be dangerous. Well, you can't say I didn't try, but I can see I'm wasting my time. I should have known." He leaned back with a sigh. "What do you want from me?"

"I'm going to have to establish a false identity. I've never done that. To my knowledge the task force has never sent an investigator undercover. I figure I'll need a driver's license, a Social Security number, and a credit card. You know more about what I'll need than I do."

"Shouldn't be too hard to arrange. What name are you using?"

"Rena Rainier," she said with a grin.

He stared. "Rena Rainier! Sounds like a pseudo-French hooker or a B-movie actress!"

Casey grinned. "But that'll fit right in, you see. That's where I'm going to be from. A production assistant for an independent film producer, in Sedona scouting a location for a big, important film. Perfect cover, don't you think?"

"No, I don't think," he said with a shake of his head. "I'll see what I can do."

"When? How long will it take? I want to get started right away."

"Can't wait, can you?" he said in a grumbling voice. "I should have all the documents by, say, noon tomorrow."

"Will they stand up under a close check?"

"The driver's license will. If a call comes in about Rena Rainier, it will be routed to a woman in the know and she will verify that a Rena Rainier has a valid California driver's license. As for the fake Social Security number, it will take time to run that to ground; they're pretty chary and slow about giving out information over there, and then usually only to a properly identified law enforcement officer. And by that time, you should be in and out of this. As for a credit card, that also takes time, and it will also take time for me to get you one."

"I may not need one. I'm taking along a good chunk of cash from task force funds. The first thing I'll do in Sedona will be to open a checking account for Ms Rainier. I know, nowadays people look upon a person without a credit card with suspicion but I'm going to cultivate an image as a certified eccentric."

He scrubbed a hand across his face. "You know I'm going to be worried sick about you every minute you're gone."

Smiling softly, she reached across the table and stroked his cheek with her fingers. "That's sweet of you, darling."

"Yeah, right." He glowered at her. "And I'll expect you to call me at least once a day."

"Depend on it," she said and winked.

"And from a pay phone, not from the hotel, or any other place where the call can be traced."

"Of course, Detective. Do you think I'm stupid? Give me a little credit."

"You're a smart investigator, babe, but sometimes you take stupid risks, yes. And this strikes me as a situation where the risk of your doing that is very high."

"I'll be careful, Josh. I promise."

"I wish I could believe that." He added gruffly, "I love you, Casey. Probably too much for my own damned good."

She took his big hand between hers and squeezed. "I know that, Josh, and I appreciate it, probably more than you'll ever know."

The next day, shortly before noon, Casey left Phoenix for Prescott in the Cherokee, with Donnie in the front seat beside her. It would have been difficult for anyone who didn't know her well to recognize her; at least she hoped so. Her hair was now a coppery red, with a dramatic white streak sweeping back from her left temple, and had been cut in a short shag. She wore blue contact lenses, an assortment of jangling jewellery, and a bright blue silk jumpsuit, cinched at the waist with a wide, curved, studded belt that accented her narrow waist. Her goal had been to look brassy but expensive, and she thought she had attained it.

Certainly Donnie had been startled, even a little disapproving of her new look. Yesterday, when she had told him about going to the ranch, he had been too delighted about the pending visit to Dan Farrel's ranch in Chino Valley to wonder about the details; but this morning, on seeing her new persona for the first time, he had said dubiously, "Why are you made up like that, Casey? I don't think Uncle Dan is going to like it very much."

"He probably won't," she said ruefully. "But this isn't for him to approve or disapprove. I haven't had a chance to tell you yet, kiddo, but I won't be staying at the ranch. I'm going on to Sedona, on a case."

He squirmed in excitement. "You're going to go undercover!"

"You hit it, kiddo."

"Can I go, Casey? Huh, Casey?"

"You know better than to even ask."

"Aw-w." He looked over at her. "I'll bet it's about those three murders in Sedona, huh?"

She looked at him with a shake of her head; sometimes, for a boy of twelve, Donnie amazed her with his knowledge and perception. "How did you know about that?"

"It was on TV last night," he said absently. Then he clapped his hands. "The Tourist Killer!"

Casey had to laugh. Donnie had taken to naming the more sensational cases she was involved in: The Dumpster Killer; The Rodeo Killer; The Honky-Tonk Killer; et cetera. The names had been very apt, had stuck, and almost immediately had been picked up by the media.

"You're too smart for your own good, kiddo," she said.

"A word of warning here, Donnie. Only you and Uncle Dan and Aunt Alice are to know about this, so don't go blabbing it around. Understood?"

"You think I'd do that? I'm not a snitch," he said scornfully.

"Snitch?" She shook her head with a sigh. "What am I going to do with you, kiddo?"

"But Josh knows, doesn't he?"

"Yes, Josh knows." She laughed. "But he's not going to tell anyone. He's not a snitch, either."

"Aw–w, Casey!"

A little over an hour later they passed through historic downtown Prescott, and then on out into Chino Valley. About three miles beyond the small town of Chino, Casey turned left onto a gravel road. It had been a relatively dry winter, and the monsoons had yet to arrive. The fields they passed were brown, with patches of sparse grass. The cattle were all collected around the spots of green.

Halfway to the Farrel Ranch she passed the entrance to the Dyce Ranch. She shuddered; a little over a year ago Donnie had been held captive there by a half-mad Darrel Dyce and it had taxed her resources to free Donnie without harm. Darrel Dyce and his son, Barney, were now serving prison sentences, and his daughter, Melissa, had moved in with the Farrels, while she bore their grandson.

Another mile down the road, and she turned through a gate with a wooden arch over it. She clattered over the cattle guard and drove another half mile until she topped a small rise. From there they could see main ranch house, corrals and outbuildings.

The house was long, low, and Spanish, with a wide veranda across the front. Its walls gleamed white in the afternoon sun. Shade trees sheltered the front, and a cement-paved turnaround offered parking places for several vehicles. As she parked the Cherokee alongside Dan

Farrel's old pick-up, she saw her uncle step out of the house onto the veranda, his rolled-edge, sweat-stained Stetson tilted back on his head. She had called him before leaving Phoenix.

Dan Farrel was tall, lean, in his sixties, wearing faded jeans and worn cowboy boots. His face was weathered, and craggy. His pale blue eyes regarded them, warm with welcome.

Donnie was out of the Cherokee first, running at Dan full-speed. He cried, "Uncle Dan!"

Dan came down the steps, opening his arms, and Donnie ran into them. Casey followed more slowly.

As she reached them, Donnie pulled back. He said excitedly, "Is Brownie okay?"

Dan laughed. "Fine as rain, fat and sassy. Waiting for you in the corral."

"All right!" Donnie started at a run for the corral.

Dan gazed after the boy for a few moments, smiling fondly. Casey took the opportunity to study his face. She was happy to see that some of the sadness was gone; he had been devastated by the murder of his son, Buck. Although Buck and Melissa Dyce had not been married, Dan had gladly taken Melissa into his home. Apparently the birth of his grandson, Dan Jr, had eased the sorrow of losing Buck. That was the last time Casey had seen him, when she and Donnie drove up from Phoenix several months ago for the birth.

Now Dan looked at her, his gaze searching. "I'm happy to see you, Casey, but my God, what have you done to yourself?"

She motioned dismissively. "It's all a part of the case I'm working on. I'd rather not discuss it, the less you know the better." Her glance went past him. "Where's Aunt Alice and Melissa? Melissa *is* still here, isn't she?"

"Oh, yes. I've talked her into staying, more or less permanently. Little Dan needed a nap, and she's napping with him. You didn't say what time you'd be here. And Alice is busy in the kitchen, cooking up a storm for dinner. She'll be happy to see you."

Casey shook her head. "I'm sorry, Uncle Dan. I can't stay. I have to get to Sedona as soon as I can. Maybe when I wrap up the case, I can stay on for a few days." She drew a deep breath. "And I have another favour to ask of you, besides looking after Donnie."

"Heck, that's no favour. We're delighted to have him. So what do you need?"

"A ride back to town. Drop me off at the airport. I'll rent a car there. I can't drive my own car. I'll leave it here, if that's all right with you."

"Of course it is. But this is all so mysterious, Casey. Can't you tell me?"

She shook her head sharply. "I'm sorry, Uncle Dan. It's better all the way around if I don't. As I'm sure you realize, I'm going to be working undercover. The fewer people who know about it, the better. Will you drive me to the airport?"

Frowning, he slowly nodded assent.

Chapter Three

At the car rental desk inside the Prescott Airport, Casey rented a medium-sized vehicle. She showed the woman behind the desk the fake driver's license Josh had gotten for her.

"I'll pay cash in advance for a week, although I may be staying longer."

The woman across the counter glanced up, her gaze coloured with suspicion.

Casey said with a smile, "All my credit cards were stolen a few days ago. They haven't been replaced yet. Should come through in a few days. The minute they do I'll come out and show them to you."

The woman still looked dubious.

"I know it's unusual to pay cash these days, but I couldn't wait. I'm pressed for time. I'm here to scout locations for a very important, big-budget movie."

At that the woman relaxed, her face brightening, as Casey had hoped. The clerk said, "Oh, a lot of movies are shot here. Not so many lately, since Westerns kinda died down. But I guess Westerns are coming back. Is this a Western?"

"Well . . . let's just say it's a modern-day Western."

The woman smiled widely. "Is Clint Eastwood going to star in it?"

"How did you know?" Don't overdo it, Casey told herself. She added quickly, "That's the reason time is short. To get Mr Eastwood to commit to the picture, we have to move on it in a hurry."

The paperwork was finished and pushed across the

counter to Casey. She signed her new name where required, paid the week's rental, counting out the bills. The clerk eyed the money askance before finally picking it up.

Casey took the proffered key, went out to where the rental was parked, and drove it back to the small airport building to pick up her luggage from where Dan Farrel had unloaded it in front.

The drive to Sedona would only take about an hour, and Casey decided to go over Mingus Mountain and through the old copper mining town of Jerome. This route took a little longer, but there was more to see and enjoy. The day was fine, the view exceptional, and Casey felt that she needed to relax a little before starting her new role. She was as keyed up as an actress about to go on stage for the first time. She had brought some of her tapes with her, and soon the evocative flute of Carlos Nakai and the scenery were doing a good job of calming her.

Driving through this part of Arizona always made Casey think of her Hopi grandmother, She often wondered what Grandmother would think of her now, of what she was doing? Would it seem strange to her, as it did to Casey's uncle, Claude Pentiwa, that her granddaughter, little Nessehongneum, was spending her time trying to catch the white man's killers? Uncle Claude certainly did not approve, and made no bones about telling Casey so; but Grandmother had been a different kind of person; Indian to the core, but deeply steeped in the Hopi belief in tolerance. She had accepted Casey's white blood as a given fact. Casey remembered her Grandmother's words: "A butterfly will always be a butterfly, and there is no use expecting it to be a crow," and smiled to herself.

By the time the monumental red rock formations of Sedona came in sight, she was feeling relatively calm and in control. The Enchantment was located several miles out of town. Thinking of her promise to call Josh once a day, Casey stopped at a pay phone in town, and called Josh. It was after five, and since he was working the day shift, he should be home. He answered on the second ring.

"Hello, Detective."

"Casey!" His voice flooded with relief. "Is everything okay?"

"So far, A-okay. I'm in Sedona, on my way to the Enchantment. I'm calling from a pay phone."

"Well, at least you're thinking like an undercover cop," he said approvingly. "Keep it up, and you may get out all in one piece."

"How about that credit card in the name of Rena Rainier you promised me? Doing business with a car rental agency and paying in cash is a drag. The woman behind the counter looked at me as if I were demented. I anticipate the same reaction at the hotel."

"I'm working on it, babe. I think I'll be able to pick it up tomorrow. When I get my hands on it, I'll express it right up to you."

"Good! I have to hang up now, Josh. I've had a long day. By the time I check in, I'm going to be ready to collapse."

"Wait, wait! What are your plans? How are you going about this thing?"

"At the moment I have no plan; I'm just going to play it by ear."

"That way lies disaster, babe," he said in a grumbling voice.

"Goodbye, Josh. I'll call you tomorrow." As she started to hang up, she heard his fading voice say, "Love you, babe . . ."

As she turned off Highway 89A a short time later, onto Dry Creek Road, the sun was low in the sky. As she left the residential area and drove farther into the canyon, the view ahead of her was breathtaking; the red and pink sandstone of the canyon could have been painted by a cosmic artist.

As she entered Boynton Canyon, she could see Capitol Butte rearing up to her right; nearer at hand, also on her right, was Chimney Rock. Although she knew it had stood there for thousands of years, it seemed in imminent danger of toppling.

It was easy to understand why, with its magnificent scenery and brilliant colours, Sedona and the Oak Creek Canyon area were so famous, drawing tourists from all over the world. But there was a downside to this fame; over the past few years explosive growth, with its attendant traffic congestion and overbuilding, was slowly eating away at the natural beauty; and the feet of thousands of tourists were destroying the fragile ecology of the desert and the area along Oak Creek itself.

And now, with the recent murders, violent crime had come to Sedona. Which was logical, she supposed, since crime always piggy-backed on population growth. However, the feeling had been growing in her that that was too simple an explanation for the three murders; she sensed something far more sinister at work here.

It was necessary to pass through a guard gate to gain access to the hotel. Casey gave the guard her name; he consulted a list, then gave her a large, coloured card with the name, Rainier, on it, to place on her dashboard. Casey nodded her thanks and drove a quarter mile to the lobby building. On her right, as she drove, was a golf course, lushly green. Several golfers were playing the course. On her left were a number of tennis courts, with high screens; she could hear the thump-thump of tennis balls being whacked as she passed. She parked the rental and went into the lobby.

There were two couples at the registration desk. Casey waited her turn, then gave the desk clerk the Rainier name and filled out the card given to her.

"I'll pay cash for two nights," she told the clerk. "I've lost my credit cards. I should have a replacement tomorrow or the next day."

The woman behind the desk nodded. "That will be fine, Ms Rainier. You'll be staying with us for two weeks?"

"I would imagine so, I'm not sure. I'm not really here on vacation." Casey raised her voice. "I'm here scouting locations for a movie."

This one didn't react as had the rental clerk at the airport. She merely nodded without any display of interest. Casey supposed she was accustomed to movie company people staying here; because of the scenery a great many movies were filmed in the area.

The clerk said, "Enjoy your stay with us, Ms Rainier. Your room is Number 304. The key is in here." She handed Casey an envelope and pointed to the concierge's desk at the entrance to the lobby gift shop. "Dave will show you to it and handle your luggage."

As Casey turned away from the desk, a man in his forties, dressed in Western clothes, stepped in front of her. "I couldn't help overhearing, ma'am, about you being here scouting locations for a movie. Could I have a minute of your time, maybe buy you a drink?"

She studied him for a few beats. He was of medium height, powerfully built, with a deeply tanned face and deep black eyes. His hair was thick and black, combed straight back. His nose was as thin as an axe blade, over a mouth that curved in what Casey always thought of as a salesman's smile, sincere as a counterfeit twenty dollar bill. She said, "I'm sorry, but I've had a long day, and I . . ."

He interrupted smoothly, "All the more reason you should relax over a drink." His deep voice turned coaxing. "Please humour me, it'll be worth your time." He held out a hand. "Glenn Cabot. I have a business here in Sedona, have had for some time. I know Sedona in and out and sideways. I think I can help you in your project."

She took the extended hand. His grip was strong, his flesh dry and cool.

"Rena Rainier, Mr Cabot. All right, just one drink."

"Great, Miss Rainier!" The wattage of his smile increased. "You won't regret it, believe you me."

"Just let me have a word over here." Casey walked over to the concierge's desk and spoke to the young man, who couldn't have been much more than sixteen. "I'm Rena Rainier, checking into 304. But I'm going to have a drink with this nice gentleman. I won't be long, then I'll need someone to handle my bags and show me my room."

The young man beamed. "No problem, Miss Rainier. If I'm not here, someone else will help you."

The bar was located to the left, just off the lobby. There were a half-dozen people at the tables. Cabot guided Casey to a corner table and beckoned imperiously to the waitress. Two walls of the bar were glass, and from where she sat she could see the rays of the lowering sun glancing off the walls of the canyon.

She said, "You staying here at the hotel, Mr Cabot?"

He laughed heartily. "Heavens, no! I was just playing a round of golf with a friend of mine who's staying here for a week."

"Dressed like that?" She gestured to indicate his Western garb.

"Hardly." He laughed again. "I changed in my friend's room."

The waitress came. Casey ordered a vodka tonic, and Cabot ordered a double Wild Turkey on the rocks.

"I own Canyon Jeep Tours, Miss Rainier," he said expansively. "I provide Jeep tours through the canyons, with a driver-guide, and I also rent Jeeps to people who like to drive themselves. That's one of the ways I could be of assistance to you."

"And just how is that, Mr Cabot?" she asked, all innocence.

"Well, there've been movie companies here before, and they often rent my Jeeps to get around in. They'll go over rugged terrain, you know, places where no other vehicle can go. And you might like to use one yourself, to scout the canyons for locations."

The waitress came with the drinks.

Cabot picked up his glass, toasted Casey with it. "Here's to the success of your movie. May it be a box office smash. It would help me help you, if I knew what kind of a movie it is. Most of the movies shot here are Westerns."

"*Canyon* isn't a Western, per se, although it could be called a modern-day Western, I suppose," she said, improvising wildly as she went along.

Cabot grunted. "Tell me, Rena, is this pretty much a done deal? I've had some experience with movie companies, at least with people claiming to represent movie companies. They roll in here, talking big, then leave town, after being courted, wined and dined, and we never hear from them again." He gestured. "Of course, I understand that about eighty percent of all proposed movie deals never get made."

"You understand correctly, Mr Cabot," she said quickly, "but this is a firm deal. The financing is set, we have a distribution deal, and most of the lead roles have been cast."

He took a sip of his drink, his gaze intent on her. "Perhaps if you told me a little about the story, I could be of more help."

She took a deep breath and decided to go all the way. "I don't have a copy of the script to show you. It's being rewritten even as we talk. Scripts often are, right up until shooting starts, and even beyond that. I'll tell you a little about the story, but I must swear you to secrecy, Mr Cabot. The story is very topical, one may say right out of the headlines."

"I'll be like a clam." He placed his right hand over his heart. "I'm all ears."

"Well, the script was started months ago, but in the most amazing coincidence, the storyline follows what has happened here in Sedona, the three murders that took place, the last one just two nights ago. That's one reason the script is being rewritten." She gazed at him intently to gauge his reaction. "In the script the murders are committed by the members of a satanic cult, as sacrifices."

He stared at her for a moment, then shook his head in disbelief. "Lady, you're right about keeping quiet about that. It's a damned touchy subject around this town, and getting touchier by the minute. If I were you, I'd be damned careful about who you mention it to."

"Why is it so sensitive?"

"It's giving Sedona a bad name, and it's starting to have an effect on the tourist trade. Tourists are the lifeblood of this town."

"What do you think, Mr Cabot?"

"About what?"

"About some cult being responsible for the murders?"

"I really don't have an opinion. That's a matter for the police."

"Surely you must have discussed it with others. What do they think about it?"

He gave a shrug. "Not as much as you might think. It's a taboo subject around town."

"But there are cults around, I've read about them off and on for years. How about the medicine wheels? The New Age movement? Things like that?"

"Sure, there are always the loony fringes. But I'm not the one to ask about that, and I suggest you be careful about who you talk to. People here unroll the welcome mat for movie companies. It means dough, good business, good publicity." His gaze was piercing. "But if you go around asking questions like this, doors are going to slam in your face. Why *are* you asking all these questions, anyway? I thought you were here scouting locations, not doing research."

Realizing she was going too far, Casey backed down. "Well, we do want the script to be as authentic as possible. The writer asked me to look into it if I had time."

"Well, Miss Rainier, I'd advise you to soft-pedal the questions. You'll get more cooperation that way." He took a card from his pocket and slid it across the table to her. "There's my card. You call me any time and I'll be glad to help you in any way I can." He grinned. "Of course, I'm hoping to do some business with your company. That's what it's all about, isn't it?" He slid his chair back and got to his feet. "Glad to have met you, I'm running late for an appointment."

"Thanks for the drink, Mr Cabot," she called after him.

Without looking back he waved a hand and continued on. Casey glanced at the card: "Canyon Jeep Tours and Rentals," followed by a telephone number.

She finished her drink, staring after Glenn Cabot. Had she gone too far, been incautious, with her questions? But how else could she learn what she needed to know? Questions were an integral part of the investigative process; she would just have to be a little more careful.

She left the bar and went back to the lobby. The young man at the concierge's desk took her down to the rental in his cart. She started the car and followed his cart back down to the main road, then up a narrow lane for a hundred yards or so. He motioned for her to park off to the left.

He said, "This is as far as you can drive, Ms Rainier. I'll take you and your luggage the rest of the way in the cart."

As the cart drove down the narrow, cement walk that connected the individual buildings that were the "rooms", Casey thought about what had happened since Dan Farrel had dropped her off at the airport. She had started lying to the woman at the car rental, and had been lying steadily ever since. Casey had never been a good liar; she had always had a firm belief in telling the truth. Yet, for someone who always tried to tell the truth, she seemed to be doing pretty well. She could only hope she didn't get caught at it.

She laughed aloud, then became aware that the cart driver was looking at her curiously.

"Just a private joke," she said, and had to laugh again.

Chapter Four

A knock on the door awoke Casey the next morning. She opened her eyes and was surprised to see sun streaming in through the windows. A glance at her watch on the bedside table told her it was after nine. She never slept this late!

She called out, "Yes?"

"Maid service."

She cleared her throat. "Sorry. Come back in an hour or so."

She got quickly out of bed, shed her pyjamas and did a few stretching exercises. Normally, at home, she would have run a few miles, but it was too late for that this morning. Usually, when staying in a hotel or motel, there were noises: the sound of television and people's voices from adjoining rooms and in the hall; the clatter of cleaning carts; the sound of cars as people drove in or left the parking lot. But here there were only one or two rooms to a unit, or *casita*, and the only access was by foot or the nearly silent electric carts. The quiet during the night had been fantastic, no sounds at all, and she had slept soundly. She was going to have to leave a wake-up call if she was going to get any kind of a decent start in the mornings.

She laughed aloud. She could easily become accustomed to this luxury. Last night, after unpacking, she had ordered dinner from room service. It had been expensive, but some of the best food Casey had ever tasted. She had fully intended to order breakfast in this morning, but it was a little late for that.

Bob Wilson would have a cow when he got his first look at her expense sheet for this case. The thought brought another smile to her face as she went in for a shower.

When she was dressed, she left the room and walked quickly to where the car was parked, then drove to 89A, turned left and headed toward town. She stopped at a small, white diner for breakfast; the place looked like something out of the Thirties, down to an old-fashioned juke box, with a small coin box at each booth. There was even a drive-in set-up along one side, no longer in use. After breakfast she pulled into a shopping mall, found a pay phone, and called Bob Wilson's office in Phoenix.

When she got him on the line, she said, "Hello, Bob," knowing that he hated to have her call him by his first name.

He fooled her by answering calmly, "Well, it's Miss Undercover. Do you have anything to report, Farrel?"

She laughed curtly. "How could I? I just got here early last night. The moment I have anything, Bob, you'll be the first to know."

"That'll be a switch," he said sourly.

"The main reason I'm calling, I just thought of something last night before I went to sleep. Since I'm undercover, I can't go around asking too many questions, especially of the Sedona police. It'll arouse suspicions. We need another investigator up here, one who can work in the open, nose around asking the questions I can't. We can meet in secret, exchange notes. Since all this is at the Governor's instigation, there should be no trouble sending another investigator in."

There was a silence on the line before Wilson said slowly, "I suppose that can be arranged. All right, I'll send someone up today. Call me late this afternoon and I'll tell you where he's staying. You can get in touch with him."

"Who are you sending?"

"You let me worry about that, Farrel," he said sharply.

"First, I have to see who's available. Whoever it is I'm sure you two'll get along just fine."

There was a note in his voice she didn't like, but she said, "Okay, Bob, I'll call you this afternoon. Wait, I ordered some cards printed at one of those quick print places. They promised to have them today. Could you have the investigator you send bring them up when he comes?"

Wilson said he would take care of it, and Casey gave him the name and address of the printer.

Walking to the rental, Casey wondered whom he would send. The only surety was that it would be a man, for Casey was the only woman out of the six investigators on the task force. She gave a shrug as she got into the car. No need to worry about that now; she would find out tonight.

For the rest of the morning she drove around Sedona and the surrounding area, refamiliarizing herself with the locale. She didn't want to approach anyone else until she had the cards, verifying who and what she was supposed to be. After a quick lunch she drove to the Sedona Public Library on Jordan Road and buried herself in back issues of the *Sedona Red Rock News*. It would probably have been easier to do it at the newspaper offices, but she would have attracted more attention there; at the library she was just another browser.

It was a more tedious job than she had calculated; the back issues weren't on film, so she had to go through the papers one by one, hunting for what she wanted. The library was small, and crowded; but the staff was pleasant, cooperative, fetching the old newspapers for her without showing any curiosity.

She spent the rest of the afternoon searching for coverage of the murders and anything on cults. The information on the murders was scanty, which Casey knew was either the result of little information being available or a police cover-up. She suspected the former.

Well, she couldn't very well go to either the Sedona police

or the two sheriff departments involved and pester them; that would have to be up to her partner, when he arrived.

In the newspaper coverage of the first two murders, she came across a few references to possible cult involvement, but reading between the lines, she surmised that it came from rumour, with no concrete evidence to back it up. She also found several articles mentioning instances of vandalism in the area, which, according to the Forest Rangers, were believed to have been committed by New Agers conducting their rites. Yet no arrests had ever been made, so again it was mostly guesswork.

She went through issues of the Red Rock news dating back almost three years. Her back was aching, and she was stiff from sitting so long, her fingers were black from newsprint, and her eyes burned. She glanced at her watch for the first time in hours and saw that it was almost four. God, had she been here that long? She had to call Wilson if she hoped to get him before he left the office.

She thanked the woman who had brought her the stacks of newspapers in brown grocery sacks and went outside. The bright sunlight almost blinded her. Hastily she donned sunglasses, got in the rental, which was hot as an oven, and drove off the parking lot in search of a pay phone.

"Beginning to think you weren't going to call, Farrel," he said when she could got through to him. "Anything to report?"

"Not yet. How about that investigator I asked for?"

"He's on his way. In fact, he should be checking into his motel right about now. He'll be staying at the King's Ransom Quality Inn. Quite a bit cheaper than where you're staying, I might add. Some people don't feel they have to throw the taxpayers' money around to do their jobs."

Casey ignored the jibe. "Who?"

"Gabe Stinton."

"Name doesn't ring a bell, and I thought I knew all of our investigators."

"Gabe's a new man, just hired a few days ago."

Casey hesitated, then said: "Do you think it's wise to send a new man on an important case like this?"

"Stinton's a good investigator, or I wouldn't have hired him," Wilson said in a growling voice. "Everybody else is tied up."

"Well, I'll call now, see if he's arrived yet," she said and hung up.

She looked up the number for the King's Ransom and asked if Gabe Stinton had arrived yet. She was put through to his room.

"Mr Stinton?"

"Speaking."

"This is Rena Rainier."

There was a slight hesitation, then a pleasant male voice said: "Yes, I was expecting your call."

"Are you familiar with Sedona?"

"This my first time here."

"Not too far from where you're staying is the Tlaquepaque Shopping Village, to your left just off 179, just after you cross the bridge over Oak Creek. In the centre of it, just as you come in off the parking lot, is a courtyard. Could you meet me there in a half-hour?"

"Of course. But since we've never met . . ."

She laughed. "I suppose I could ask you to wear a rose in your lapel, but that would be a little much, wouldn't it? I have red hair, with a white streak – at the moment – and am wearing tan slacks and a pink blouse. I'll be sitting on a bench just inside. Oh . . . do you have the cards I ordered?"

"Yeah, I have them."

"Be sure and bring them along."

When the tall, lanky young man appeared in the courtyard entryway, blinking at the sprinkle of tourists and visitors, Casey immediately knew that he was Gabe Stinton. He looked, she thought, very much like a young James Stewart. Hardly the image of a hardened investigator.

When he saw her, his face lit up and he walked toward her. His gait was unusual, sort of an awkward lope, as if he found it difficult to control those long legs and arms.

"Uh . . . Miss, uh . . ." He smiled suddenly, a shy, charming smile. "Miss Rainier?"

"Yes, Mr Stinton." She rose and hooked her arm in his. "Let's walk up the street and gawk at Oak Creek, like tourists. We can talk better, without being overheard."

He looked around in alarm. "You mean . . .?"

Dear God, what has Wilson stuck me with? she thought in dismay. She said, "I don't mean anything. But it's better not to take chances."

Outside the complex, Casey motioned, and they started walking to their right. Casey said, "You've only been with the task force for a few days I understand."

Gabe nodded. "I was hired this week."

"What experience have you had in law enforcement?"

"Not a hell of a lot," he said somewhat sheepishly. "I was in the Army for four years after I got out of law school . . ."

"Law school? If you're a lawyer what are you doing taking a job with the task force?"

"I never passed the bar. Oh, I probably could have," he said with a shy smile, "but I became disillusioned with the system. It seems to me that lawyers have become a part of what's wrong with the country today."

At least he knows law, she thought; that should be a help. She said, "You've got that right. So what happened after the Army? You're what . . .? About thirty?"

"Thirty-one, actually. For the past five years I've been working for a mall security firm in Phoenix."

Casey barely managed to suppress a sigh. "Why did you leave there?"

"I only took the job as a stopgap, until I decided what

I really wanted to do with my life. Frankly, I got bored. I had been thinking for some time of applying for the Phoenix Police Department, but I wasn't sure that's what I wanted. The police strike me as being as regimented as the Army."

Casey smiled. "Wait until you've been around Bob Wilson for a while." They had crossed the bridge, and now stood waiting for a break in the traffic. When it came, they crossed to the other side of the street, and Casey led Gabe up past a building on the left to a spot where they could walk into the trees and see the creek. They stood gazing quietly for a few minutes looking down at the water racing below them.

Casey said, "Did you bring the cards?"

"Of course, Ms Farrel." Dipping into his pocket, he took out an oblong box.

Casey said, "Rena, please, Gabe. Get used to calling me that until this case is finished. For my benefit, as well as yours. I don't want anybody overhearing you call me Casey Farrel, and I want to get used to my undercover name."

She broke the seal on the box, opened it, and took out a white card with black letters embossed on it: Rena Rainier, Production Assistant, Minot Productions. There was a Los Angeles phone number down at the bottom.

Gabe said, "Is there such a company?"

Casey grinned. "If someone calls this number, they'll be told there is. I can only hope no one checks beyond that." She faced him. "Gabe, did Wilson tell you what you were to do here?"

"Well, he told me what you're investigating, and he told me that I am to keep in close touch with you. He told me I was to check with the Sedona police and the two sheriff's departments involved, since you won't be able to do that. I'm supposed to tell them that the task force is coming into the case because the Governor is afraid the murders are going to scare away the tourists."

She nodded. "That's right. See if they have any new leads."

He looked at her keenly. "Do you think they're cult killings?"

"I don't know what I think yet," she said with a sigh. "But I have a feeling about it. As for keeping a close check on me, forget about that. I'm undercover here. We'll see each other, talk to each other, as little as possible. I'll call you maybe once a day. If you have anything to report, we'll arrange to meet. But whatever you do, do not call *me*, or come out to the Enchantment to see me. Is that clear?"

"Clear, Rena." He grinned. "See?"

As they started back to the shopping village, Gabe said, "I can't tell you how excited I am about working this case, and about working with you."

"Just don't get too excited, Gabe," she said dryly.

"I've read about all those cases you've solved, Rena."

She made a dismissive gesture. "Don't believe everything you read, Gabe."

Casey wasn't necessarily a happy camper as she drove back to her hotel. What had Bob Wilson been thinking of, hiring Gabe Stinton? He was a nice enough guy, certainly intelligent, but he was woefully inexperienced. Probably Wilson had hired Gabe because he was a lawyer. Or almost a lawyer.

But a security guy for a shopping mall? Jesus!

Chapter Five

Early the next morning Casey donned her jogging clothes and ran for a half-hour, up beyond the lobby building, then stopped off at the desk on her way back. There was a Federal Express envelope waiting for Rena Rainer.

"My credit card replacing my lost one," she explained to the woman behind the desk.

The woman smiled meaninglessly.

It's like peeling an onion, Casey thought as she jogged back to her room, only in reverse. She had to keep applying layers of deceit to conceal her true identity.

In the room she took a quick shower, ordered a hearty breakfast from room service, then got dressed in the clothes she intended to wear for the day.

A knock on the door announced the arrival of her breakfast. Room service at the Enchantment was the most efficient she had ever encountered.

Before she left the room she made sure she had a good supply of the cards Gabe had brought up from Phoenix; with them, and her new credit card, she now had something to back up her assumed identity.

In town she drove past the Y intersection of 89A and 179, parking a couple of blocks in front of the office of Canyon Jeep Rentals. There were several open Jeeps parked before the building, all painted the deep red of many of the huge rock formations towering over Sedona. One Jeep was just pulling out, carrying two couples and the driver.

Inside was a small waiting room, with chairs and a long

counter bisecting the room. The counter was manned by two women, neither older than thirty, and both wore bright Western garb. One of the women was engaged in booking a couple of tourists for the next available Jeep tour.

The other woman smiled brightly at Casey. "May I help you?"

Casey said, "I'd like to see Mr Cabot, please. Tell him it's Rena Rainier."

"I'll check and see if he's available." She picked up a receiver and spoke into it in a low voice.

After a few moments she hung up, went down to the end of the counter, and swung open the gate. "Mr Cabot will see you."

Casey followed her to a door set in the back wall. Cabot's office was small, with an ancient desk, a couch and chairs arranged before it. The walls were covered with posters and blow-ups of photographs depicting the scenery around Sedona. The picture window behind the desk gave out on a view of Oak Creek below.

Cabot got to his feet, flashing his salesman's grin. "Miss Rainier! Didn't expect to see you quite so soon. What can I do for you?"

"First, I forgot to give you one of my cards the other evening." She handed him one of the cards.

Cabot took it, spared it a quick glance, and motioned to the couch. As she sat down, he said, "So, how goes the location search?"

"Frankly, I haven't really looked yet. I spent most of yesterday driving all over the area, orienting myself. Also, doing a little gawking at the scenery. It's absolutely beautiful here."

"We think so." He laughed lightly. "Unfortunately, to the thinking of many, especially the long-time residents, too many people have discovered us and are moving here in droves. As for me, that's fine. Good for business."

"Yes, I understand a great many people from California

are moving into Arizona. Can't say I blame them too much." She cleared her throat. "The main reason I dropped in, is to see if you can direct me a little. Tell me the best places to look, the best people to see."

Cabot's gaze rested on her curiously. "Best people? How do they figure in your movie?"

"Well, we're going to be shooting some scenes inside, certain stores, a restaurant or two. The owners will be well paid, of course, but I need to feel them out, find which ones will be willing to cooperate." Casey had been giving this some hard thought. Since three murders were involved, in the same area, it seemed likely that the murderer, or murderers, were residents of Sedona or Oak Creek. This would be one way to speak to some of the residents, without arousing suspicion.

Cabot was speaking. Casey brought her attention back to him. "I'm sorry, I was lost in thought there for a moment. What did you just say?"

"There's a party tonight, given by our mayor, Claudine Thornton. A number of business people will be present, as well as city officials. Would you like to attend?"

"That would be great, but I hate to party crash."

"You won't be. You can go with me, as my guest. My wife is out of town for the week. I was planning on attending alone." Cabot laughed. "Don't worry. You'll be welcome. Except for a few die-hards, most people in Sedona are delighted to see a movie company shoot here . . ."

The phone rang on his desk, interrupting him. He scooped up the receiver. After a moment he put his hand over the mouthpiece, and said, "Rena, this is long distance, I'll be a while. The party starts at seven, drinks, food, the whole nine yards. Our place is open late. Why don't you drop back shortly before seven, and we'll go out in my car?"

"That'll be fine, Mr Cabot. And thank you . . ."

He was already back on the phone. With a wave of her hand Casey left the office.

For the next hour or so she drove around Sedona, stopping at random at various businesses. In each she stated her purpose and left one of the Rena Rainier cards. Since it was summer, vacation time, all the shop owners were harried, but most of them were more than willing to spare her a few minutes. She told them that the movie would require some scenes shot in shops; any shop so used would be compensated generously for their time and the use of their premises. Everyone appeared willing, even eager, to cooperate.

But she learned nothing to advance her investigation. She knew it would not be wise to discuss the murders, at least not at this stage, and with Glenn Cabot's warning in mind, she didn't mention anything about cults. All of which limited her questions. How *was* she going to learn anything this way? Perhaps at the mayor's party tonight she would be given a chance to dig into it a little. There would be alcohol flowing freely, she was sure, and alcohol loosened tongues and made people incautious.

After a leisurely lunch she headed out of town on Highway 179. About a mile from the Y she saw an antique shop on the right. She pulled in and parked. There was a sign beside the entrance: "No rest rooms available." Not very customer friendly, she thought. Of course it would be a chore to provide such facilities for a steady stream of browsers during the heavy tourist season . . .

"You thinking of using the potty?" a voice said from behind her.

With a start, Casey wheeled around. Standing behind her was a small, plump man of perhaps fifty. His face was round, shaded by a huge, straw, plantation hat. Bright blue eyes peered at her inquisitively from underneath the hat brim. He held a miniature white French poodle cradled tenderly in short arms.

The man's mouth, lips red as if rouged, pursed. "Because if you are, you're out of luck. We have a firm rule. If you make a purchase, you get to use the potty. If not, forget it."

"I gathered that from the sign." Casey gestured. "You said 'we'. I gather you're the owner?"

"Half-owner. Rob, my partner, is minding the store right now. I had to take Pookie here for her morning stroll." He hefted the dog, which emitted a couple of sharp yips. "I'm Wesley Strom."

"Rena Rainier." Casey extracted one of her cards from her purse.

Wesley Strom took it, flicked his gaze over it, then pursed his mouth at her again. "Oh, one of those."

"'One of those'? I take it you don't approve?"

"You take it correctly, but don't take it personally, darling. I just wish you movie people would choose some place else."

"I thought you'd be pleased. Most people seem to be. A movie company brings in business."

"I've lived here since before the boom, and I was perfectly happy with Sedona the way it was. People see how lovely the area is in your movie, they come in droves, not only as tourists, which wouldn't be so bad, but to live. We have far too many people as it is. But don't mind me, I'm just a crabby old queen." The blue eyes twinkled at her. "And there's nothing I can do to stop you, dear. What exactly is your function?"

"Oh, I'm here scouting locations. We'll be using some businesses, interior scenes, in the movie. One scene, for instance, takes place in an antique shop. But from what you just said, I gather . . . ?"

"You gather correctly, darling. But again, nothing personal. As a matter of fact, from what I've seen of you, Rena, I think I like you. Drop in any time, just don't expect me to do movie business with you."

He held out a small, plump hand, and Casey took it.

Laughing, she said, "I may just do that."

Wesley took back his hand, and jiggled the poodle. "Say goodbye to the nice lady, Pookie."

The poodle obliged, yipping twice. Wesley marched into the store, the straw hat set squarely on his head.

As Casey got into the rental car, she had a disturbing thought. It hadn't occurred to her that someone could be killing off tourists in the hope of discouraging them from moving to Sedona. Was that possible? It struck her as pretty far-fetched. But still . . .

At any rate, Wesley Strom might be worth cultivating. He appeared to be the talkative sort, and, as a long-time resident, was sure to have a wealth of local information.

Casey spent the next two hours dropping her cards off at various other establishments, and discussing movie locations. Almost everyone she talked to expressed enthusiasm for the project and promised cooperation; although a few agreed with Wesley Strom.

She learned nothing useful for her investigation, but she wasn't at all discouraged. She had known going in that it wasn't going to be quick and easy. At four she decided to call it a day, so that she would have time to prepare for the Mayor's party.

On the way back to the resort, she stopped at a phone and called Gabe's motel on the off-chance that he was in. He was.

"Gabe . . . You learn anything pertinent today?"

"Well, yeah, I did." His voice sounded excited. Casey smiled to herself.

"Great. What have you got?"

"A couple of items of interest. First, they've discovered the spot where the last victim, the lady from California, was killed."

"Where?"

"Strangely enough, not too far from where you're staying, on top of a mesa not far from Chimney Rock."

"How can they be sure?"

"Well, a park ranger found this boulder splattered with blood. Tests matched the blood with that of the victim. Apparently, the boulder was in the shape of a crude altar . . ."

Casey felt a pulse of excitement. "Then I was right, it *is* a cult murder!"

"They're playing it cagey, but the opinion seems to be that it might be. The weapon used in all three cases was a knife, wasn't it?"

"Yes. That's right. Gabe . . . Tell me the exact location of the spot where the blood was found."

"From what I gather there's a hiking trail leads off Boynton Canyon not too far from the entrance to the Enchantment."

"Yes, I know where it is. Every time I drive past there are always cars parked there."

"According to my information, there's another trail which branches off to the left, a little over a mile up. That eventually takes you to the mesa where . . ." He broke off. "Casey . . . uh, Rena, you're not thinking of going up there, are you?"

"I'm not thinking anything yet."

"Don't go up there alone. It could be dangerous!"

"You mean, the killer might revisit the scene of the crime? That hardly ever happens, Gabe, believe me."

"Let me go with you."

"No!" she said sharply. "The less we're seen together the better." As he started to speak again, she shut him up. "Don't forget, Gabe, that I'm the senior investigator here. I'm giving the orders!" She softened her tone. "But I appreciate your concern, and you've done a good job of work on your first day on the job. Call you sometime tomorrow."

Before he could speak again she hung up.

*   *   *

On her way to the Enchantment she stopped off at a hardware store and purchased a powerful flashlight. She stopped again a few hundred yards short of the resort entrance gate. There were a half-dozen vehicles already parked at the beginning of the hiking trail.

Casey walked up the well-worn trail for a short distance. She had already determined that later tonight she was going to go up to the spot where the blood had been found. It was probably taped off, but she doubted very much that there would be an officer guarding it; it was likely all the evidence had been collected by this time.

And it wasn't very likely that she would find something the other investigators had overlooked. Still, she had learned that it was often valuable to visit the scene of a homicide, even well after the fact. It was rare that she discovered any physical evidence, but she liked to get the feel of it. Often she would flash on something, an almost psychic feel for the murderer; sometimes she even felt that she inhabited the killer's skin and mind for a few moments. It could be, and often was, an eerie, frightening feeling, but valuable nonetheless.

Yes, she thought, as she turned away back toward the car, I'm going up there tonight, despite Gabe's warning of danger. What danger could there be this long after the fact? The murder was days old. What purpose could it serve for the killer to return?

Chapter Six

The house of Sedona's mayor, Anne Caldwell, was located on the south side of Oak Creek, high on the side of the cliff that overlooked Oak Creek and Sedona. The view took Casey's breath away.

As she looked out of the window of Cabot's new Cadillac, she exclaimed, "Wow!"

Cabot grinned. "Something, isn't it? People always have that reaction the first time they glimpse the view from Her Honour's abode."

"The house isn't bad, either," she said as he parked. The house was all glass and redwood, with a deck cantilevered out over the plunging hillside. There were already a half-dozen cars parked in the large parking area before the house, which Casey judged, must be at least six thousand square feet.

"Anne had it built about five years ago, just after she moved here," Cabot said. "It'd go for at least a million and a half on today's market."

"I assume the mayor's office doesn't pay that well," Casey said dryly.

Cabot laughed. "Hardly. Brent Caldwell made his money as a developer in Phoenix. Six years ago he ran for the House of Representatives. Six months before the end of his term he suddenly died. The Governor appointed Anne to serve out the remainder of his term. She probably could have been elected for the next term, but she decided not to run. Said she hated living in Washington, so she came home to Arizona, sold all her husband's business interests, came up here, and built this house. Told me she was going to take it easy. But I guess that brief taste of politics hooked her. When a group of us got together and asked her to run for Mayor, she jumped at it. Doing a damned good job of it, too."

Casey couldn't help wondering if the connection between Mayor Caldwell and the Governor was one reason the Governor had personally requested Bob Wilson to turn the task force loose on the case.

She got out of the car and followed Cabot up the flagstone walk to the front door, which stood open. Sounds of laughter and conversation poured out of the doorway. Cabot walked right in.

Inside, Cabot began shaking hands and introducing Casey; the names and faces came so rapidly that Casey lost track quickly. The entryway opened out into a large living room, with a semicircular conversation pit around a huge, stone fireplace. The whole west wall was solid glass; it was dark now and lights twinkled like fallen stars across Oak Creek.

At the far end of the room, a man sat at a grand piano, tinkling out show tunes of the Forties and Fifties. Cabot led the way past the piano and through double doors into another room almost as large as the first room. A bar along one wall was manned by a woman bartender, and two other women in maids' uniforms circulated with trays of drinks. This room was more crowded than the great room, and the noise level was high.

A loud voice brayed behind them, "Headed for the bar, hey, Glenn?"

Cabot and Casey turned in unison. A buxom woman of fifty-odd years stood behind them. In appearance she made Casey think of a past female governor of Arizona: Blue-white hair was piled on top of her head above a Cupid's face, round, with a little too much make-up; her blue eyes, small, shrewd, peered at Casey inquisitively.

Cabot said heartily, "Hi, Annie. Annie, this is the lady I told you I was bringing, Rena Rainier, here scouting locations for a movie. Rena, say hello to Anne Caldwell, Sedona's illustrious mayor."

"Hello, Your Honour," Casey said.

"Not that, for God's sake!" Anne Caldwell brayed husky laughter. "I swore I was going to install stocks down at the Y, and the next person to call me that would be locked there all day for people to jeer at. But since you're new in town, I'll overlook it this once. Call me Annie."

Casey laughed. "All right, Annie it is then."

"So you're one of those Hollywood slicks come here to con the locals, hey?" Anne's eyes had a sly twinkle.

"Well, I certainly hope that isn't what we're doing. Usually, we leave a good feeling behind us."

Anne Caldwell raised her eyebrows. "That may be, but it isn't always that way. Last year a movie company came to Prescott, stayed for two weeks, ran up humungous bills all over town, paid by cheque. A week later all the cheques bounced like basketballs."

"I assure you that the company I work for, while an independent production company, is financially sound."

Anne's bray of laughter sounded. "Don't fret, love. I was just having you on, as the Brits say. Welcome to Sedona, Rena. Now I have to play the hostess. Take care of her, Glenn."

"Annie's quite a lady," Cabot said as he forged a way to the bar. "She has a quirky sense of humour, and she's outspoken to the point of being almost brutal at times; yet she's well liked, even by those people who don't always agree with her."

Casey asked for a vodka tonic, and while Cabot got the drinks, she looked around. The crowd had grown considerably during the short time they had been here. It seemed a congenial, relaxed group.

As Cabot handed Casey her drink, she said, "Quite a crowd. Does she give parties like this often?"

"Oh, yes, at least twice a month. Annie loves to party." He grinned. "Some call her the Perle Mesta of Sedona. And others, less cautious and more cruel, call all this," he gestured at the room, "the Sedona Mafia."

"And why is that?" Casey took a pull of her drink.

"Because almost all of the movers and shakers, the power brokers, if you will, are to be found in this house. Disgruntled voters claim that all decisions affecting Sedona are made here."

"And are they?"

Cabot shrugged carelessly. "Not really. Certain issues might be discussed here, opinions solicited and so forth, but I very much doubt any serious decisions are made here."

"Then are you one of the town's power brokers, Glenn?"

His salesman's grin appeared. "Some might think so, but I'm really not. I'm not much interested in power as such, only insofar as it might help me make money . . ."

A hand touched Casey's elbow. "So we meet again, movie lady, and so soon!"

Casey glanced around into the cherubic face of Wesley Strom. His merry blue eyes twinkled at her. He was dressed outrageously: a flowered shirt with the tails hanging out over bilious green slacks. Standing beside him was a slender man about Strom's own age; he was dressed in a conservative grey suit, complete with white shirt and a solid grey tie. His face was long, dark, and wore an expression of solemnity. The two men, on the surface at least, could not have been more different.

Casey said, "Mr Strom, I didn't expect to see you here."

Strom shrugged plump shoulders. "Oh, I never miss one of dear Annie's dos. Hi, Glenn."

Cabot nodded. "Hello, Wesley."

"This, Ms Rainier, is my bosom companion, Rob." Strom

smiled at his companion possessively. "This is the movie lady I was telling you about, Rob. Rena Rainier."

Rob nodded meagrely. "How do you do, Miss Rainier?"

Casey returned his greeting, and said, "Where's Pookie, Wesley?"

Wesley's red lips pouted. "Oh, Annie won't allow dogs in her house. Says she has an allergy. You know what I always tell her? Some of your guests give me allergies, but I never fail to show up." He giggled softly.

Casey smiled in return. "Pookie might not like the drinks anyway."

"Pookie's strictly blue collar. She only drinks beer. Which reminds me, we were on our way to get drinks." He took a step away, then wheeled back. "How goes the movie location search?"

"Little early to tell yet. At least I haven't come across anyone as adamantly against our shooting here as you are, Wesley."

"No, no, dear!" he said chidingly. "Not all that opposed, really. Most movie people I've been in contact with are arrogant, ego-driven, rude, uncouth, pushy, and puffed-up with their own importance."

Casey was laughing. "Wow! All those things, huh?"

"All those things and more. But you, my dear, aren't that way at all. You may even change my opinion of movie folk."

"Thank you. I guess I should feel flattered."

"Oh, definitely, dear. And now, I must have a drink before I perish." Taking Rob's elbow, he steered his companion toward the bar.

Glancing at Cabot, Casey saw that he was smiling. "Is Wesley a local character?"

He laughed. "*One* of the local characters. There are a number in Sedona. Actually Strom is well thought of here. He's shrewd, not at all the bubblehead he appears. He's been here for years, and he knows antiques better than anyone I know. He's active in local politics, he even served on the city council once . . ." He broke off, smiling at someone behind Casey. "Hello, Russ. Didn't know you were back from Phoenix yet."

Casey turned to see a man who appeared to be in his middle fifties, of medium height but well built, with the look of a construction worker. His dark eyes rested on Casey curiously; he scrubbed a blunt-fingered hand over a head as hairless as an egg.

The man called Russ said in a deep voice, "I got back around noon today."

"This is Rena Rainier, Russ," Cabot said. "Rena, say hello to Russell Turner. Rena is in Sedona scouting locations for a movie."

"Oh, yes, I've heard about you, Ms Rainier."

Casey shook her head. "Word sure gets around in a hurry."

Turner grinned, teeth gleaming in his deeply tanned face. "Sedona is still a small town, Ms Rainier, in spite of its recent growth. And you know how small towns are."

"And Russ is responsible for much of the growth," Cabot said. "He's a developer, he's built half the houses in Sedona."

"Not half, Glenn. Maybe a quarter. And I'm not really responsible. People come to me to build their houses, I build them. That's what makes the world go round, isn't it? And if that puts me on the side of the growth ledger, so be it."

Casey said, "Does that mean you won't object to a movie being shot here?"

"Hell, no. On the contrary. The more, the merrier." Turner's name was called from across the room. He waved a hand, and said, "I'm being paged. Get in touch with me, Ms Rainier, if I can help you in any way. I'm in the book. Turner Construction."

Casey watched the man walk across the room. He walked

with the slight swagger of a man confident of himself and his success.

To Cabot she said, "I'd say there's a man sure of himself. But I suppose he has reason, since he seems to be quite successful and well heeled."

"Well, I'm not all that sure. There are rumours."

"Rumours?"

Cabot lowered his voice with a look around. "It's said that Russ is overextended. He sank a lot of money in a chunk of land out on Dry Creek Road, hoping to build a lot of expensive homes. But there's a lot of opposition from the people trying to put the brakes on all the fast growth. I hear that he's strapped for cash. Fact is, I understand he went to Phoenix to raise a chunk of money. Coming back early like he did may mean that he didn't get it."

There was a look of slyness about Cabot, and Casey had to wonder if he was speaking out of knowledge, or concocting a false rumour out of envy of Turner's success.

Cabot looked around the room again. "I suppose we'd better circulate. Do you want me to introduce you to the other guests?"

Casey hesitated briefly. If there was to be an opportunity to ask questions about cult activity in Sedona, it might not be wise to do it within Cabot's hearing. She said, "You go ahead. I'll manage. Considering how fast news seems to spread, I imagine everybody here knows who I am anyway."

"Probably true," he said with a nod. "When you feel you've had enough, hunt me down and I'll drive you back to your car."

He moved easily into the crowd. Casey found a vacant spot against one wall, a pocket of relative quiet, and watched the crowd for a bit, sipping on her drink. She had never been totally at ease in a social situation such as this, and even less so with a mob of strangers.

She doubted very much that she would learn anything of

value here, but at least she could acquaint herself with some of the players.

Finished with the drink, she launched herself into the crowd. Over the next hour she met a number of people, storing the names and faces in her memory. By that time she was beginning to think of finding Glenn Cabot for the promised ride.

And then, leaning against the wall with her second, and last drink, of the night, she overheard a snatch of conversation that sent up an alert. To her left were two people, a man and a woman, both clearly feeling the effect of their drinks.

The woman was speaking, ". . . don't know how you can think that, Vernon, I've never heard of a single incident where any New Agers were involved in acts of violence. Maybe what the park rangers call vandalism, but not murder, for God's sake!"

"Vickie, any cult attracts the lunatic fringe. You're an intelligent woman, you should know that." The man spoke in a lower voice, with a guarded glance around.

Casey, her interest caught, studied the pair covertly. The woman was in her late thirties, early forties. She wore a colourful, flowered dress that almost swept the floor. The man wore faded jeans and a sports shirt. Despite their casual attire, there was an air of affluence about them. Ageing yuppies, Casey thought, then chided herself for making snap judgements.

The man half turned, and Casey got a better look at him. He was short, sturdy, with a powerful build. He had piercing black eyes, over an aquiline nose. His skin was dark, with a reddish cast. Although he appeared to be around fifty, he had a full head of black hair, with no trace of grey. As he gestured with one hand, Casey noticed an expensive watch on his right wrist, with an ornamental band that she recognized as Indian craftwork. And, she belatedly realized, he was a Native American.

The woman was leaning against the wall, her face toward Casey. She was a blonde, a little on the plump side, with rather heavy features, rather too theatrically made-up. Her green eyes, now somewhat fierce in contention, protruded slightly.

The woman was speaking again. "Speaking of intelligent, that's a sweeping statement for you to make. You're lumping all cults together, Vernon. There are many people out there today who are simply seeking some centre to their lives, some guidance."

Vernon laughed scornfully. "People like that need a keeper more than they need guidance. For years they have been stealing our sacred artifacts – you can see them in museums and shops all over the country. Now, they are stealing our ceremonies, our culture! You speak of vandalism: they are desecrating the sacred ground of our people, ruining our holy sites so that we can no longer use them. They have no shame. Anyone who would do that could easily commit murder."

"You have a small mind, as well as a closed one, Vernon!" Vickie said angrily. "I agree that they shouldn't use your sacred ground, but maybe they don't know that. And yes, there are some bad, even evil, cults, I know that. And I know that some of them are accused of making animal sacrifices, but . . ."

"And human sacrifices, while you're admitting things."

The woman hesitated, her expression showing annoyance. "Yes, even human sacrifices – but that's not common. What I'm saying is that most of these groups, the New Agers in particular, are just looking for a code to live their lives by. Their motives are good, even if their actions may be a little thoughtless."

"And what I'm saying is that good motives or not, they are doing wrong in trying to usurp our beliefs, ceremonies and rituals; and destroying the local environment to boot. Also, some of them are mixing our sacred lore in with a lot of damn crap, including witchcraft and Satanism. But what's the use in talking to you. You're just like the others. You don't listen!"

The woman's green eyes misted with tears. "The question is, why am I wasting my time talking to *you*?"

Vernon turned on his heel and strode away. Vickie stared after him. She raised the glass in her hand and took a drink.

Casey edged closer. "Pardon me, but I couldn't help overhearing. Your conversation about cults intrigues me."

The woman turned an angry glare on her. "Who are you?"

"I'm Rena Rainier." Casey took a card from her purse and offered it to the woman. "I'm in Sedona scouting locations for a movie."

The woman took the card and glanced at it. "Oh, I've heard about you. I'm Vickie Steele. What do cults have to do with your movie?"

"The storyline involves a cult. One of the lead characters is a cult member."

Vickie's interest quickened. "Villain, or one of the good guys?"

"The audience won't know until the very end, but actually he's one of the good guys," Casey improvised.

The other woman nodded, smiling brightly. "That's great. The New Agers are getting trashed in the media, a lousy reputation they don't deserve."

"How about other cults?"

Vickie's face took on a wary expression. "There may be others. I'm not all that up on cult activities. Why do you ask?"

Casey spread her hands in a shrug. "No particular reason, except I'm always curious about new things. I've attended various meetings in Los Angeles. Some were quite interesting, others were a little far-out for my tastes. To be frank, I'm looking for a group that I can really get into, something that might give me a direction in my life. So if there's something like that here, I might like to attend a session or two. I gathered from the conversation I overheard that you might know of something along those lines."

Vickie glanced around, and lowered her voice. "I might, if you're really serious, if I knew you weren't just interested in exploiting what you learned. We've . . . They've learned to be very, very careful."

"Oh, I would never do that." An inner voice cautioned Casey not to push too hard this early, but she felt a pulse of excitement, sensing that Vickie Steele just might be the contact she was looking for. She said casually, "I gather that the man you were talking to is against all cults."

"Oh, Vernon!" Vickie gestured dismissively. "He's an idiot about such things. He believes everything bad about cults, ready to blame them for everything under the sun. That was Vernon Bornfield. He publishes a small weekly Native American newspaper. He's been on this anti-cult kick for some time, claiming the cults are destroying his people's sacred grounds. He's hoping that if enough feeling can be raised against the cults, they will all pack up and leave Sedona. Unfortunately, many other people believe the same way. The murders have them frightened."

"Yes," said Casey casually, "I heard Mr Bornfield mention the word 'murder'. What's that all about?"

Casey watched the woman withdraw. "Some local murders that haven't been solved."

"And he thinks a cult was involved."

The woman shrugged. "I'm afraid so. Well, it was really nice talking to you . . ."

"Nice talking to you too." She was losing her.

Casey put her hand on the other woman's arm. "By the way, Vickie, what do you do?"

"I own and operate a beauty shop in town, the Steele Magnolia." She smiled, obviously relieved to be back on safe ground. "We're busy right now, but if you need any work done, call me and I can get you in without an appointment."

"Thanks, I just may do that."

Casey watched the other woman disappear in the crowd, feeling high on excitement. Something could come of this, she felt sure.

Leaving the security of the wall, she went in search of Cabot, reflecting that she could easily have a complete movie script worked out before she left, the way she kept improvising bits and pieces of it as she went along.

It was almost eleven o'clock by the time Casey drove along Dry Creek Road toward the Enchantment. She slowed and parked in the area at the start of the hiking trail. There was only one other vehicle in sight, parked a hundred yards up, dark and silent. Either a hiker who was delayed up there, Casey thought, or one who liked to hike at night, which could be hazardous to the health.

She changed into hiking boots, got the powerful flashlight out of the car, turned it on, and followed the beam to the head of the trail. Although the moon was full, a heavy cloud cover had moved in, probably the advance guard of an early monsoon, and the night was dark.

The vaulting rock formations, including Chimney Rock, loomed ominous and eerie, their bright colours muted by the darkness.

Casey trudged along, afraid to walk too rapidly. Even with the powerful beam of the flashlight, the rocky trail was treacherous, especially when it began to climb steeply. An eerie quiet shrouded the canyon; even the night birds were silent.

Casey felt chilled, even though the air was warm. At the foot of the towering cliff, another, fainter, trail branched off to the left. Following Gabe's directions, she veered left. Almost at once the trail began to climb steeply. At times it was so steep that she had to pull herself along by clutching at the branches of the trees along the side of the trail.

Finally, she topped the rise, breathing heavily. To her astonishment the beam of the flashlight disclosed a flat area about the size of a football field. And then she saw the circle roped in by yellow crime scene tape.

Quickly she switched off the flashlight, holding her breath. Had the police left somebody behind to guard the spot? She strained her ears, listening hard. Nothing, except the sighing of the wind, which was strong on the mesa top.

After a few minutes, when no alarm had been sounded, she switched on the light again and stepped over the crime tape. Immediately inside that was a large circle of stones, and inside that was a pentagram, also outlined in stones. In the exact centre of the pentagram was a large, flat boulder.

As she stepped inside the pentagram, Casey stopped short, feeling a cold that seemed to penetrate to her very bones. She shivered, hugging herself.

Slowly, she advanced to the boulder, shining the light on it. Dark stains splotched the surface, running down the sides. Clearly this was where the latest victim had been killed, spread out on this crude altar, the knife plunging toward the heart.

Had it been a cult sacrifice, or something else entirely?

It seemed evident that some kind of dark ceremony had taken place here. But what kind, and for what purpose?

Casey closed her eyes, emptying her mind as much as possible. Into the void rushed a feeling of enormous evil. She felt the pressure from all sides; and imagined she could feel the sides of the pentagram contracting from all points, trapping her within walls of cold stone. In her mind she could hear the horrifying screams of the woman on the rock as the knife pierced her heart, and her last, dying breath gushed from her.

So intent was Casey on trying to call up a vision of the terrible scene, that she lost all contact with her surroundings.

Now she heard something behind her. The soft scuffle of feet? Ragged breathing?

She started to whirl, and powerful arms wrapped around her from behind. Hands gripped her throat like iron bands, squeezing.

She fought for breath, but couldn't draw in air. Her lungs began to burn. Streaks of light darted across her eyes. She tried to kick back at her attacker, driving her elbows into unyielding flesh.

The hands tightened and tightened, and she slumped in her attacker's grasp, consciousness ebbing.

Chapter Seven

Casey swam slowly up to consciousness. She opened her eyes to almost total darkness. For a few moments she was disoriented. She tried to swallow and found her throat sore; then full awareness flooded, and she sat up with a cry of alarm, her hand going to her neck.

She looked around quickly. There was no one there, and the only sound was the whisper of the wind. She was still on the mesa, sitting within the stones forming the pentagram.

Why was she still alive? Had the attack been only a warning? And who had attacked her? Had her assailant been lying in wait for her, or come up here in search of something left behind at the time of the murder?

All pertinent questions, to which she had no ready answers.

An urgency seized her. She had to get out of here. She got to her feet with an effort and took a few stumbling steps before she remembered the flashlight; she would have a devil of a time getting back down the steep trail without the light. She had been holding it, switched on, at the moment she had been attacked. Could her attacker have taken it?

She moved a few steps in each direction, feeling for it with her feet. Then her right foot collided with it. She stopped down, retrieved it, pushed the switch. She felt a rush of relief when the light sprang to life.

Hurrying now, wishing nothing more than to get back to

the car, she headed down the path, expecting any second that a threatening figure would spring at her out of the surrounding darkness.

She made it back to the bottom of the trail and the road without incident. When she reached the car, she looked toward the spot where she had seen the other car. It was gone. More than likely the vehicle had belonged to her attacker, who must have been on the killing ground when she arrived.

Perhaps her attacker had assaulted her so he could make an escape without being seen or recognized. Somehow she didn't think her attacker had been female; there had been great strength in those squeezing hands. If it had been a woman, she possessed exceptional strength.

Casey hurried to her car, got in, locked the doors, and drove on toward the Enchantment with great relief.

The next day she met Gabe Stanton mid-morning at Midgley Bridge where it spanned Oak Creek on Highway 89, north of town. It was a popular tourist parking spot situated high over the river below.

When she arrived there were several vehicles already in the small parking area off to the left of the highway. Casey got out and walked to the edge of the small canyon, where it was shady and she could look down at the water. Gabe arrived a few minutes later.

As he parked and came toward her, Casey motioned with her head. He followed her down the narrow path leading to the creek. At the bottom, Casey led Gabe down the stream until they reached a place relatively isolated from the camera-snapping tourists.

"Good morning, Rena," Gabe said. "I got a call from Bob Wilson early this morning, just after you called and asked me to meet you here. He wanted to know what progress you were making."

She sighed. "I've had hardly enough time to turn around

and he's demanding progress. What does he expect, miracles?"

Gabe laughed. "Probably. I told him to cool it, give us some time. Also, he said if he didn't get a report from you soon, he'd call your hotel. I told him that I thought that wouldn't be wise." He grinned. "I'm sure he knows that, but I figure he's one of those people who feels he isn't doing his job if he doesn't apply pressure."

Casey sighed. "You've got that right. For someone who hasn't been working for the task force long, you have him pegged pretty good, Gabe."

"In the Army you meet types like that all time, always riding your ass with the idea that's the best way to get a job done," he said with his shy grin.

"Gabe, did you tell anyone aside from me about the murder site on the mountain?" She watched his face intently.

"Of course not! Why do you ask?"

"Well, I went up there late last night . . ."

"You didn't!" he said in dismay.

"I wanted a look at it, without the tourists. Sometimes you can get vibes."

"What happened, Casey? Something happened, didn't it?"

She sent a fast look around. "Rena, remember? And yes, something happened. Somebody sneaked up on me from behind and tried to strangle me."

"I warned you about going up there! You could have been killed! I should have gone with you."

"Any investigator runs a certain risk," she pointed out. "It's a part of the job. Look, as it stands, in case it comes up, I could always say I was scouting the mesa for a location for the movie. I might not be believed, but at least it's a possible explanation for my being there. Now suppose you were along. How could I explain being up there with a task force investigator?"

"Do you think your attacker is our killer?"

"I have no idea," she said with a shrug. "But it's a distinct possibility."

"Who else could it have been?"

"It could have been some person with more curiosity than good sense, getting a thrill from visiting a crime scene."

"Then why try to kill you?"

"I don't know that killing me was the intent. Whoever it was could simply not have wanted it known that he, or she, was there. After all, I could easily *have* been killed, but the attacker didn't finish the job."

"I think it *was* the killer," he said stubbornly.

Privately, she agreed with him, but didn't voice the thought.

"Anyway, my main worry is eased. If you didn't tell anyone else, no one could have even suspected I was up there. Which means my cover isn't blown. My attacker was up there for some purpose other than waiting to waylay me."

"I fail to see how much comfort that is," he said in a grumbling voice.

"It is to me. Well," she said briskly, "I have things to do. You wait here for a bit before you leave. The less we're seen together, the better."

As she started off he called after her, "Be careful now, you hear?"

She waved a hand over her head without turning, and continued on.

Casey walked briskly into the Steele Magnolia shortly after one o'clock. Vickie, wearing a green smock almost the exact shade of her eyes, was leaning on the counter by the cash register, talking on the telephone. Her gaze travelled to Casey, and she smiled in welcome, as she said something in a low voice into the receiver and hung up.

"Well, Rena! I didn't expect to see you so soon."

Casey said, "I thought I'd take you up on your offer. I'm

pretty much free this afternoon. I badly need a shampoo and set, and a manicure. If you can take me, that is, without an appointment?"

"I said I would, didn't I? I'll squeeze you in. In fact, I'll do you myself." A certain slyness invaded the other woman's eyes. "Maybe if I do a good job, I could land a bit part as a beauty operator in your movie."

"That's always a possibility." Once again, Casey improvised. "As it happens, there is a brief scene in the movie with a beauty operator. So far as I know, it hasn't been cast yet."

"Then come on, Rena, let's do it." Vickie led Casey to the last empty chair in the place.

Casey was glad to see that all the occupants of the other chairs had their heads buried in hair dryers, leafing through magazines in their laps.

When Casey's hair was washed and rinsed, and Vickie had begun the set, Vickie said: "How's the search for your locations going?"

"Quite well, so far," Casey said easily. "Of course, I've only started. I'll be here at least another two weeks. This is an important project for my producer, I want to be absolutely certain I've got it right."

"You must enjoy your job, going to different places all the time," Vickie said wistfully, head bent over Casey's nails. "I'm stuck here, never get away except for a week or so's vacation every year."

"It has its good points," Casey said. "On the other hand, it's a rather nomadic existence, one place for a few weeks, then on to the next. It would be nice to stay put for a change, get to know everybody, know what's going on."

"Believe me, I'd give all that up for a job like yours."

"Must be some aspects you like about your life here. For example, last night you mentioned something about some group you belong to. That sounds interesting."

Vickie's hands stopped moving, and she looked up warily. "Did I say that?"

"Well, yes, more or less. Do you think it's possible I could attend a meeting or two?"

Vickie hesitated. "I don't know, we're very careful who we take in, or even let attend."

Casey said casually, "What's it called, your group?"

Vickie hesitated again. "Children of the Enlightenment."

"Is it part of the New Age movement?"

"Not really, although it may have started out as that. I've only belonged for little over a year. I understand most members belonged to the New Age movement once, but it didn't give them what they needed. Children of the Enlightenment does."

"And what exactly is that?" Casey asked, trying to keep the excitement out of her voice.

Vickie spoke softly, busy again on Casey's hair. "Something we all seek. Like the name says, we seek enlightenment, how to direct and control our lives, how to get the things we want in life."

"And have you gotten all those things?"

"Some, not all. But I will, our Leader assures me that I will!" Vickie looked up, her eyes burning with a zealot's fire. "Other members have. It just takes time, is all!"

"Your leader? Who is that?"

Again, Vickie darted a furtive glance around, then leaned forward. "We don't know who he is: he always wears a mask."

"A mask?" Casey said in astonishment. "Why does he do that?"

"He tells us it is better we don't know his identity, that we can be more at ease if he remains anonymous."

"You keep saying *he*. Your leader is male then?"

Vickie thought for a moment. "I've always thought so, but I'm not one hundred percent sure."

"What exactly do you do at your get-togethers?"

Vickie shook her head vehemently. "Oh, I couldn't tell you that." She giggled. "That's secret. Only members are allowed to know that."

"Then how do I go about becoming a member?" Casey hoped she wasn't sounding too eager. Was it too much to hope that she would be allowed to join this quickly? Of course there was no assurance that the Children of the Enlightenment were involved in anything other than just what Vickie had said; but at worst she might, through them, connect with other groups.

Vickie was speaking. "Well, you have to be interviewed by the members of the council. They don't just take *anyone*, you know. And I don't think you should mention what you told me last night. You know, about one of the movie characters being a member of a cult. Despite the bad reputation cults have, our group doesn't do anything *really* bad, but some people might be shocked by some things we do."

"Such as?"

"Oh, we're pretty lax about sex. We're encouraged to be . . . well, free about it." She laughed archly. "Our Leader says that the way the blue-noses look on sex is silly. A person should feel free to do anything that gives them pleasure and joy."

Casey kept her gaze fixed on Vickie's face. "Many cults have sacrifices, I understand."

Vickie shrugged. "Oh, we sacrifice a chicken now and then, sometimes a goat . . . Oh!" Vickie clapped a hand over her mouth. "I told you I'm not supposed to tell you any secrets, and here I am blabbing away. But I feel like I know you so well, that you're already a member, Casey."

"That's okay, Vickie. I won't tell a soul. Will you help me?"

"Yes, I'll talk to one of the council members, at our next meeting, and get back to you." Vickie sat back. "There! All done."

A few minutes later Casey stood outside the beauty salon, blinking in the fierce glare of the sun. Putting on her sunglasses, she walked to her car.

She felt a sense of accomplishment. Of course, it still wasn't firm that a cult was behind the murders, and certainly nothing pointing to the Children of the Enlightenment. However, it was a beginning, a foot in the door.

As she drove away, her thoughts jumped back to Vickie Steele.

Casey had watched carefully when Vickie responded to the question about sacrifices and had detected no guile when the woman said the cult's sacrifices were only animals. Casey was almost sure that Vickie hadn't been lying. However, there was always the possibility that only the most trusted members, the inner core, so to speak, were privy to human sacrifices.

It was only the middle of the afternoon, but Casey decided to call it a day. In her estimation she calculated she had accomplished a great deal, and she needed a little downtime to think about and digest what she had learned; so she drove directly to the Enchantment.

As she stopped at the gate to let the guard examine the coloured card on the dashboard, she wondered just how secure she was here. Anyone could steal a hotel card and pass the guard's inspection without incident. Aside from that, it would be easy enough to bypass the gate on foot and approach her room through the trees.

Driving on, she gave vent to a soft snort. What reason would anyone have to do that? Insofar as she could tell, her cover was still intact. On the other hand, look at what had happened to her on the mesa last night.

She drove on with a shake of her head, parked as close to her room as she could, about fifty yards distant, and walked to the unit. She hadn't left anything that might indicate the presence of an intruder during her absence – a hair somewhere on the door, clothes hung a certain way in the closet, items stacked a certain way in the drawers, et cetera. What would be the use? The maids always came in to clean after she left in the mornings.

She shook her head again. She was becoming paranoid!

Inside the room she shucked her clothes and quickly got into her running suit. She left the room and jogged easily down the hill to the main road, turning left toward the main building. Running was not only good exercise, but she could clear her mind, concentrating only on putting one foot before the other. She often did her best thinking during a hard run.

It was a hot day, probably in the low nineties, and people observing her would likely think she was nuts. But the heat here was nothing compared to Phoenix in the summer, so it didn't bother her. She slowly picked up the pace. There were people on the golf course, and she heard the thunk of tennis balls on the courts to her left as she passed. Maybe it was too warm for others as well; tennis was more strenuous than running.

She ran for a half-hour. By the time she made it back to the road leading up to her room, she was soaked with sweat and breathing heavily, and by the time she made it up the hill to the room her thighs were trembling.

She passed the swimming pool on the way up and had noticed that it was empty. Mind occupied by how pleasant a swim would be about now, she failed to notice that her door was ajar until she had her key out. She froze, a chill racing down her spine. Who was inside? The room had been cleaned when she returned. She was debating what to do, when the sound of a footstep wrung a startled cry from her.

One of the bellmen appeared in the doorway, carrying a bucket of ice cubes. She said angrily, "You startled me!"

"I'm sorry, Miss Rainier. I was just bringing around the ice. We always do it around this time of the day."

"I didn't see your cart around anywhere."

"It's parked down behind the other units." He indicated the two rooms about thirty yards down the slope. "These are the last two rooms, and I thought it'd be easier than to drive up."

"Here, give it to me." He handed her the bucket, and turned away. She called after him, "Sorry I was sharp with you."

"It's okay, Miss Rainier," he said without turning.

It's not okay, she thought, as she went into the room and closed the door. She really *was* being paranoid, seeing danger behind every tree.

It wasn't like her to be so easily spooked. But there was something about this case, a feeling of dark evil, that she had never experienced before.

Chapter Eight

After a good night's sleep Casey had a light breakfast and left her room early; she needed to make two phone calls.

First, she called the Farrel Ranch in Chino Valley. Dan Farrel answered the phone.

"Uncle Dan?"

"Is that you, Casey?"

"It's me. How is everybody?"

"Fine, fine," Dan Farrel said heartily. "Donnie has been in the saddle so much, his skinny little butt is sore. Alice is fine, and so am I. I can't tell you how much we enjoy having Donnie stay with us, Casey." His voice changed. "How are you? How's the case coming along?"

"Slowly, Uncle Dan," she said with a sigh. "I was hoping it'd be a fast-breaker, but I've already realized that it's not to be."

"You aren't in any danger, are you?" he asked in a low voice.

She laughed lightly. "Nope, at least I hope not."

"Well, you be careful up there."

"I always am, Uncle Dan."

"That's not what Sergeant Whitney says."

"I know what Josh says, but Sergeant Whitney is a fuddy-duddy."

"Well, I know you want to talk to the boy. We're just finishing breakfast. Here he is."

Donnie said breathlessly, "Casey?"

"How you doing, kiddo?"

"I'm okay, Casey. I've been riding and all sorts of things."

"I'll just bet. Well, long as you're having fun."

"It's always great here, Casey. You catch the bad guy yet?"

"Not yet, kiddo. Give me time, will you?"

"You'll nail the perp soon. You always do."

"Always good to hear your vote of confidence," she said dryly. "I just wanted to check in with you. I'll call again in a day or so. You behave, mind Uncle Dan and Aunt Alice, you hear?"

"Aw, Casey. You talk like I'm just a little kid."

"Well, excuse me. I'd forgotten you're matured and all," she said. "Bye, kiddo. Talk to you soon."

She hung up, smiling, then immediately punched out Josh's home number in Phoenix, hoping to catch him before he went on shift. He answered on the second ring.

"Hello, Detective."

"Casey!" His tone was warm, intimate, and she felt good just hearing his voice, as she always did. "How goes the investigation, babe?"

"Not as fast as I'd hoped, but moving along. One thing I'm pretty convinced of now, a cult *is* involved. Gabe told me yesterday that the locals have evidence that the latest victim was killed on a mesa, on a crude altar in the centre of a pentagram . . ."

"Whoa, back up a minute. Who's Gabe?"

"Oh, didn't I tell you? Gabe Stinton's a new investigator Wilson hired. He sent him up to help me."

"Let me guess here. He's stalwart, handsome, and single, right?"

She had to laugh. "About single, I don't know, but the other two, yes. How'd you know?"

"Because you somehow always manage to wind up working with some good-looking stud."

"Do I detect a hint of jealousy, Detective?"

"You're goddamn right you do," he said in a grumbling voice. "How do you do it?"

"Just lucky, I guess."

"So how is this guy supposed to *help* you?"

"He's to be my conduit into the local police investigation. Since I'm undercover, I don't want to make myself known to the locals. Not just yet, anyway."

"You mean, one of them may be a rogue?"

"I don't think that at all. But haven't you heard the old saw? A secret known to two people or more is no longer a secret? Too many people already know about this particular secret, Josh."

"Why do I have the feeling you want something from me, that you didn't just call up to tell me how much you miss me?"

"But I *do* miss you, Josh. I always do when I'm away."

"Yeah, right."

"But I do need a favour. You happen to know anyone on the Sedona police?"

"Yeah, I know a guy. He once worked homicide with me here. Said he was fed up with all the blood and gore splashing the streets of Phoenix, wanted to work in a small, quiet town." Josh snorted laughter. "Now look at him! Three murders on his plate."

"Could you call and get some information out of him?"

"Now why should I do that? This ain't my case, I'm not paid to do chores for the Governor's Task Force on Crime."

"But we worked on the honky-tonk murders," she said teasingly. "I thought we did well together."

"Sure, until I ended up in the hospital, and you went on to solve the case, getting all the glory. So come up with another reason, babe."

"Because we're buds."

"Buds? Hah!" She heard his sigh over the line. "All right, all right. What do you want to know?"

"I need to know where the first two victims were killed. All I can learn from the press coverage was that it is believed they were killed somewhere other than where they were found."

"Why don't you get this Gabe guy to handle it?"

She hesitated, then said, "Gabe is far from an experienced investigator, Josh. The locals might wonder why he's digging for information not released yet. It might antagonize them, and close off all lines of communication."

"And my nosing in wouldn't?"

"It wouldn't really matter too much, would it? It's not your case."

He snorted. "There are a lot of flaws in your reasoning, babe, but I'll see what I can learn. If nothing else, it'll stop you from bugging me. Hopefully."

"I knew you'd come through. Old Reliable. Gotta go now. Love and kisses, Josh. Bye now."

She hung up, smiling softly. She always got a lift talking to Josh, and she could use a boost in her spirits right now. But if he ever found out about her going alone to the hilltop crime site last night, he'd bite her ear off and spit it out!

The next stop was the police station on Forest Road. Although she could not present herself as an investigator for the task force, it would be logical under her cover to introduce herself to somebody on the police force. The station was located in a small wooden building that resembled nothing so much as a fast food place, hardly in keeping with the present size and affluence of Sedona. She recalled reading somewhere that a larger, more fitting building was in the planning stages.

After showing her card to the woman at the reception counter, a tall, lean man in his forties, in a suit and tie, opened the single door and motioned her inside. The room was small, cramped, with a desk and two chairs.

The man held out his hand. "I'm Lieutenant Martin, Ms Rainier."

His handshake was warm, strong. Cool grey eyes set in a strong, deeply tanned face, studied her calmly.

Casey said, "I thought I'd pay you a courtesy call, Lieutenant. I'm here in Sedona scouting . . ."

"Scouting locations for a movie," he said with a spare smile. "News of your arrival has preceded you. I probably knew about it before you'd been here more than a few hours. Please be seated."

He motioned to the chair and went around behind his desk. "Now, how can I help you, Ms Rainier?"

Casey cautioned herself to tread carefully; this lieutenant was sharp. One slip and she'd be in excrement up to her knees.

"If you're looking for a permit to film," he continued, "that's not my department. But you shouldn't have any trouble in that regard. Most people are delighted to have a movie company here." The spare smile again. "It brings in money."

"Oh, it's a little early for that. I just thought I'd check in with you, get your input."

"Input regarding what?" he asked bluntly. "Does your movie involve the police? I hear it's not a Western."

Time to improvise again. "One of the main characters is a local policeman, yes. The story involves a woman fleeing from her husband, who is a psycho. She lands in Sedona, and asks this policeman for assistance."

His look was dark. "But how does a cult figure in your story?"

Casey blinked. "The Sedona grapevine is effective, isn't it?"

"It wouldn't be because of the recent murders, would it? If so, I'm afraid . . ."

"No, no," Casey said quickly. "The husband, see, was involved with a black cult back in California, where they lived as man and wife. So he gets in touch with a local cult, in the hope they can help him find his wife."

Lieutenant Martin, face expressionless, regarded her impassively for a few moments. "Then your movie isn't going to exploit the killings?"

"No, no, not at all. The suspense is all supposed to come from whether or not the husband can find the wife and kill *her*."

The officer appeared to relax a bit. "Then I can't see much harm in that."

"One thing I'm curious about," Casey said. "From what limited research I've done on Sedona, I've found a rather strange thing. The town is located in *two* counties, Yavapai and Coconino. Isn't that unusual? I don't recall running across that before."

Martin nodded. "Yeah, it is unusual."

"But doesn't that present problems? In law enforcement, I mean? You have two sheriff departments to contend with."

"Not that much of a problem. What happens within the city limits is handled by us. And both sheriff departments cooperate with us fully. Of course, I suppose you're referring to these murders. With a serious crime like that the sheriff's department comes into it. Frankly, we don't have the facilities to handle an investigation such as this. And this time both departments are involved, since two bodies were found in one county, the third in another. And we're using the lab facilities and other departments out of Flagstaff."

Casey spoke without thinking. "But you haven't made much progress toward solving the murders, have you?"

Martin reared back, his face turning hard and cold. "We're making progress. An arrest is imminent."

Police talk for no progress, Casey thought. As Josh had told her more than once: "When you're stumped, stonewall. Tell 'em you expect an arrest any day."

"Well, thank you for your time, Lieutenant." She got to her feet. "I'll get out of your hair."

Martin said curtly, "You're welcome, I'm sure. Good luck with your movie."

Leaving the police station, Casey found a camera shop and purchased a video camera. Then she drove up 89A to Slide Rock State Park. How could a movie be made in Sedona without a scene shot at Sedona's most scenic location?

The park was located on Oak Creek, the colourful rock formations soaring up from the creek bed. The clear water flowed over a series of small falls. None of the falls were high, and they created a natural water slide that provided an ideal place for children and adults to slide down to the stream below.

There was a fair crowd in the park, some enjoying picnics, others observing the water sliders and a large number taking pictures. The children and adults alike screamed in delight as they caromed down the watery rocks.

Casey strolled along the rocky banks of the creek, filming, working her way upstream. Soon, the river narrowed somewhat, and the rock slides were behind her. It was far less crowded here, although some people dawdled along, some striking off onto the many hiking trails. There were a few people fishing along the stream. She noticed one man out in the middle of the fast-running water, wearing waders, casting his line into the water. She stopped to watch him for a few moments. He was a slender man, probably in his late forties. He was wearing a fly caster's hat, with a casting flies stuck in the crown; the hat was pulled down so she couldn't see his features.

She turned the camera on him, filming, just as he turned and saw her. He raised a hand and yelled, "Hey, what are you . . .?"

He was interrupted by a shrill scream from upstream, and he spun around to look. Casey followed his gaze.

About thirty yards upstream a teenager in a skimpy bathing suit was standing staring down, hands over her mouth. She screamed again.

The man in the waders started splashing toward her, as did Casey. The man was closer, and he could go in a straight line, while Casey had to take a more circuitous route to avoid the water.

By the time she reached the spot, the girl in the bikini had turned, her face buried in the man's shoulder, sobbing wildly.

Breathless, Casey stopped beside the man, and stared down into a shallow pool, formed by creek water flowing between two smooth boulders.

A man, dressed only in shorts, lay on his back in the water, staring sightlessly up at the sky, his torso pale, except for a dark wound over his heart.

Casey shivered, hugging herself. The body had a waxen look. The man must have bled profusely, but the flowing water had long since washed it all away.

Chapter Nine

Someone had called the police, and a screaming siren could be heard in the distance, growing ever closer. A crowd had gathered within moments of the girl's scream.

Because of the crowd, Casey had managed to film the body without, she thought, attracting undue notice.

But the man in waders noticed and drew her to one side before the first cop car arrived. He motioned to the camera.

"You press?"

"Oh, no. I'm here . . ." She took out a card and gave it to the man.

He glanced at it. "Rena Rainier, is it? A film company?"

"Yes, I'm scouting locations for a film to be shot here." She added wryly, "I'm surprised you haven't heard. Everybody else seems to know."

"Nope, hadn't heard, but then I haven't been out much the past couple of days." He squinted at her from shrewd grey eyes set in a weathered face, and she revised her earlier estimate of his age. He was in his fifties somewhere.

"I saw you filming the body." His eyes held a suspicious glint.

She shrugged. "Just habit, I guess. Film people, carrying a camera, film everything in sight."

"Earlier, just before the girl screamed, I caught you filming *me*."

She gave him a smile she hoped was sincere. "First time

I've ever seen a fly fisherman in complete gear. How could I pass up the opportunity?"

He frowned at her for a moment, then a smile broke across his craggy face, relieving the stern cast of his features. "I'll accept that . . . just so long as I don't appear in your damned movie."

"I promise," Casey said solemnly.

He stuck out a hand. "Alex Haydon. I own the Haydon Stables, out on Dry Creek Road. Horses, riding lessons, the whole nine yards. Your movie an oater?"

"I'm afraid not."

"Just as well," he said with a shrug. "Don't much favour movie folks. Had a couple of bad experiences with them. Rubber cheques bounced all the way from here to Hollywood. Nothing personal."

"Nothing personal," she said gravely.

"But if you want to rent a horse, be glad to accommodate . . ." He broke off as the approaching siren died. "I see the cops have arrived." His gaze came back to her. "My guess is you don't much favour chatting with them. Questions could tie you up for hours."

"I'd just as soon not."

"Then I'd suggest you step over there and join the gawkers. Me and the little girl who found him can answer all their questions. No need to involve you."

"Thank you, Mr Haydon."

She moved over to join the growing crowd of onlookers. Looking up the creek, she saw that a second car had joined the first, and watched as Lieutenant Martin got out. All the police were heading this way. Casey moved back farther into the crowd, hoping the lieutenant wouldn't spot her.

The thought uppermost in her mind was, when had the body been placed here? She was positive that, like the other three, the victim had been killed somewhere else. But when? Late last night would be her guess, when the park was deserted. But how had it remained unnoticed all this time? With all the people walking around, it should have been noticed long before now. Of course, with all the near-naked bodies wandering about, anyone seeing it might have thought it was just someone sunbathing, or resting after some exhaustive time spent on the water slides. Also, in today's climate of "don't get involved", it was quite possible that some people had seen the dead body and decided it was best to just ignore it.

She decided it was time to leave. Lieutenant Martin and the other cops were all gathered around the body. The lieutenant was talking to Alex Haydon, and no one was looking her way. She slipped out of the crowd and started back toward where her rental was parked, and almost ran head-on into Gabe Stinton.

His eyes widened in astonishment. As he opened his mouth to speak, she shook her head slightly and walked on without breaking stride, resisting a powerful impulse to turn and look back.

Casey called Gabe several times that afternoon and evening, but was unable to get through to him. She spent a nervous night speculating on why he had been at the park, and what, if anything, he knew. There had been a brief mention on the TV news last night of an unidentified man's body found in Oak Creek, but the information was sketchy.

Casey finally got through to Gabe at his motel room early the next morning and a meeting was arranged at the bridge again.

Gabe was already there when Casey arrived, standing on the edge of the canyon, looking down. He acknowledged her with a slight nod and started down the winding trail to the water. Casey let him get a good lead, then followed him down. At the bottom he turned right, walking along the rocks. He stopped at a spot isolated from the occasional tourist.

When Casey stopped beside him, he said, "Sorry, Rena.

I'm sure you've been calling, but I didn't get back to the motel until nearly midnight last night." He looked at her. "What were you doing down there anyway?"

"Nothing more than a coincidence. I certainly didn't know a body would be found there. Why were you there?"

"I was at the station when the call came in, and they let me tag along. I'm getting in pretty thick with the guys there, and with the Coconino County Sheriffs, too. They let me attend the autopsy on the victim. Had to go all the way to Flagstaff for that. That's why you couldn't reach me."

"What did you find out?" she asked eagerly. "He was stabbed in the heart, right? Just like the other three victims?"

"You've got it!"

"Then clearly they're all connected."

"That's my opinion, yeah. But the cops aren't admitting that publicly as yet. Afraid there'll be a panic." Gabe grinned, faintly smug. "But there is a definite connection between this victim and the last one, Barbara Stratton. It seems that Stratton and the dead man worked together."

"But how can they know that so soon? All the victim had on was his shorts!"

"They got lucky. He flew into Sedona two days ago, and stayed at a motel. His name was Leo Thornesburg, and he was a vice president in charge of sales for Camden Industries. Apparently, he was highly suspicious about Stratton's death, and decided to come up here and look into it personally. He told some associates about his suspicions, as well as his wife. He also told his wife that he would call her every night before midnight. And if he didn't call, she should contact the police. Well, midnight came and went last night and he didn't call. She rang the motel, had them check his room. He wasn't in; so she then called the police station here and reported what her husband had said. They weren't too concerned, thinking it was just a case of an out-of-town husband picking up some bimbo and spending the night with her; but when the nameless body was found yesterday alarm bells went off. Lieutenant Martin immediately faxed a picture of the dead man to LA, and the wife identified the victim as her husband."

Casey said thoughtfully, "Do you suppose he was killed because he got too close to the killer or killers?"

Gabe shrugged. "If so, he must have been a hell of an investigator; he was only here two days. Of course, it may be simply a coincidence. They've never been able to come up with any connection between any of the other victims."

"A homicide cop I know says there's no such thing as a coincidence," she said with a grin.

He shook his head. "Still, I can't get past the fact that the last two victims *were* connected. It has to mean something.

"Thornesburg may have only been here two days; but what if he already knew something, something he had learned back in Los Angeles?"

Casey's eyes widened. "Maybe you're onto something," she said slowly. "We'll have to look into that." She gave him a wide smile. He smiled back, looking pleased.

"Did you learn anything else of interest?"

Gabe shook his head. "No, that about covers it. But I'm working closely with the locals now. Lieutenant Martin is very cooperative, and I'm sure he'll pass on anything he learns; which I'll admit surprises me. I've heard that locals usually resent the hell out of a task force investigator nosing in."

"Often, that's true. But not always. It often depends on the situation and the personalities involved. Also, in this case, the local investigators have been handed a hot potato. Serial murders are something new for Sedona, and they're probably happy to accept any help they can get. Keep in close touch, Gabe." She smiled warmly. "You're doing great."

His quick shy grin came. "I'm just glad it's you working with me, Cas . . . uh, Rena, instead of someone else."

She arched an eyebrow. "Even if I'm a woman?"

He became grave, his gaze holding hers. "Especially because you're a woman."

She felt a rush of warmth, and she recalled Josh's question. She started to ask Gabe if he was married, then angrily shoved that thought out of her mind and got back to business.

"I suppose that this last victim, too, wasn't killed where he was found; have they found the spot where he *was* killed?"

He shook his head. "Not so far as I know, but they do think that at least one of the other victims was killed at the same place the woman was. There were two types of blood smeared on that stone."

Casey nodded. "Well, that's something. You're doing a great job, Gabe. Thanks."

He looked as if he was about to say something, but she looked away, down at her watch. "Okay, Gabe, I'm going now. You stay down here for a few minutes, give me time to get well away."

With a nod she turned on her heel and made her way up the steep path for the parking lot and her car.

At the Steele Magnolia, Vickie was busy with a customer in the back, but when she saw Casey she said something to her customer and made her way to the front, her face lighting with a smile.

"Rena! Good morning. What can I do for you? All the chairs are occupied at the moment, but I can slip you in shortly."

Casey smiled back. "No, nothing like that. It's just that I may have to fly back to Los Angeles and have a meeting with my producer, and I wanted to let you know that I'd be gone for a few days."

Vickie made a sound of dismay. "Oh, you're not leaving?"

"No, no, I'll be back. A day or so at the most. But I was

wondering . . . Is your group meeting soon? And have you found out if I'd be welcome to attend?"

"The next meeting won't be until next week, Tuesday night."

"Good. I'll be back by then."

"As for your attending, I haven't been able to confirm that yet, but I'm sure there'll be no problem, so long as I vouch for you, and that I'll be more than happy to do. I just know you'll be a welcome addition to our group."

"That's nice of you to say, Vickie. And I do appreciate it. I'll call you the minute I get back."

Vickie's face assumed a worried look. "I hope there's no problem, something that may have changed their minds about shooting here."

"Oh, no, nothing like that. Just that a few changes have been made in the script, necessitating some additional locations. That's always happening with movies. We'll film here, don't worry."

Vickie clapped her hands. "I certainly hope so." She added wistfully, "Will you see if I can be worked into the film? Maybe just a few lines. I've always felt I could act in movies."

You and just about everybody else, Casey thought. She said, "I'll do my best for you, Vickie. After all, you're doing me a favour, the least I can do is to return it."

Deep in thought, head down, Casey left the beauty salon and almost collided with a figure just outside. She glanced up into the smiling face of Wesley Strom. His blue eyes twinkled merrily at her. "I was driving past and thought I saw you enter Vickie's, Rena. Thought maybe I'd catch you and say hello." His left hand stroked Pookie, cradled in his arms. "I was taking Pookie to the vet's for his semiannual shots."

"Hello, Wesley," Casey said warily. Had he really been driving past, or had he been following her? Or was she getting paranoid again?

Wesley continued, "I was wondering how your location hunt is progressing."

"It's progressing. Slowly. My boss wants it to be the best movie he can make, so I'm supposed to make sure of the best locations for every scene."

Wesley bobbed his head in approval. "Glad to see dedication in movie folk. All too often they go at everything slipshod, and it shows up in the finished product."

"In fact, I may be flying back to Los Angeles for a day or two. There have been some script changes, new scenes written, requiring additional locations."

"But you'll be back."

"Oh, yes, definitely."

"I guess you heard about the latest murder?" His bright eyes peered at her inquisitively.

"I heard, it was on the TV news last night."

"Terrible, terrible." He shuddered theatrically. "I don't know what Sedona is coming to. The result of all this uncontrolled growth, I say. Too many people come in, the crime rate goes up."

"I'm not sure you can blame it on population growth, Wesley. From what I gather, it's probably a serial killer, and they can pop up anywhere."

"My, my, Rena, you sound like you know about serial killers."

Casey shrugged. "Not that much. But I have read a lot about them, novels and such. Serial killers seem to be the phenomenon of our time."

"That's true, unfortunately." He sighed, squeezing Pookie's neck until the animal yelped. Wesley said contritely, "Sorry, sweetheart. I guess I'd better take her for her shots, before she pees on me." He waved a hand airily. "Nice to run into you, darling. Be careful in LaLa Land. It's a wicked city out there."

The rest of the day Casey spent driving around the area, taking a great many shots of various possible locations for filming. She had a quiet chuckle over that. She was really into her role as a location scout; at least she should be convincing to anyone who might be watching her. She kept an eye out for anyone shadowing her, but she didn't see anyone. Of course it was difficult to be sure, what with all the tourist traffic.

All the while she was mulling over what she had just told Vickie and Wesley, and the idea that Gabe had put into her mind. It was obvious that, without really deciding it, she was going to LA. She wasn't certain that there was enough of a reason; but somehow it felt right. There was a connection there, she knew it in her gut!

The trouble with this undercover assignment was that she couldn't go about her investigation the usual way. In LA she could again become Casey Farrel, task force investigator, if only for a little while.

Here in Sedona, at the moment, she was spinning her wheels. In this particular case the only lead they had was the possible cult connection. She could only learn about cult activity by joining or attending a meeting of such a group; and that appeared to depend on Vickie. Since the next meeting of Vickie's group was not until next Tuesday, Casey felt that she should be doing something useful. Great rationalization, kid! She smiled to herself.

Late in the afternoon, before heading back to the Enchantment, she stopped at a pay phone and called Bob Wilson in Phoenix.

"Los Angeles!" he bellowed. "Why in God's name do you have to traipse off to LA? Last big case you were on you had to go all the way to Nashville! Or so you claimed."

"I did have to. And I solved the case, didn't I?"

"Damnit, Farrel, you know how tight our budget is," he grumbled. "And I suppose you'll want to stay at the Beverly Hills Hotel!"

She smiled to herself. To hear Wilson rant, one would think all expense monies came out of his own pocket. She said, "I'll make do with a medium-priced motel this time. I think I may be able to pick up a lead or two, Bob. There's a connection between the last two victims; they both worked for Camden Industries. Therefore, it will be worth my time, and your expense, to make the trip."

"Not *my* expense, damnit, Farrel, the taxpayers'! When will you get that through your head?"

"Soon, I'm sure. You've told me often enough." Of course, she knew very well that Wilson didn't give a hoot for the taxpayers' money; he just trumpeted about it to everybody who would listen, hoping that the word would get back to the Governor about how thrifty he was with the State's money.

"Okay, okay, go to Los Angeles," he said now in a grumbling voice. "But you'd better show some results, or I'm not going to be at all happy."

"I'll watch every penny, Bob. Trust me."

"Yeah, sure."

"Will you call Gabe Stinton and tell him I'll be out of town for a couple of days? I want to keep all contact with him at a minimum."

"Yeah, yeah, I'll take care of it."

Casey hung up, smiling broadly. It always raised her spirits considerably when she got the best of Bob Wilson; it happened all too seldom.

On the way to the Enchantment she passed by a wooden archway over a road to her left. On the archway wooden letters spelled out: Haydon Ranch. She slowed and found a place to turn around about a hundred yards down the road. It was still early; she had time to see if she could talk to Alex Haydon. The fact that he had been there, in Oak Creek, when the body was found, kept nagging at her.

She rattled over the cattleguard and drove about a half mile down a gravel road before reaching a large clearing.

A fairly new redwood ranch house sprawled to the right and low horse barns and corrals were to the left. Several vehicles were parked by the corrals, and several people were perched on the top rail of one corral. She parked the rental and got out, carrying her camera. She began filming before she got to the corral.

Then she hung the camera around her neck and peered in through the corral rails. There were two horses in the corral. Alex Haydon stood by one animal, a young woman beside him. Haydon was gesturing and talking to the woman. A saddle had been thrown on the horse, and Haydon was tightening the cinch. After listening for a few moments Casey gathered that he was demonstrating to the woman the fine points of saddling a mount.

Finished with the saddle, Haydon gave the woman a hand up onto the horse. A youth wearing a stained, rolled Stetson and worn cowboy boots, swung open the corral gate. The woman on the horse flicked the reins, and her mount trotted through.

Haydon came through the corral gate, his boots kicking up dust. The youth closed the gate behind him. Haydon took off his Stetson and used a red handkerchief to mop the sweat from his face. Then his gaze found Casey. His grey eyes widened, he returned the Stetson to his head, and came over to her.

"Miss Rainier, ain't it?"

Casey nodded. "That's right, Mr Haydon. How are you?"

"I'm fine, young lady. And how goes your search for filming locations?"

"Getting there. This could be ideal for a couple of scenes." She swept her hand around. "Working ranch, catching the flavour of the area."

Haydon smiled sparely. "Not a working ranch in terms of cattle. About the only cattle ranches you'll find are up on the Rim. This is more in the nature of a dude ranch, although I don't provide anything other than horses, or a guide if required."

"I think it might do for our purposes." She met his gaze squarely. "I wanted to thank you for keeping me out of the loop yesterday, so I wouldn't be tied up with questions."

He blinked at her lazily. "No reason you should have been. You didn't know anything that would help their investigation, did you?"

Casey shook her head. "No, nothing. Did you happen to know the victim, Mr Haydon? I understand he's been identified. Leo Thornesburg, from Los Angeles."

"Nope, didn't know the poor guy," he said blandly. "Complete stranger to me."

"Speaking of strange, didn't it strike you as odd that a dead man wearing only shorts could have lain there all that time without anyone noticing."

He studied her for a moment, then nodded. "Yes, you're right. It is strange, but not without precedent. In today's society, a dead body could lie for hours on a busy street, and no one would acknowledge it."

"Unfortunately, you're right." Uneasily, Casey noticed that Haydon was staring at her intently.

He said, "I thought yesterday that you looked familiar, today, even more so. Have we ever met, Miss Rainier?"

Casey's heart gave a lurch. After several successful investigations Casey had gotten considerable media coverage. She had been interviewed on television, and her picture had appeared in various newspapers and magazines. She had known, going in, that there was some danger of her being recognized, but she had hoped, with the considerable change she had made in her appearance . . .

She forced a laugh. "I've never met you before yesterday, Mr Haydon." Then she added another falsehood to the long list. "Maybe you saw me in a movie once. I did a few bit parts before becoming 'legitimate'."

"No, that wouldn't be it. I stopped going to movies when

they started splashing blood and gore and having sex right up there on the screen." He shrugged. "Well, it doesn't matter, does it? Maybe you look like someone else."

Still shaken, she was happy to make her escape.

Back at the Enchantment, she stopped at the desk and informed the clerk that she was making a two-day trip to Los Angeles but wanted to retain her room. If Bob Wilson found out, he would have a hissie, but she didn't want to chance losing it.

In her room she called the airport and made a reservation for an early flight to Phoenix for the next morning. Then she called Phoenix and reserved a seat on a late flight to Los Angeles. She needed a few hours in Phoenix before continuing on.

Chapter Ten

From Sky Harbour Airport in Phoenix, Casey took a cab to the condo she had recently purchased. Josh had loaned her the money for the down payment, for which she would always be grateful. The building was located in a nice residential area in North Phoenix only a twenty-minute drive from Josh's house. She had left most of the clothes she had been wearing in Sedona in her room at the Enchantment. Now she wanted to shed her Rena Rainier persona and return to being Casey Farrel.

Arriving at the condo, she first called Josh at the station. He wasn't available, so she left a message for him to call her. She had taken a shower and changed clothes and was in the process of packing a bag for the Los Angeles trip when he called back.

"Casey! How come you're back so soon? Have you broken the case already? Not that I'm not glad you're back, babe."

"No, I haven't broken the case. I have to make a quick trip to Los Angeles."

"Los Angeles?" he echoed in disbelief. "Why in hell do you have to visit the city of nuts and fruitcakes?"

"How about buying me lunch and I'll fill you in?"

"I'd love to buy you lunch, babe." He injected a leer into his voice. "Maybe we could do a little something *before* lunch to work up a strong appetite?"

"I already have a strong appetite, Detective," she said tartly.

"I was afraid of that," he said with a sigh. "Pick you up in about an hour."

"I'll be packed and ready. Then you can drive me to the airport after we eat."

They ate lunch at a coffee shop.

As they ate hamburgers in a booth across from each other, Josh beamed happily at her. "Good to see you, Casey. How goes the undercover bit?"

"All right, I guess. One thing I didn't realize, you have to lie a lot."

Josh threw back his head and laughed heartily. "That you do, that you do. I thought about that, knowing how you like always to tell the truth, no matter whose gonads get caught in the crusher in the process."

"Did you learn anything from your friend on the Sedona police?"

"Not a whole hell of a lot, I'm afraid. It seems there's not much to learn. Oh, I did find out that they haven't located the murder scene of the first two victims. The third one, yeah . . ."

"I know about that. Gabe told me."

He squinted at her. "Gabe did, did he? You mean, he might make a good investigator?"

"He'll do," she said cryptically. She wondered if she should tell him about her encounter on top of the mountain, but only briefly; she knew very well how he would react to that.

"Then if this Gabe is so damned good, you don't need any help from me," he said, assuming an injured tone.

"Now don't start that again, Josh!" she said in exasperation.

"Okay," he said, grinning. Then he sobered. "I heard about the fourth murder."

"That's the reason for my quick trip to LA."

He finished chewing a bite of hamburger, and leaned back, now intent. "Suppose you tell me about it, Casey."

Quickly, she sketched in the connection between the last two victims. "It's the only connection that's been found," she said.

Josh shrugged. "Besides the fact that all four have been affluent, and all had important positions."

Casey nodded. "There's that, of course, but if that's relevant, I have yet to figure it out. What I'm hoping to learn in Los Angeles is, did either Stratton or Thornesburg let drop any hints there that might provide a clue. I particularly want to talk to Thornesburg's wife. Thornesburg told her that if something happened to him, she should immediately contact the Sedona police. He may have told her more than that. After all, he went to Sedona because he was suspicious of *something*."

"But surely someone there asked her about that."

"I'm sure they did. But from what Gabe told me, they learned nothing more."

Josh grinned. "And you think she'll talk to you?"

"It's possible. Haven't you told me that a face to face with a witness is always better than a telephone interrogation? And, as you've also pointed out, women are more likely to talk to other women."

"Did I tell you that? I've got to watch it, you're always throwing my words back in my face," he said with a laugh. "But you're right, of course. It could even be that Thornesburg said something that his wife might not regard as important."

"And he could well have done the same to someone else in the firm. The thing is, I hate it when I have to interrogate someone who has just lost a loved one. It always strikes me as ghoulish."

"It goes with the territory, babe. Besides, I'm sure the wife will cooperate fully. Certainly she'll want her husband's killer caught."

Finished with his burger, Josh took a last drink of his Coke. "Do you still believe that some cult is behind the murders?"

"More so than ever. In fact, I have to get back to Sedona fairly promptly. I've met a woman who's a member of this group, the Children of the Enlightenment. I've made friends with her, and she's promised to get me into a meeting so I can see if I want to join."

"The Children of the Enlightenment, huh?" Josh snorted laughter. "Sounds like something we could all use, enlightenment. Want to bet it's just a bunch of nutcases gathering to bay at the moon, maybe have a little kinky sex. Hey, babe, you'd better watch it. They may have you engaging in all kinds of orgies."

"I've never believed that sex is a group sport . . ."

"I know, that's one thing I've always liked about you." He reached across the table to take her hand. "A one on one kind of woman. *My* kind of woman. Depend on it."

She let her hand remain in his grasp. "Although I have few details yet, I think this group is a little more serious than that. I've done quite a bit of reading on the subject. Many authorities believe there are a number of satanic cults active, and that some of them kill humans as sacrifices, to solicit favours from the Devil. There was that group in Mexico – they performed a mass killing, remember. It was in the papers. And some teenagers in the mid-west that killed another boy. It's not that far-fetched."

Josh shook his head. "I know. That's why I warned you to tread carefully. If you're right, and they find out who you really are, *you* may end up as one of their sacrifices, Casey. Depend on it."

Casey felt an icy shudder slide down her spine. "Believe me, I fully intend to be careful." *Sure* you are, a small voice hooted in her mind; like going up alone to the killing ground the other night?

Josh picked up the cheque. "Well, if you're going to catch your plane, we'd better get going."

The last thing he said to her at the boarding gate was,

"Luck out there, babe. And think about stopping off overnight, huh, on your way back through Phoenix."

"I'll think about it, Detective."

She put her hands on each side of his face, pulled his head down, and kissed him on the lips.

A half-hour later the plane had reached cruising altitude. Casey unbuckled her seat belt and adjusted her seat more comfortably. She accepted a vodka and tonic from the flight attendant and took a sip, her thoughts moving ahead.

Los Angeles.

Black memories flooded her mind. She hadn't been back to Los Angeles since leaving there four years ago, when she had sworn she would never return.

Of course what had happened couldn't be blamed on the city. She had been young, naive and a virgin, just graduated from Northern Arizona University in Flagstaff. Her mother, a full-blooded Hopi Indian, had died when Casey was fifteen, and her father, a pilot, had died in a crash over the Grand Canyon four months before Casey graduated. She had no brothers or sisters. The only relatives she had known about at the time had been on her mother's side, all living on the Hopi Reservation; and bad blood existed there because her mother had married a white man.

After graduation, she found that jobs were scarce in Flagstaff. Since there was no place else she really wanted to be, she thought she would try Los Angeles, where, she had read, there were good jobs available, and lots of sunshine.

And LA lived up to the promise. She soon found a job in Beverly Hills, as assistant to the head of a large private investigative firm.

Always an avid reader of mystery novels, especially Chandler and Hammett, she associated excitement and glamour with the business. Actually, there was little that was exciting connected with the work, which consisted mainly of credit and background checks, divorce cases, and investigative work for insurance firms.

Despite this, Casey found that she had a knack for the work. She had a logical and deductive mind, and found herself intrigued by the more complicated cases. Solving a crime, she found, was often like solving a puzzle, with the added reward of knowing that she was, usually, helping someone.

Another attraction was the owner of the firm, a handsome, charming man, with a rakish bent, in his forties. He was obviously taken with Casey, and she fell in love with him, her first love, her first affair. It ended in disaster. She became pregnant, and her lover, refusing to accept any responsibility, had taken another lover the week Casey told him about the pregnancy.

Crushed, Casey quit her job, and returned to Arizona, this time opting for Phoenix, where there was more work than in the smaller towns.

Then came the abortion! It had been an agonizing decision, but at the time she could see no viable alternative.

After the abortion, she felt that she had lost control of her life, it was slipping away from her. Not many months after returning to Arizona, she found herself temporarily jobless, without funds, reduced to sleeping in her car. One night, sleeping in an alley, she had witnessed a serial killer dropping one of his victims into a dumpster. This had resulted in her meeting Joshua Whitney and Donnie, whom she later adopted. In effect, Josh had rescued her; he had been instrumental in her getting the job as investigator for the Governor's Task Force on Crime. She owed him a great deal.

In the end things had turned out all right. She had Donnie and her job, and Josh, if she could ever decide she wanted to marry him. Even the experience in Los Angeles had given her something: experience at investigative work.

Yet the memory of Los Angeles was still bitter. No matter

how right she may have been about having the abortion, she was never completely free of guilt. Donnie's arrival in her life had helped, but sometimes when she looked at him with love, she couldn't help thinking about what her baby, her own flesh and blood, would have been like.

She was aroused from her reverie by the announcement of their imminent arrival at LAX. As she sat up, buckling her seat belt, she knew she still experienced a reluctance to return to LA. She could, she told herself, wait in the airport and book the first flight back to Phoenix.

But when she walked through the boarding gate she headed directly for the car rental counter; all she had brought with her was a carry-on bag.

The flight from Phoenix had been a short one, so there was plenty of daylight left when she drove out of the airport. Camden Industries was located in Beverly Hills. The Thornesburg residence was also located there, only a few miles from the office building.

Casey had forgotten about the horrendous traffic in LA and all adjoining cities. It was now into the evening rush hour, and vehicles were lined up bumper to bumper. Drivers in Phoenix were always complaining about the terrible traffic on the freeways and surface streets, but in Casey's estimation it was nothing like LA traffic. It took her almost two hours to make it to the motel on Pico Boulevard, where she had made reservations, and it was close to the dinner hour by the time she was checked in and shown to her room.

Perhaps it wasn't too late to arrange a meeting with Evelyn Thornesburg. The number was listed in the telephone book. Before Casey did anything else, she called the number.

A woman answered. "Hello?" The voice was raw, husky.

Casey said, "Mrs Thornesburg?"

"Yes, this is Evelyn Thornesburg."

"Mrs Thornesburg, my name is Casey Farrel. I'm an investigator with the Governor of Arizona's Task Force on Crime. We're investigating your husband's death. I realize this is a very bad time for you, and I'm sincerely sorry for that. But time is of the essence on cases such as this. I need to ask you some questions. Can you spare me some time? Perhaps tomorrow?"

"I don't know what I can tell you," the woman said dully.

"It would be most helpful if you could spare me an hour, no more than that."

"Are you calling from Arizona?"

"No, I'm here, in California. I'm at a motel not far from you."

"Could you come over this evening?"

"That would be great, if it's no imposition."

"I want to do whatever I can to catch the bastard who killed Leo!" Evelyn Thornesburg said vehemently.

"What time should I be there?"

The woman was silent for a moment. "Well, a neighbour is here now, helping me fix dinner for the kids. It might be better if we wait until they're bedded down for the night. Would ten be all right, or is that too late? I won't be able to sleep anyway."

Casey's voice quickened. "Ten will be just fine."

The other woman gave terse directions on how to find her house before hanging up.

Casey quickly unpacked, shucked her clothes, and took a shower. She had noticed a restaurant a few blocks away. She would have time for a relaxing drink and a leisurely dinner before keeping her appointment.

At least Evelyn Thornesburg seemed willing, even eager to cooperate, Casey thought with a feeling of relief. Often, she had found that not to be the case. Sometimes a close relative of a murder victim was too overcome with grief to talk to anyone, much less the police.

Chapter Eleven

Although there had been some changes in the areas surrounding it, Casey found Beverly Hills as gracious as she remembered it: the large, beautifully landscaped lots; the gracious homes; the up-scale shopping areas; all exuded an aura of elegant gentility.

The Thornesburg residence was located in a large lot set back from the street. Casey drove up a curving driveway and stopped before a low, sprawling, Spanish-style house with a red-tiled roof. Off to her left, on the south side of the house, separated from the driveway by a redwood fence, she saw light glinting off a swimming pool.

She estimated the house was easily worth a million, even in the current depressed real estate market in Southern California. But then Leo Thornesburg had been a vice president at Camden Industries, so he probably drew down a more than ample salary.

The house was dark, except for a faint glow coming through the stained glass panels of the front door. Casey mounted the steps to the porch and pressed the bell. She could hear it ringing inside: deep, mellow tones. A full minute passed. She pressed the bell again.

This time she heard the shuffle of footsteps. The door opened a crack, held in place by a chain. She saw the pale glow of a face in the crack, and a strained voice said, "Yes?"

"Mrs Thornesburg? I'm Casey Farrel. We have an appointment?"

The door closed, Casey heard the chain being slipped out of the slot, and then the door opened fully. A light went on in the foyer.

Casey stepped inside, and the woman admitting her immediately closed and rechained the door.

She turned a pale face to Casey. "I'm sorry for being so careful, but after what you told me on the phone, I'm frightened."

"I don't think you need to be, Mrs Thornesburg," Casey said reassuringly, "but it doesn't hurt to be careful."

They studied one another for a moment. Evelyn Thornesburg was in her mid-forties, Casey judged, slender, too thin, dressed in tan slacks and a wrinkled, cream blouse. Her face was narrow, and would have been pretty except for the lines of strain and signs of recent weeping. Her brown hair was stringy, unkempt.

Suddenly, her brown eyes flooded with tears. She half turned away, bringing a sodden piece of tissue to her eyes. In a choked voice she said, "I . . . I'm sorry. I can't seem to stop crying."

Casey said sympathetically, "It's understandable. It must be a terrible shock."

Evelyn Thornesburg made a visible effort to get her emotions under control. She said, "I really don't know what I can tell you that will help in any way."

Casey smiled. "I've often found that people know more than they think they do."

"Well, let's go into the living room where we can talk in comfort." She started off to the left, and Casey followed her. Evelyn said back over her shoulder, "Would you like anything? A drink? Or I have a pot of coffee on."

"Coffee would be just fine."

The living room of the Thornesburg house could have been taken right out of a woman's magazine. It was large, with a picture window in one wall overlooking the swimming pool. The furniture was Spanish in style, heavy pieces upholstered in soft leathers. The room was immaculate, nothing out of place, all furniture surfaces polished to a high gloss.

It should have been a comfortable looking room, but it struck Casey as being too perfect, too neat, as if it had been cleaned only minutes ago.

Evelyn motioned to the couch. "Please have a seat. I'll get the coffee. Cream and sugar?"

"Black, please."

The woman nodded and disappeared through an archway to the right. Casey sat down with a sigh. She was tired; it had been a very long day. Evelyn was gone for quite a while. When she finally returned, carrying a tray with a pot of coffee and two cups, Casey noticed that she had occupied part of the time making some repairs to her appearance. She had run a comb through her hair, and added a touch of colour to her lips. She put the tray on the coffee table before the couch, filled the cups, then sat down.

As Casey picked up her cup, Evelyn said brightly, "That's pure Columbian, I ground the beans myself."

Casey gazed down into the cup. The aroma was rich and flavourful. Casey took a sip. "Very nice." She set the cup down and faced the woman sitting next to her. "First, Mrs Thornesburg, I understand from our investigator in Sedona that you told the police your husband said he believed there was something strange about the death of Barbara Stratton."

Evelyn pursed her lips. "I don't know about strange, but Leo told me he didn't believe Barbara was the victim of a serial killer."

Casey nodded. "And I also understand he told you that if you couldn't contact him in a reasonable length of time, you were to call the Sedona police. Is that substantially correct?"

"That's what he told me, yes." Tears misted Evelyn's eyes again, and she looked away.

Casey waited a decent interval for the woman to get herself under control before continuing. "Then he evidently knew, or at least suspected, that he might be placing himself in some danger?"

"Yes, he did."

"Did he explain why he thought that?"

"No," Evelyn said with a shake of her head. "I tried to get more out of him, but that's all he'd say. I told him that if he thought he might be harmed, he shouldn't go. I told him he should think first of me and the children . . ." She broke off, looking away. "All he would say was that he had to do this, that he owed it to Barbara."

To change the subject for a moment, Casey said, "How old are your children?"

Evelyn brightened. "Brian is fourteen, Diana twelve. I don't know what we're . . ." She broke off, giving her head a fierce shake. "Without Leo I don't know how we're going to manage."

"Surely he had insurance? And he had a good paying job."

"He'd only been VP for five years, and most of the money he's been earning went into the house and . . . things. There *is* an insurance policy, but I don't know how much it's for."

Another family where the man handled all of the business, Casey thought to herself. It was always surprising, in this day, to find women who knew nothing about their husband's business, or the family finances. Casey had seen it before: intelligent women, capable women, who had no idea what their husbands made; how much was invested and where; how much was owed. If the husband died, the woman was left not only with that sorrow, but the worry and work that was necessary to unscramble the family finances. Sometimes, families who had thought themselves well off, found that they had been living in a house of cards, which came crashing down when the man was no longer there to prop it up. The victim of a homicide was often not the only victim; wives and children also suffered greatly.

She said, "Getting back to something you said a moment ago, you told me your husband believed that Stratton wasn't the victim of a serial killer; did he explain that?"

"No, he didn't," Evelyn said slowly. "I asked, but all he'd say was that I didn't need to know. He said the less I knew the better."

Casey felt a tug of disappointment. She'd been so hopeful that this trip would provide vital information. Was it all a waste of time? She said, "He could have meant that you might be in danger if he told you."

"I came to that conclusion, thinking about it after I learned he'd been . . . been killed." Evelyn was silent for a few moments, gazing off. Then her glance came back to Casey. "But I'm convinced that all this is connected with something here. Something that had happened, or was about to happen. The cause of both Barbara and Leo being murdered, I mean."

Casey leaned forward alertly. "What makes you think that?"

Evelyn gave a helpless shrug. "I don't know! I've thought about it and thought about it, but . . . It's just a feeling I have."

"Sometimes feelings like that are valid. Such feelings, hunches, intuition, whatever, have often helped me solve a case. Maybe if we think about it together, it'll become clear. Now, do you think it might have something to do with his job at Camden Industries?"

"It must have. If the two deaths are connected, it must have something to do with Leo's job. That's the only contact Leo ever had with Barbara. The only times we ever saw her outside the office were at a couple of Christmas parties, and once at a company Fourth of July barbecue."

"What did you think of Barbara Stratton, Evelyn?"

"I didn't like her one bit," the other woman said vehemently. "She was a cold bitch, arrogant, considered herself several notches above any of the Camden wives. She was ambitious, willing to step on anybody's face to get ahead."

"Did she have a husband, children?"

Evelyn shook her head. "No, although I understand that she was married once."

"Did she play around? Have affairs with any of the officers in the company?"

Evelyn hesitated. "I don't know for certain, but there was talk that she had. It seemed to be common knowledge that she was promiscuous."

"How many officers, vice presidents, at Camden?"

Evelyn hesitated, rolling her eyes ceiling-ward. "Let's see . . . Three, aside from Leo and Barbara."

"I don't even know what Camden produces."

"Electronics. They're very big in electronics."

"How about the president of the company? Who is he?"

"Grady Camden. He started the company about forty years ago, just in time to get in on the big boom in the industry."

"How old a man is he?"

"Oh . . . Mr Camden must be seventy, if he's a day."

"Do you happen to know if he ever had an affair with Barbara?"

"Not that I ever heard about. But it wouldn't surprise me a bit. Of course he's pretty old. His wife died about five years ago."

Casey hesitated for a moment, before saying slowly, "I don't know just how to put this, Evelyn, but it must be asked. To your knowledge did your husband ever have an affair with Barbara Stratton?"

"Oh, no! He'd never do that," Evelyn said with a small cry. Then her hand came to her mouth, her eyes widening. "Would he?"

"Did the possibility ever cross your mind?"

"Of course not! Leo wasn't that kind of a man. He didn't even *like* Barbara. I don't know how many times he told me that."

"I've found that sexual attraction often has little to do with liking. And your husband *was* a Camden VP, in a position to help Miss Stratton, but . . . No matter." Casey waved a hand. "The other Camden vice presidents . . . Do you know them well?"

"Not too well. Met them at company parties and such, and Leo and I traded off dinners with them from time to time, simply fulfilling social obligations."

"Do you know of any reason why one of them might have killed Miss Stratton, *or* your husband?"

"None that I can think of. Leo was well liked in the company. I wouldn't have put it past Barbara." Evelyn's voice stung with hatred. "But then she was already dead, and you shouldn't speak ill of the dead. My mother always told me that."

Casey had to wonder if there *had* been an affair between Stratton and Thornesburg, and if Evelyn knew about it.

She leaned back, finishing her coffee, which had grown cold.

Evelyn reached for the coffee container. "Here, let me warm that up for you."

"Never mind." Casey gestured. "I have to be going. I've imposed on you enough. One more thing . . . What are the names of the other three Camden vice presidents?"

Evelyn tugged at her lower lip. "Let's see, there's Sam Porter, head of Research. Martin Smith, head of Engineering. And Paul Tate, Accounting."

Casey jotted the names down, then looked up. "No other women vice presidents then?"

Evelyn shook her head. "No, Grady is sort old-fashioned in that regard. He believes that women belong in the home, or at least confined to clerical or secretarial jobs. He doesn't much approve of women seeking careers."

"But he did hire Barbara Stratton," Casey pointed out.

Evelyn's eyes widened. "He did, didn't he? I've never really given much thought to that. So maybe Mr Camden and Barbara did have an affair. Maybe that was the reason he gave her the job." She got a thoughtful expression. "I just thought of something. Leo told me, oh, three months or so back, that Mr Camden was thinking of retiring as head of the company, turning it over to someone else to run, while he remained as chairman of the board. And Leo told me there was a rumour Barbara was in line for the job."

"Camden has no children?"

"Yes, three, two girls and a son. But according to Leo, none of them has the slightest interest in running the company, so long as the money keeps coming in. All the stock in the company is in the hands of Mr Camden and his children."

Casey said thoughtfully, "Do you think it's possible that Stratton was blackmailing Camden? Maybe because of an affair they had?"

"Anything was possible with Barbara." Evelyn blinked. "You're not thinking that Mr Camden killed her to put a stop to her blackmailing him?"

Casey smiled slightly. "That's a reach, but it's not impossible."

"But how would that explain Leo being killed?"

Casey nodded. "There's that. Maybe he was killed because he knew something, but we may never know what. Of course this is all speculation, with no foundation whatsoever. I'd appreciate it if you didn't discuss this with anyone. It could very well start a vicious rumour, with absolutely no basis in fact."

Casey recalled a piece of advice Josh once gave her: "Never hurts to get a good juicy rumour going in a murder investigation, babe. It usually rattles a few cages. It may not be ethical, but then neither is murder."

Evelyn was saying, "Oh, I would never do that. Mr Camden

has been very nice to us, and I wouldn't want to do anything that might harm him."

Casey closed her notebook with a snap, and got to her feet. "Well, I'll stop bothering you now, Evelyn, and I want to thank you for your cooperation."

Evelyn also got up, saying hopefully, "Do you think anything I told you will help you find Leo's killer?"

"I can't answer that just yet, but it was helpful. It cleared up some things, and opened up some lines of investigation that may prove to be fruitful. Goodbye, Evelyn. My sympathy for your loss, and rest assured that we will do everything we can to bring your husband's killer to justice."

What pompous bullshit, Casey thought, as she drove out of the driveway. But maybe her parting words were of consolation to the widow.

It was now close to midnight; it was a week night, and the streets were relatively free of traffic. Yet, as she cautiously drove away from the Thorneburg home Casey noticed a pair of headlights reflected in the rear-view mirror. The other vehicle was following too closely, but she couldn't speed up here, it was too dangerous. When she reached Pico Boulevard, she speeded up to fifty, ignoring the thirty-mile-an-hour limit. The headlights of the car behind dropped back briefly, then grew closer, until they were about two car lengths behind her.

Was she being followed? On the trip up the traffic had been much heavier, and she hadn't taken note of a possible tail.

Now she dropped back, this time well below the speed limit. The following headlights also dropped back, and the vehicle made no effort to pass.

It seemed pretty obvious that she had a tail; either that or the driver of the following car was using her car as a guidance vehicle. She knew that some overly cautious drivers, especially the elderly, did exactly that.

She shrugged. There wasn't much she could do about it

at the moment. Her thoughts circled back to the interview with Evelyn Thornesburg. Had she learned anything that would be a threat to anyone? She didn't see what it could be. True, the revelation of Barbara Stratton's ambition, her willingness to do just about anything to get ahead – at least so said Evelyn Thornesburg – opened up some possibilities. But if the roots of the last two homicides lay at Camden Industries, how could the two earlier homicides tie in? Both victims were from cities far removed from Los Angeles, so how could they connect with the last two? It just didn't scan, and it made Casey's head hurt to think about it. She was tired, her thoughts fuzzy; she was ready for bed.

She spotted the blinking neon sign announcing her motel on the right, ahead. She glanced into the mirror – the trailing lights were still there. She signalled for a right turn and drove into the motel driveway, stopping before the office, her gaze pinned to the mirror.

The car drove right on by. She only caught a quick glimpse of a dark-coloured vehicle, possibly of a foreign make, before it passed from sight.

Casey drove on back, parked before the room she had rented, and went inside. She didn't turn on the lights immediately, but stood at the window in the dark, the blinds cracked just enough for her to see out. She stood like that for a full fifteen minutes, her gaze riveted on the driveway from the street. No cars appeared.

Finally, she turned away with a heavy sigh. She was being paranoid again.

She turned on the lights and went about preparing for bed. But just before she got under the sheets, she turned out all the lights and peered outside again. The same eight cars that had been there when she parked were still there, no new additions.

Chapter Twelve

Casey was in no hurry the next morning. She wanted all the Camden executives in their offices and settled in before she invaded their privacy. She didn't call for appointments. She wanted to catch them unprepared; she had long since learned that she got better results that way.

Of course, she had no real jurisdiction in California, but that was usually no problem. The proper procedure was to contact the local police, inform them of her presence, and ask for an officer to accompany her. If the locals learned she was here without touching base with them first, they would be ticked off at her.

But this time, since she was working undercover in Sedona, the fewer people who knew about the task force, and her involvement, the better. She could only hope that Grady Camden would readily cooperate with her since two of the victims had been Camden employees, and then instruct the three remaining VPs to cooperate as well.

She ate a light breakfast before heading out. As she drove away from the restaurant, she kept a close watch in the rear-view mirror for signs of a tail. As far as she could ascertain, no vehicle was following her.

The corporate offices of Camden Industries were located just off Santa Monica Boulevard.

Casey parked in a slot marked "Visitor", and went inside, out of the heat which was beginning to build. The inside was air-conditioned. The reception area was large and attractively furnished. The only distraction Casey noticed was the piped-in music: bland music several years out of date.

She approached the reception desk. "I'd like to speak to Grady Camden, please." She placed one of her cards on the desk.

"Do you have an appointment?"

"No, but I'm sure Mr Camden will wish to see me." Casey gestured to the card.

The receptionist picked-up the card and scanned it, her eyes widening. She had a friendly, open face. Now the blue eyes searched Casey's face in growing apprehension. "What is this about, please?"

"As the card says, I'm an investigator from Arizona, with the Governor's Task Force on Crime. I'm investigating the murders of two Camden vice presidents, Stratton and Thornesburg."

The receptionist paled slightly. "That was a terrible thing! All of us here are just shocked."

"I'm sure you are. Now if you'll let Mr Camden know I'm here, please."

The receptionist picked up a phone, turned half away, and spoke in a low voice. After a moment she hung up and looked up at Casey. "Ms Wheaton, Mr Camden's personal assistant, will be right down to escort you upstairs." She gestured to a couch nearby.

Casey sat down composedly. She wondered what consternation her sudden arrival was causing among the executive suites. She had hoped to catch them all by surprise. Now that was all by the board. If Grady Camden didn't call and inform the other executives, the receptionist and/or Camden's assistant would spread the word as soon as she was closeted with Camden.

Ten minutes later a tall, handsome brunette came striding toward Casey, who got to her feet.

The woman said coolly, "How do you do? I'm Janice Wheaton. Mr Camden will see you now."

She turned, and Casey followed her out of the lobby to an elevator around the corner. The third floor hallway was carpeted, and their footsteps made no sound. In fact, there was a hush that was almost funereal. No music intruded, and there was no sound coming from behind the closed doors they passed. Ms Wheaton opened the last door at the end of the corridor and motioned Casey in.

The assistant said, "Ms Casey Farrel, Mr Camden."

The office was large, and the outside wall was made of glass. At first glimpse, the man behind the large desk in front of the huge window seemed only a shadow.

A melancholy voice said, "Thank you, Janice. You may leave us. Come in, Ms Farrel. Please be seated."

Casey took a seat before the desk, and Camden resumed his own seat. Now Casey could see him clearly. He was of medium size, a little on the heavy side. He had a thick head of hair that was almost theatrically white. Gray eyes swam behind thick-lensed glasses. His round face seemed a few years younger than the age Evelyn Thornesburg had given him. But there were lines of strain around his eyes, which looked tired, faintly sad, and the red flush to his round face hinted at a dangerously high blood pressure.

He said, "I wasn't informed that the task force was involved in this case." He added quickly, "Not that I'm not pleased. Every agency involved in catching the bastards who killed Barbara and Leo, the better."

"We try to keep as low a profile as possible. I'm surprised you even knew the task force exists."

"Oh, we try to keep current, even way out here, in California," he said in a dry voice. "I even knew about you. You've gained a certain amount of fame, Ms Farrel, and I'm glad you're on the case."

So much for anonymity, Casey thought wryly.

Camden leaned forward. "I'll be happy to cooperate any way I can."

"A few questions have come up. I had a long talk with

Mrs Thornesburg, and she mentioned a few things that need clarification."

Camden sighed. "Ah, yes, poor Evelyn. This has all been quite a shock to her, I'm afraid." His look became guarded. "What things are you speaking of, Ms Farrel?"

"It seems that her husband had some suspicions about Barbara Stratton's death. He went to Sedona in the hope of clearing them up. What do you know about that?"

"Yes, Leo said something like that to me," Camden said with a nod. "I don't know as I'd qualify them as suspicions. Mostly, he seemed to doubt the police line that Barbara was killed by a serial killer."

"He seemed to think that the reason for her murder originated here. Do you know why he thought that?"

Camden looked startled. "Nothing of the sort! Certainly, he didn't mention that to me. How did you reach that conclusion?"

"From what he told his wife."

"Are you implying that someone *here* killed Leo?"

"Not implying," Casey said cautiously. "But it's a possibility that must be considered."

"Utter nonsense!" Camden said with a snort. "Certainly not myself, or any of my executives. We can all alibi each other. We had a meeting that afternoon that ran through dinner and afterward."

Casey said alertly, "You mean, for the time of the murder? How could you know that? So far as I know, the time of death is yet to be established."

Camden shook his head. "Not the time of death, no, but the period that began when he left his motel, a few minutes short of eight that evening. I see from your expression that you didn't know about this."

"I'm afraid not."

"I talked to a Lieutenant Martin about an hour ago. He said that Leo was seen leaving the motel at that time with another man. The lieutenant is proceeding on the theory that the man was Leo's killer, that he either abducted Leo at gunpoint, or lured him to accompany him, and then killed him shortly after. In any case . . ." Camden spread his hands. "You can see that none of us could have killed Leo. Besides, what reason could we possibly have? It's ridiculous to even consider such a thing."

Not all that ridiculous, Casey thought. They could all have conspired, one of them making a quick trip to Sedona to kill Thornesburg, while the other four lied to give him an alibi. Who would find it easier to lure Thornesburg from the motel than one of his fellow vice presidents? Of course, that would be really reaching, especially at the moment, so she shared none of her thinking with Camden. Instead, changing the subject drastically, she said abruptly, "Mr Camden, there is a rumour that you once had an affair with Barbara Stratton. Is it true?"

"What!" He reared back, his face reddening even further. "Where did you hear such a rumour?"

"I never reveal my sources, Mr Camden. Answer the question please."

"Evelyn, wasn't it? Of course it was."

For a moment or so he stared at her in defiance. Then he slumped slightly. "Yes, it's true. Barbara was an attractive woman, sex personified. My wife passed on some time ago, and I was lonely. But the affair with her was short-lived, over at least three years ago." He leaned forward, his attitude almost pleading. "You have to understand something about Barbara. In some ways she was amoral. She enjoyed sex, and she was very good at it."

"And apparently not averse to using sexual wiles to get ahead in the world," Casey said in a dry voice.

Camden nodded. "That, too."

"And yet I understand that now that you are considering retirement from active participation in the company, Stratton was being seriously considered for your position."

"Yes, that's true." Camden sighed. "All the executives

were under consideration, but I will admit that Barbara was probably my choice."

"Why was that, Mr Camden?"

"Because she was damned good!" he snapped. "In the time she took over Sales, volume of sales increased over forty percent. Her morals aside, she was an asset to the company."

"Was it possible that, as a result of your affair with Barbara Stratton, she was blackmailing you to get the position?"

"Absolutely not! Absolute rubbish." His face was now dangerously red, and Casey wondered if he was on the edge of a heart attack.

"Of course, you have only my word for that. Believe what you like, I can't stop you." He slumped, tired lines appearing in his face. "I would be a poor subject for blackmail of any sort. My wife is dead, and my children . . ." He took a handful of tissue from a desk drawer. "Frankly, they couldn't care less, so long as the company remains prosperous, and their dividends are paid on time."

Despite herself, Casey felt a tug of pity for the man. What would it be like to be as successful as Grady Camden, and yet have no one who really gave a damn about him as a person, as a father?

She pushed the thought away, and asked, "How about the other executives? Were any, or all of them, sexually involved with Stratton?"

He sat up, a disdainful look on his face. "You will have to ask them that. Whatever else, I'm not a . . . what is the word you cops use? An informant, a stoolie?"

"I fully intend to ask them. How about Leo Thornesburg? Did he have an affair with her? I can't very well ask *him*, now can I?"

He said stiffly, "I know nothing about the lives of my executives beyond the office. Their private lives are none of my business."

Casey knew he was lying, but it would serve little purpose to antagonize him further. Besides, if Thornesburg had had an affair with Stratton, the other executives would almost certainly know about it, and probably be happy to talk about it, to direct any heat away from themselves.

She said, "Well, that's enough for now. I'd like to talk to your other executives now, please."

"There's only two available today. Paul Tate, Accounting, took the day off. His wife is in the hospital having a baby." He stared at her in some alarm. "I hope you'd have the decency not to confront Paul at a time like this?"

"Will he be in tomorrow?"

"I'm sure he will be."

"Then I'll see him then."

Camden scooped up the phone and spoke into it at length in a low voice. After a few minutes he hung up and turned to her.

"Sam Porter, head of Research, is back down the hall on the right. He's expecting you. Martin Smith, Engineering, is out at the moment. But I'm sure he'll be back by the time you've finished with Sam."

Casey started for the door. Halfway there she turned back. "There's one thing I forgot to ask, Mr Camden. Why did Barbara Stratton go to Sedona?"

"She was exhausted. She wanted a week off. I was more than happy to give her the time. She'd earned it."

"But why Sedona? Had she ever been there?"

"Not to my knowledge. As for the reason she chose Sedona, I . . ." He fell silent for a moment, frowning in thought. "I think someone suggested it to her. She said something along that line."

"She didn't tell you who?"

"No, she didn't."

"Could it have been someone here?"

"I suppose it must have been, but I have no idea who."

Sam Porter seemed rather young to be the head of a department; especially one as important as Research, which would be very important in a business. On the other hand, he could be a boy genius.

A short, wiry man, dressed casually, he got to his feet at her entrance, keen blue eyes studying her warily. He ran a long-fingered hand through abundant brown hair, ruffling it, making him appear even younger.

"I'm Casey Farrel," Casey said. "I assume Mr Camden told you why I'm here?"

Porter nodded. "He mentioned that you were an investigator from some Arizona task force, looking into the deaths of Leo and Ms Stratton."

"That's substantially correct."

Porter motioned to the chair drawn up before his desk, and waited politely until she took it before sitting back down himself. "I really don't know how I can help." He added hastily, "Not that I'm not willing, but they were murdered in Arizona." He arched an eyebrow quizzically.

"That's true, but both victims worked here."

"And you're thinking the cause of their deaths stems from here?"

"That's what I'm trying to learn, Mr Porter."

"I don't see how that could be, but . . ." He spread his hands. "What do I know? I'm hardly a detective." He smiled slightly, as if to point out how ridiculous that was. "From what I gather, I thought the theory was that a serial killer was responsible, that two other murders had already taken place."

"That is the most popular theory, but consider the odds against a serial killer selecting two consecutive victims not only from out of the state, but living in the same area, and working together."

His smile turned rueful. "Pretty heavy against it."

"That's right. Now, I won't take up much of your time, Mr Porter. Only a few questions."

He spread his hands again. "Fire away."

"How well did you know Barbara Stratton?"

Something flickered in his eyes, but his voice remained steady. "About as well as anybody knows anybody they work with."

"It didn't go beyond that?"

"I'm not sure what you mean, Ms Farrel."

"Oh, I think you do, Mr Porter. I have been told that she had affairs, of whatever duration, with all the executives in the company."

A spark of anger lit his eyes. "Who told you such a damned lie?" Then he spread his hands, looking away from her probing eyes. "Oh, what the hell! You'll find out, anyway. Yes, we had a . . . relationship. It didn't last long, and it's been over for some time."

"You're married, Mr Porter? A family?"

"What does that . . .? Yes, I'm married. I have three children. We have a generally happy marriage. But you have to understand . . ." He leaned forward intensely. "Barbara was a damned attractive woman. When she came on to me, I was flattered, and I had a few weak moments."

"Then she came on to you?"

"Absolutely! Frankly, she intimidated me. I would never have had the guts to make a move on her."

"Did she ever hold the affair over your head, try to blackmail you, ask favours of you?"

"No, no." He wagged his head. "She would never have done that."

"How about the other executives? Did she sleep with them?"

His face closed up. "You'll have to ask them."

"I've already asked Mr Camden. He admitted it."

"He did?" Porter asked in astonishment. "I had always suspected, but I never really knew."

"How about Leo Thornesburg? It's already confirmed," Casey said, bending the truth a little, "so you may as well tell me."

"Yes, she got Leo in her clutches." Porter sighed. "Poor Leo. He was such an innocent as far as women were concerned. He mooned around like a lovesick teenager. When it was over, when she dumped him, he was crushed."

"He must have still felt something for her. He went to Sedona to look into her death."

Porter shrugged. "I know nothing about that."

"He didn't confide in you his reasons for going."

"Nope, first thing I knew about it, was the report of his death."

"You know of anyone here who might have reasons to kill them?"

"Good heavens, no!" He shot forward. "Why would one of us do something like that?"

"That's what I'm trying to find out," Casey said dryly. "It's my understanding one of the five Camden executives was about to become president of the corporation when Mr Camden resigns. What do you know about that?"

"Only the rumours," he said with a shrug.

"I should think you'd be more interested, since you're also a vice president with a shot at the spot."

He shook his head vehemently. "I've been here the least time of any of the others. No way would I have been considered."

"I've been told that the odds favoured Stratton."

"That's quite likely true. Barbara was as much a ball of fire in business as she was in bed. In my opinion, she would have been a dynamic head of the company."

Casey looked away for a moment in thought. "One more question, Mr Porter, and I'll get out of your hair. Mr Camden told me that Stratton was going to Sedona for some R&R, and he vaguely recalled that someone in the office recommended Sedona as a good vacation spot. But he can't remember who made the recommendation. Do you know, by any chance?"

Porter said, "Nope. I haven't a clue."

Martin Smith was a different kettle of fish entirely. He vehemently denied being sexually involved with Barbara Stratton.

"I'm a happily married man, Miss Farrel, with two children. We're a Christian family. I teach Sunday school every week. I believe in family values, in the Bible and its teachings. I adhere to the Ten Commandments."

Casey studied the man for a few moments in silence. She knew he was lying, and suspected that he knew she knew. It had been her experience that people who so strongly denied any wrongdoing were often up to their armpits in whatever they denied. But experience had also taught her it was very difficult to break through such stonewalling, unless she possessed some hard facts contradicting the lies she was being told. In this case she didn't.

Smith was in his late fifties, with thinning hair, suspicious brown eyes, and a narrow face stern with righteousness. She suspected that he was completely humourless.

"I see," she said slowly. "I gather that you didn't approve of Barbara Stratton then?"

Thin lips set in a straight line, he snapped, "It is not my place to approve or disapprove. Ms Stratton was an excellent executive. Her private life was beyond my scope."

"She was being strongly considered to become Mr Camden's replacement when he retired, I understand. Did you approve of *that*, Mr Smith?"

"Again, it was not my place to . . ."

She nodded, sighing. "To approve or disapprove, I know. How long have you been with Camden Industries, Mr Smith?"

"Twenty years."

"Then you surely would be in the running for Camden's position when he retires, wouldn't you?"

"Perhaps. But Paul Tate has been here longer than I, and seniority is not the only consideration in these matters."

Casey nodded. "Yes, I understand that, but it seems to me that it would be only human for the rest of you to be a bit resentful."

His pale face reddened slightly. "The matter was not yet decided; there had been no announcement . . ." He broke off, staring at her hard. "Surely, you're not suggesting that *I* killed Barbara because I wanted the presidency! That is utterly ridiculous! And Leo as well?" He sneered. "What motive could you offer for my killing Leo?"

"None, Mr Smith. At the moment."

He rode over her, "Besides, I was in a meeting with Mr Camden and the others the evening Leo was murdered."

"Yes, I'm well aware of that. You claim you didn't have an affair with Stratton, Mr Smith. How about the other executives, including Leo Thornesburg?"

He answered without hesitation. "They were all involved with Miss Stratton."

"Including Grady Camden?"

"Yes, he also had an affair with her."

Sanctimonious bastard, she thought; denies having anything to do with Stratton, but doesn't hesitate to point the finger. And it's obvious that he resented being passed over for the big promotion, or he wouldn't be so quick to point that same finger at his boss.

Casey had had more than enough of Martin Smith. Obviously, he was not going to be of any help. She would have loved to have some evidence proving he'd been involved with Barbara Stratton, so she could turn the heat up.

She got to her feet abruptly. "Thank you, Mr Smith. I may want to talk to you again." She had no such intention, but maybe the threat would worry him a little.

It was just short of noon when she left Camden Industries. She had a whole afternoon and night to kill. She considered going to the hospital to interview Paul Tate, but barging in on a man and wife having a baby would be pretty shoddy. She even considered bypassing Paul Tate entirely and catching a flight back to Phoenix this afternoon. But she didn't really give it serious thought; Tate might be able to contribute something of value.

Instead, after a leisurely lunch, she found a movie theatre and watched an action movie that had little connection with reality. For two hours she watched a world that was divided into sharp black and white, and where good – or what passed for good in these things – always triumphed. It would be nice if real life was always so tidy.

It was growing late when she left the theatre. She drove back to the motel for a shower, a change of clothes, and a few phone calls. She needed to call Gabe in Sedona and confirm Grady Camden's startling statement that Thornesburg had been seen leaving his motel with a man shortly before his death, and she had to call Josh and Donnie.

Before going to her room she stopped at the soft drink alcove and got a bucket of ice and a Coke from the machine.

Consequently, she was juggling her purse, the room key, bucket of ice, and the Coke when she stepped inside the room. The curtains had been drawn, and the interior of the room was dark. Hands full, she used her hip to close the door.

As she turned back, she heard a furtive movement, and had time only to realize that someone had been waiting behind the door, before an arm went around her, and a rag was slapped over her mouth and nose. Her lungs filled with a sickly sweet odour she recognized as chloroform.

Dropping what she was holding, she used both hands to

claw at the hand and rag clamped over her mouth. She struggled fiercely for a moment or two, then slumped as the anaesthetic swept away her consciousness and dropped her into darkness.

Chapter Thirteen

Casey awakened to confusion and pain, with no idea of how long she had been unconscious. She felt rumpled and dirty, her mouth had a foul taste, and her head ached abominably. She was lying where she had fallen, just inside and to the right of the door. She got shakily to her feet, bracing herself against the wall.

She groped along the wall for the light switch. The overhead light flared, and she uttered a sharp cry as splinters of pain pierced her skull. She covered her eyes and leaned against the wall until the pain lessened.

Finally, she gazed around the room. All the drawers on the night table were pulled; her one small bag had been turned upside down, and all the drawers of the dresser had been emptied. She saw that the change of clothes she had brought along had been dumped on the floor, all the pockets turned inside out, and her purse had been emptied on the bed.

After a brief examination she concluded that nothing was missing; even her credit cards and cash had been left strewn across the bed.

She felt certain that her assailant had been searching for any material she might have on the investigation.

Fortunately, the only notes she had were the names of the Camden executives that Evelyn Thornesburg had given her. She was graced with a near-perfect memory, and rarely took notes during the interrogation of suspects or witnesses.

She made a stab at straightening up the room, but her

heart really wasn't in it. She finally stopped, shucked her cloths, and stepped under a very hot shower. She stayed under the stream of almost scalding water for a long time.

When she finally emerged, she felt better. She felt clean again, and the hot water had taken the edge off the fuzziness and nausea left by the chloroform.

Sitting on the edge of the bed, the phone in her hand, she thought about reporting the attack to the local police, but immediately dismissed the idea. It would only alert them to her presence here, and would accomplish nothing.

She called Stinton's motel in Sedona. To her relief he answered on the second ring. "Hello?"

"Call me at this number from a pay phone," she said crisply, and read the phone number and room number off the phone. "Read the number back."

There was a stunned silence, then he read the number back to her. Casey hung up without another word.

The phone rang ten minutes later. "Yes, Gabe?"

"Uh . . . Rena. Where the hell are you?"

She smiled slightly. "You may call me Casey for the duration of this phone call. Just don't make a habit of it."

"You just took off without a word to me. I thought something had happened to you. I called Mr Wilson, and he told me you were okay, but that I didn't need to know where you were."

She sighed. "I'm in California, Gabe. I'm out here talking to some of the people Leo Thornesburg worked with."

"Find out anything?" he asked eagerly.

"I'm still sorting it all out. I'll fill you in when I see you. What's happening there? Grady Camden, president of the company, tells me that the police have learned Thornesburg was seen leaving his motel the night of his murder with a man, probably his killer. Is that true?"

"Yes, there was a witness staying in the same hotel."

"Any identification? And are they sure that it *was* a man, not a woman?"

"Nope, they haven't identified him. And the witness is fairly sure that it was a man." He added in a rush, "But something else happened this afternoon, Casey! They arrested Vernon Bornfield for the murders! You know, the Indian activist."

"Yes, I know who he is," she said slowly. "Why did they arrest Bornfield? What evidence did they find?"

"Nothing all that concrete, in my opinion. I understand he's been under suspicion almost from the beginning because of his strong vocal opposition to the cults. He claims they are destroying the holy grounds of his people. The police line is that he killed those people in the hope that the various cults would be blamed, forcing them to close up shop and leave the area."

"That's pretty weak, seems to me."

"They also found footprints matching his boots on the mesa where Barbara Stratton was killed. And they got a warrant and searched his house, where they found a knife hidden. Analysis of blood specks on the knife match Stratton's blood type."

"Did Bornfield confess, or admit anything?"

"No, he denies everything. Oh, he admits to being on the mesa, but on a night after the murder. Said he was just up there checking because it's a sacred Indian site."

Casey flashed on the attack that night on the mesa. Had Bornfield been the attacker? "And the knife?"

"Claims it isn't his, never saw it before. He claims it was planted, that he's being framed."

"Seems stupid of him, if he is the killer, to hide a murder weapon in his own house."

"I'll tell you what I think, Casey. I think the police are getting desperate for an arrest. The media pressure is heavy on them. And this is the first decent suspect they've come across. Even if Bornfield isn't the perp, this buys them a little time."

"Then your read on the situation is, they're not closing the book on the investigation?"

"No, far from it. In fact, I've become pretty close with Liutenant Martin. He told me, privately, that he's not all that convinced that Bornfield is their guy. He's certainly not about to stop looking."

"That's good," she said absently. "I'll probably be back in Sedona sometime late tomorrow. We'll talk more at length then. Right now I'm hungry. Haven't had my supper yet. Bye, Gabe."

She hung up, ignoring the squawk of protest issuing from the receiver.

Casey reluctantly began her next two calls. She was in no mood for chatting, and she didn't intend to tell either Donnie or Josh about what had happened. Donnie had no need to know, and it would only get Josh angry and upset, and trigger his lecturing mode.

However, she was in luck: she caught Donnie in the middle of watching an old Western movie with his uncle, and he was only too happy to be put off with a few words of affection; and Josh, thanks be to the Gods, wasn't home. Gratefully, she left a message on his machine.

Casey was tired and grumpy when she awoke the next morning. She had slept poorly, awakening several times during the night, sure that the intruder had returned and was in the room with her. She made a phone call and reserved a seat on an afternoon plane to Phoenix. After the interview with Paul Tate she would have no reason to linger in California.

She packed quickly and checked out. Driving out of the parking lot, she kept a sharp lookout for any possible tail. She didn't spot anything. After a hearty breakfast at a fast food place she drove to Camden Industries, arriving shortly before ten.

This time, at the reception desk, she was told to go

directly upstairs – Mr Tate was expecting her. That gave her pause for a moment. Tate was expecting her? A bit strange.

So the first thing she asked him was, "You were expecting me, Mr Tate?"

"Of course, Ms Farrel. I called Mr Camden yesterday from the hospital to tell him about the birth of my son. An eight pound baby boy!"

"Congratulations, Mr Tate," she said dryly. "When was this?"

He gave a puzzled frown. "I beg your pardon?"

"What time did you call Mr Camden?"

"Oh . . . let's see. The baby was born around eleven yesterday morning. I called Grady about two hours later."

So this man knew I was here, *why* I was here, in plenty of time to get to my motel room and lie in wait for me. But then that could apply to the other three executives. Maybe I should ask him if he could alibi his whereabouts around that time.

But would a man who had spent the morning with his wife while she bore him a son, then rush from her bedside to render an investigator unconscious and search her belongings? It didn't seem very likely, but Casey had known stranger things to happen.

She studied him for a few moments. Tate was an accountant, but he certainly didn't fit her preconceived image of one. She had expected a conservative looking, serious type, But this man looked like a well-dressed jock, tanned, broad-shouldered and trim, with beautifully styled dark hair and merry hazel eyes that twinkled warmly at her from an almost classically handsome face. He said something, and Casey blinked. "I beg your pardon?"

"I said, would you like some coffee, a soft drink?"

"No, thanks, I just came from a huge breakfast."

"Well, then." He beamed at her, scrubbing his hands together. "What can I do to help you?"

"First, how long have you worked here?"

He smiled. "Thirty years. I guess I've been with Grady longer than any of the others." At her look of surprise he laughed heartily. "I know, everybody tells me I don't look my age. Connie, that's my wife, is almost twenty years younger than me, and she's always telling me it isn't fair. I'll be fixty-six my next birthday, Ms Farrel."

"Then it would seem that *you* would be the logical one to be promoted to Mr Camden's position when he retires. Correct?"

His eyes narrowed, and the cheery expression deserted him momentarily. "My, you have been the busy one, haven't you?"

"It doesn't seem to be much of a secret around the company that Barbara Stratton had the lead position in the race for Mr Camden's job," Casey said.

He smiled slightly. "I suppose not. To answer your question, yes, when the subject was first broached, I thought I would be top contender; but then I've been in the corporate world long enough to know that in cases like this, there is never a sure thing. There are always many things to be considered, and, after all, Grady Camden owns the company, it's his decision to make."

"Did you talk to Mr Camden about it?"

"I fail to see what that has to do with our murder investigation." He moved uncomfortably. "But, yes, I asked Grady. Just last week, as a matter of fact, how soon he expected to make a decision, but all he would say was, that no final decision would be made, not until Barbara returned from her vacation."

"Weren't you the least bit resentful that you might be passed over?"

"Resentful? I wouldn't go that far. I wasn't crazy about the idea. But then I have a good job, a good salary. Camden Industries, and Grady Camden, have been good to me."

"About Barbara Stratton's vacation . . . Mr Camden told me that he thought someone in the company suggested Sedona. Would that be you?"

"Well, I don't know as I *suggested* it. My wife and I visited Sedona on our last vacation, and loved it. I do remember discussing this with Barbara, but whether or not that's why she went, I don't know." He laughed. "Barbara was a strong-minded woman, certainly not one for taking suggestions."

"What was your opinion of Barbara Stratton, Mr Tate?"

He stared at her warily. "My opinion? That can go several different ways, Ms Farrel."

"Professional opinion, for starters. Was she an asset to the company?"

"Oh, definitely an asset. Sales almost doubled during the time she was in charge."

"Then she was good at what she did?"

"Damned good. Now don't get me wrong." He held up both hands. "I have to be honest here. Besides, I'm sure others have told you this. Barbara could be a cold bitch, arrogant and ruthless. On the other hand, she could be warm and friendly, when it served her purpose."

"Like in bed, for instance?"

He reared back, smiling broadly. "I was warned that you'd get around to that question eventually. So, I won't bother denying it." The smile disappeared. "In fact, I'm deeply ashamed. It's not something I'm proud of. But Barbara was an attractive woman. *Very* attractive. Connie was pregnant, and it's been a difficult pregnancy from the very beginning. And a man has needs . . ." He looked away. "Why revert to a cliché? I lusted after her like a dog near a bitch in heat." He laughed ruefully. "And I guess you could say that's what Barbara was. But I'm not blaming her. It takes two to tango, to employ another cliché."

"Then I gather it happened recently?"

"Yes. It began about four months ago, and ended the week Barbara left for Sedona."

"Did Barbara end it?"

"I'm ashamed to admit that she did. I was perfectly willing to continue, but she said it was time. Oh, I probably would have ended it now, with the birth of my son. Again, I might not have." He gave a bark of laughter. "Barbara told me that she never kept a lover very long, that after a certain time they became like week-old coffee, stale and bitter to the taste."

Casey said, "Not a very nice woman, was she?"

"Nope. I knew that going in, but I was so hot for her that it didn't matter."

"Weren't you the least bit resentful that she broke it off so abruptly and cruelly?"

"You're fond of that word, aren't you? Yes, I was resentful at the time. But I'm beginning to realize that it was for the best . . ." He broke off to stare at her. "My God, you're not thinking that I would kill her because she dumped me! Are you?"

"Oldest motive in the world," she said calmly. With her hands she drew quotes around the next words. "'Jealousy and hate. Spurned lover kills paramour.' You see headlines like that every day."

"But my God, to believe that! Look . . ." He shot forward. "You're not going to Connie with all this, are you? She's had a hard time of it, and to have the fact of my affair laid out, along with your accusation, would be too much!" He waved a hand dismissively. "I know, I know what you're thinking. I should have thought of her before I got involved. The trouble is, Ms Farrel, men all too often do their thinking with their pricks, if you'll pardon my language. We all know it, but can't seem to stop it."

"I've often found that to be unfortunately true," she said gravely. "But don't worry about it, Mr Tate. I see no reason to trouble your wife. At least not at this stage of the investigation. But that may all change in the future, that's all I can promise at this point."

"I suppose that's all I can ask," he said with a sigh.

"How well did you know Leo Thornesburg?"

Tate spread his hands. "We weren't buds, if that's your question. But we were on good terms. Leo was a capable guy."

"The way I understand it, Mr Thornesburg was suspicious of the circumstances surrounding Barbara Stratton's death. That was the reason he went to Sedona. At least so he told his wife. Did he talk to you about that?"

Tate shook his head, smiling slightly. "Leo wasn't a confiding sort of guy. He was rather reticent about his private life."

Casey said quickly, "What makes you think this concern had something to do with his private life?"

Tate got a startled look. "Why, I just assumed . . ."

"Because he had an affair with Stratton?"

"So you know about that too?"

"I know that all the executives here had sexual relations with her at one time or another. It seems Ms Stratton was a busy lady."

Tate said ruefully, "You might say that."

"But from what you told me, your affair with her was the most recent. So if their affair was in the past, long over, why would Thornesburg still be personally involved? Unless their affair was starting up again?"

"I doubt that very much. Another one of Barbara's little axioms she lived by. I quote, 'Jump-starting an old love affair is like eating warmed-over toast. Tasteless.'"

"Ms Stratton's sayings were rather colourful," Casey said dryly.

"You could say that." Tate laughed. "That's only a small sample. Many aren't quotable in mixed company."

"Did she talk to you about her trip at all?"

"No. But . . ." He hesitated, obviously weighing something.

"But what?" she prompted.

"She *did* call me from Sedona."

"When?"

"The night before she was killed."

"What was the call about?"

"She was all excited. She told me she was invited to attend the meeting of some cult."

Casey felt a pull of excitement. "A cult? She was interested in cults?"

"Oh, yes. She'd heard about how some cults indulged in sex orgies. Now *that* would interest Barbara! She'd noodled around with a few in this area, but they were all too tame for her."

"Did she name the cult?"

Tate shook his head. "Nope. I'm not sure she even knew the name."

"Did she tell you *when* she was going?"

"Sorry, she didn't say. We only talked for a minute or two."

"But why would she call you in particular?"

"I haven't the least idea," he said with a shrug. "Barbara often did things on impulse, for no reason. Maybe she thought it would shock me."

"And that's all she said?"

"That's it."

"Why didn't you tell somebody about this call, Mr Tate? The Sedona police might be interested."

"Nobody asked me. Besides, I'm telling you, aren't I?" He stared at her intently. "You think it might be a cult murder?"

"I don't know," she said curtly, getting to her feet. "Thank you, Mr Tate, for being so frank with me. I may need to get back to you."

Casey was back in Sedona by early evening. Her flight from Los Angeles International had arrived back in Phoenix just in time to catch the shuttle. She knew that Josh would be pissed that she hadn't stopped off to see him, but she was driven by a sense of urgency.

She called Gabe's motel from the airport and was lucky enough to catch him in the room. She told him to meet her as soon as he could make it.

Chapter Fourteen

The Sedona Airport was located on a mesa, named aptly enough Airport Mesa. On the way back down the hill, on Airport Road, was an overlook, a parking area with a spectacular view on the spread of Sedona below. That was where Casey had told Gabe to meet her.

She retrieved her rental car from the airport parking lot where she'd left it and drove to the overlook. She was relieved to see that it was empty of cars. She knew that it was a popular spot for lovers to park, but it was probably too early for lovers.

Gabe arrived fifteen minutes later. He parked nearby and crossed over to her car, peering in. She leaned over to open the passenger door. He slid in, looking at her closely before closing the door.

"It's great to have you back. I was worried about you out there in LaLa Land. How did it seem to you?"

Casey smiled. "A bit like a foreign country. I guess I've been away from it for too long to take it for granted."

"Well, at least it didn't shake while you were there." He looked out the window.

"I hear that this is a favourite spot for lovers." He looked over at her. "You know, it would be a perfect cover for us to pretend to be lovers. And I might add, most pleasant."

"Let's not get too involved in role-playing here, Mr Stinton," she warned.

"Maybe it wouldn't be role-playing, at least not on my part."

"Whoa, Gabe." She held up a hand. "Didn't I tell you? I have a friend in Phoenix. He's a big sucker, and jealous as hell." She grinned impishly.

"You can't blame a man for trying, can you?" he said with his shy smile.

"All right," she said briskly. "What's happened since I talked to you earlier?"

"Nothing much has changed, that I know about."

"Vernon Bornfield is still under arrest?"

"As far as I know. They have him in jail in Prescott."

"Their investigation isn't stopping there?"

"Oh, no. As I told you, the lieutenant isn't completely satisfied that Bornfield is the perp."

"I'm not, either. In fact, I'd bet on it." She dropped into thought for a moment. "About this individual who was seen leaving the motel with Leo Thornesburg, is there any kind of physical description?"

"Some, but nothing very helpful. The woman who saw him was maybe fifty yards away, across the swimming pool from Thornesburg's room, and just happened to be looking out her window when she saw Thornesburg leaving with this other man. It was twilight, and the stranger had his back to her, so she never got a look at his face. He was shorter than Thornesburg, who was over six feet, by the way, but otherwise unremarkable."

"Did she see anything else, like a gun, for instance?"

"I asked her that. She said she didn't see one. And in answer to your next question, she didn't see them get into a vehicle and drive away. They went toward the front, where the guests all park their cars, and she couldn't see the lot from where she was. But they must have driven off in this unknown person's vehicle, because Thornesburg's rental was found at the motel."

"You did good, Gabe." Absently, she reached over to pat his knee.

Gabe flinched slightly, then covered by saying quickly,

"Isn't it about time you were telling me why you took off so suddenly, and what you were doing in California?"

"It was a last minute decision, Gabe, I'm sorry. You know it's not that easy to communicate with you without risking my cover. And I went out there to talk to Thornesburg's wife, and the other Camden executives. There's just a chance that the trail leads out there." Quickly, she told him what she had learned. Finished, she said, "So you can see that I didn't learn a lot, except for the fact that Barbara Stratton wasn't all that popular at the home office, and the further fact that she was interested in cults."

He said thoughtfully, "Seems to me you're reaching, Rena. Oh, the possibility of cult involvement seems stronger, but how could it lead back to California? The first two victims were not from California, were apparently not connected in any way. And while the last two were connected, did know each other, it could just be a coincidence."

She sighed. "You think that hasn't occurred to me? But a coincidence in a homicide investigation always bothers me. Most of the time, in the end, it isn't a coincidence after all. I think when this case is solved, we'll find a strong connection to California."

"Speaking of solved . . ." He laughed. "I got a call from Mr Wilson today. He thinks it's solved. After all, he said, a suspect is in custody."

"And because of that, he thinks we should pack our bags and go home?"

"He didn't say so, in so many words, but he hinted at it. And he told me to tell you to call him 'toot suite'."

"That what he always says," Casey smiled tightly. "It's one of his favourite phrases. I'll call him tomorrow and inform him that this is far from cleared. And we'll be here until it is."

"Think he'll go along with that?"

"He has no choice. I only have to threaten to call the Governor. This whole investigation was the Governor's idea, you know, and he wants it solved. Bad for the tourist trade, you know." She shifted wearily in her seat. "Thanks, Gabe. I've had a long day, and I'm whipped. I need a good night's sleep. I think I'll have to become Casey Farrel again, and drive up to Prescott tomorrow to talk to Vernon Bornfield."

Three telephone messages awaited Casey at the Enchantment: Vickie Dalton; Glenn Cabot; and Wes Strom. She decided that it would be better to wait until she got back from Prescott. If she returned the calls now, they might wonder why she disappeared again on the morrow.

She had dinner in her room, and got a good night's sleep. She left early the next morning for Prescott. She decided to take 89A up through Jerome, the old mining town. It was a winding, two-lane road, and would take almost twice as long; but there would be less traffic on that road and it would be easier to detect if anyone was following her.

Climbing Mingus Mountain out of Jerome, her thoughts went back to a time over a year ago. On that day she had taken Donnie for a day's sightseeing in Oak Creek Canyon. It had been after dark when they left Jerome for Prescott, and they had been run off the road by a pick-up and almost killed. The driver of the pick-up had been a suspect in the case she had been working in Prescott. As she drove past the spot, she felt a chill pass over her.

By the time she had driven over the mountain she was reasonably confident that she hadn't been followed.

In Chino Valley she turned off on the side road leading to her uncle's ranch. When she parked in front of the ranch house, she saw Dan Farrel down at the corral, leaning on the fence. She got out and headed that way. Up close, she could see Donnie inside the corral, leading a dun horse around in a circle.

Behind Dan Farrel she spoke quietly, "Hello, Uncle Dan."

Dan whirled around. "Hello . . . Oh, Casey! In that get-up I had trouble recognizing you."

"That's the whole point. I can only hope others have the same problem."

"How are you, Casey?"

"I'm fine . . ."

She was interrupted by a yell from Donnie: "Casey!"

He came flying out through the corral gate and barreled into her at full speed.

Laughing, she wrapped her arms around him. "Hi, kiddo."

He leaned back to look up at her with shining eyes. "Uncle Dan said it was time I was riding another horse! He's going to let me ride Thunder!"

Casey looked over at Dan Farrel with a frown. "Thunder? That doesn't sound too encouraging. Do you think that's safe?"

Dan shrugged, his weathered face creasing in a grin. "Don't let the name throw you. The horse is well broken, and well trained. That horse the boy's been riding is fine, but he's about as spirited as an old hound dog. High time for the boy to get used to a mount with a little more fire. I'm having Donnie walk Thunder around a bit, getting them used to each other. I'll keep a close watch to see the boy's okay. He's a good rider now. He won't come to any harm, I promise you."

"Well, as long as you're sure it's okay . . ."

Donnie was tugging at her arm, and she looked down into his upturned face. He said, "You're still undercover, huh, Casey?"

She laughed. "That's right, kiddo." She ruffled his hair. "But I didn't fool you, did I?"

"Aw, Casey!" He added eagerly, "You close to the bad guy?"

"Not yet, but hopefully soon."

"I got a name for you, Casey!"

It was a game they had been playing for some time. Every time Casey was involved in a sensational murder case, Donnie would insist on giving the case a name. "And what have you come up with, Donnie?"

"The Red Rock Killer!"

"That one's easy. Anyone could think of that."

"But you didn't!" he said triumphantly.

She said gravely, "You're right, I didn't."

"But if you're not close to the killer," Dan said, "what are you doing up here? Not that me and the boy ain't glad to see you."

"There's a suspect in jail in Prescott I have to see; and I have to get going." She scrubbed her knuckles along Donnie's jaw. "You get back to your horse, kiddo. And don't get too carried away. You do what Uncle Dan tells you."

She went into the house to say hello to Alice Farrel, then spent a half-hour making herself into Casey Farrel again. She took her own vehicle, the Cherokee, into Prescott. She hoped she'd see no one she knew from Sedona. She well realized that she was taking a risk, but she felt that it was vital that she interrogate Vernon Bornfield. She certainly couldn't do it as Rena Rainier. Some risks had to be taken. And she knew that the clock was ticking. Sooner or later, Casey Farrel and Rena Rainier were going to be pegged as the same person. She could only hope that it was later instead of sooner, and she would have a firm handle on the case before it happened.

A half-hour later she was alone with Vernon Bornfield in the jail's interrogation room.

There'd been no trouble getting in to see him, but there had been one dicey moment. The sheriff's deputy to whom she had presented her credentials had given her a curious look, and said, "I thought there was a task force guy in Sedona, one Gabe Stinton, already on the case?"

Casey improvised quickly, "There is, but it was thought best that Mr Stinton remain close to the scene in the event something breaks, so I was sent up from Phoenix to interrogate the suspect you have here."

The deputy's curiosity satisfied, he ushered Casey into the room, and went to fetch Bornfield.

The room was depressing, as were all police interrogation rooms she had ever been in: one table and two chairs bolted to the floor, and walls painted an institutional green. The walls were decorated with graffiti either obscene or derogatory; a not very successful effort had been made to clean it up. The room smelled strongly of disinfectant, with underlying odours of stale tobacco, stale sweat, and old fears.

Casey stared at the man across the table from her. His dark face was inscrutable, his eyes flat and without expression as he returned her stare.

"Mr Bornfield, I'm Casey Farrel." She slid one of her cards across the table. "I'm an investigator with the Governor's Task Force on Crime."

He didn't bother looking down at the card. "It's high time somebody aside from the locals gets involved in this mess."

"It's my understanding that the locals, as you call them, have a strong case against you." She ticked them off on her fingers. "A knife with a victim's blood on it was found on your premises. A footprint matching yours was discovered at the site where Barbara Stratton was killed . . ."

"All circumstantial," he said stonily. "What reason in hell would I have to kill all those people?" His mouth assumed a satirical twist. "The days of war between the Indian and the white man are long over. Or so my people have been led to believe."

She ignored his jibe. "The knife, how do you account for that?"

"It was planted, what else?" he said with a shrug of his

broad shoulders. "You'll notice my prints were not found on it?"

"That's easy enough to explain. You could have wiped it clean, or worn gloves."

He glared at her. "Well, I didn't."

"Then you're saying the real killer framed you?"

"Exactly."

"Why? I mean, why select you to frame?"

"Because I've made no secret of the fact that I believe a cult is responsible for these killings!"

"Why do you think that? You have any proof to back up your statement?"

"No proof, no. That's a job for the cops, not me. But cult members who would use the sacred ceremonial grounds of my people for their black rites, thereby making it impossible for us to use them ever again, are capable of murder."

"I see," she said thoughtfully. "Getting back to the footprint found at the scene, you can't deny that you were there."

"No, I can't deny that," he said in a growling voice. "That was a mistake, I shouldn't have gone up there. But I went long after the woman was killed."

"We have only your word for that. But saying for the moment that I accept your word for it, *why* were you up there, Mr Bornfield?"

"I wanted to check, to see if the site had been poisoned, destroyed, if it was forever desecrated."

"And was it?"

"Yes," he said grimly. "Soon there will be no ceremonial grounds left for our people."

Casey was silent for a few moments, thinking. How Josh would hoot should he be overhearing this conversation! A serious discussion over whether or not an *aura* had been destroyed because a murder had been committed on a particular piece of earth! Yet enough of her Hopi heritage still held sway over Casey so that she wasn't at all inclined to dismiss Bornfield's concerns out of hand.

He was speaking again, "But that's not enough reason for me to going around murdering people, Miss Farrel."

"Tell me this, Mr Bornfield, the night you say you went up to the murder scene on the mesa, did you happen to encounter anyone up there?"

She could immediately sense the wariness in him. "What do you mean?"

"Come, Mr Bornfield, the question is simple enough. Was there anyone else up there?"

His glance slid away. "It was a very dark night, I didn't see anyone else up there."

Casey leaned forward. "Why do I have the feeling that you're not telling the truth here?"

His gaze jumped back to her face. "What do you mean?"

She sighed. "I happen to know that there was someone else on that mesa in the night in question. A woman named Rena Rainier. She's in Sedona scouting locations for a movie. She told me that she was up there that night, quite late. Perhaps you know of her?"

He nodded curtly. "I have heard of such a woman, yes."

"Well, she claimed that she was attacked. In the dark she couldn't see her attacker. She admitted that it was foolish of her to be up there, and alone. And since she didn't come to any real harm, she didn't report it to the police. The attacker was you, wasn't it, Mr Bornfield? Don't worry." She held up a hand. "It will be just between us. No charges will be filed, you have my word on that. But I need to know, it will clear some things up for me."

He hesitated, his gaze searching. "Yes, it was me. It was a crazy thing to do, but I meant the woman no harm. I did it in a moment of panic." He smiled tightly. "Indians *do* panic, in spite of our reputation for stoicism. I was where I shouldn't be, and I knew if I was recognized up there,

I would fall under suspicion." His short laugh was harsh. "But I'm a suspect anyway."

She sat back, smiling slightly. "If it's any comfort to you, Mr Bornfield, I believe you."

He blinked. "You mean, you don't believe I killed those people?"

It was her turn to smile. "I will tell Gabe Stinton that I'm inclined to believe in your innocence, which doesn't mean, of course, that you're not still a suspect."

"I thank you for that."

"And I appreciate your cooperation, Mr Bornfield." She got to her feet. "I want you to know that the task force is working hard on solving these murders. Hopefully, you'll be a free man soon."

Driving out of town, Casey considered what she had learned. Not a great deal, but at least one worry was eased. The attack on her that night had been done in a moment of blind panic, not by someone who knew her true purpose in Sedona, and had been lying in wait for her.

Did she truly believe Bornfield was innocent? Her gut feeling told her that the Native American wasn't the killer. Of course, her gut feelings before had been proven wrong, but not often.

Josh, of course, would have been horrified about her admitting her belief in the innocence of a man under arrest for murder. It definitely was not proper police procedure.

But then her investigative methods were unorthodox. Josh had told her that often, but at the same time admitting ruefully that they worked more often than not.

Chapter Fifteen

Casey had promised Alice Farrel that she would be back at the ranch in time for lunch. It was already on the table by the time she arrived shortly after twelve. They sat down to a sturdy, ranch lunch; she knew from experience that ranch folks, as well as farmers, ate their big meal in the middle of the day. A platter was piled high with fried chicken, and there were side dishes of mashed potatoes, fresh corn on the cob, and green beans from Alice's garden. Fluffy, golden biscuits Alice had made by hand were passed around, and frosted glasses of iced tea were served.

Donnie ate as if starved, but Casey was accustomed to that. Often, she was awed by the amount of food he could put away. In between mouthfuls he quizzed her about the Sedona murders. When he had first come to live with her, she had been appalled by his thirst for details she considered too gory for young minds; but after meeting a number of his friends and schoolmates, she found that such interests were typical of young boys. Since it seemed to do him little harm, she related many details of her current cases, editing out only the more gruesome parts. Josh had commented, "The boy says he wants to be a homicide dick when he grows up. From the interest he shows, I'd say he's got a shot at being a good one."

Casey was sure that the Farrels were horrified at the question and answer exchange between Casey and Donnie, but they said nothing.

Just as an apple pie was dished up for dessert, the phone

on the kitchen wall rang. As Dan Farrel started to get up to answer it, Donnie said with a sly glance at Casey, "That'll be Josh calling Casey, Uncle Dan."

Casey stared at him. "What're you now, psychic?"

The boy ducked his head, grinning. "I called and told him you'd be here for lunch."

"You're a big help, kiddo. Thanks a lot." She slid back her chair and went to pick up the receiver. "Hello?"

"Casey, what're you doing up there?" Josh growled. "You promised to stop off and see me on your way back from LA."

"I'm sorry, Josh, I know I did," she said in a subdued voice. "But I just didn't have the time. I had to get back to Sedona."

"Why the rush?" he said alertly. "What's happened?"

She gave him an abbreviated version of what had transpired since she'd last talked to him. "So you see, I had to get back, and I certainly had to talk to Bornfield as quickly as possible."

He grunted sceptically. "And I gather that you've decided this Native American isn't your perp?"

"Not a hundred percent, but pretty much, yes."

His sigh came over the line. "And I'll just bet you told him that?"

Casey had to smile. She hadn't told him in so many words, but she should know by now how well Josh could read her. "Pretty much."

"You know, Farrel, some day you're going to come up with egg on your face."

"But when that happens you'll be there to wipe it off, won't you, Detective?" she responded with a laugh. "Depend on it."

"You'd better hope so," he grumbled. "So when will I see you?"

"Soon, Josh, soon."

"Promises, promises."

She lowered her voice. "I love you, Josh." The words came out without any forethought, and from his silence she knew he was as surprised as she was. She added quickly, "Goodbye, Josh," and hung up before he could respond.

She got back to Sedona by mid-afternoon, Rena Rainier once again. She drove directly to the Steele Magnolia. Vickie Steele was busy with a customer in the back. She saw Casey come in and motioned for her to have a seat in the waiting area, calling out, "Be with you in a sec, Rena."

Casey sat down, leafing through an old *People* magazine. Vickie bustled up a few minutes later. The waiting area was empty except for Casey. Vickie took a seat beside her.

"Well, how did things go in LA?"

Casey smiled. "Fine. Everybody concerned is quite pleased with what I've found. They're even talking of moving the schedule up if they can."

Vickie sighed gustily, her smile flashing in relief. "Good! I was afraid they'd changed their minds."

Casey hated herself for lying, but what choice did she have? She said, "I don't think there's any danger of that, Vickie. What did you call about?"

"Oh . . ." Vickie lowered her voice even more. "We're having a meeting tomorrow night, and I was told it was okay to bring you along, so long as you swear an oath that you'll never tell what happens."

Casey felt a pull of excitement. She took a steadying breath. "You have my solemn word on that, Vickie."

Vickie smiled brilliantly. "Oh, I wasn't worried. But some of the others . . ." She shrugged. "Well, you know."

"Thank you, Vickie. What time and where do I go?"

"You can go with me. They move the meetings around from place to place. It doesn't start until late, eleven o'clock. Come by my place. Here's the address." She furtively passed Casey a folded piece of paper, and Casey put it in her purse. Maybe, just maybe, this was the break she had been waiting for.

After leaving the Steele Magnolia she drove to Wesley Strom's antique shop. The parking lot was crowded with vehicles, and the inside of the shop was packed with tourists. Wes was occupied with a customer, showing her an ancient rolltop desk. The woman was fiftyish, with blue-white hair. She wore a great deal of jewellery that jangled with every movement, and she seemed to be constantly in motion. Her voice was high and piercing as she haggled with Wes.

Casey paused just inside the door, waiting until Wes glanced her way. He beamed a smile at her, waggled a pinkie, then started toward her without a word to his customer. As he walked off, the woman turned, aiming an insulted glare at his back. The French poodle came trotting after Wes, yelping. Wes stooped without breaking stride, scooped the animal up into his arms, and came on.

"Rena!" he exclaimed. "I'm happy to see you, darling!"

"You didn't have to leave her hanging, Wes."

"Oh, her!" He didn't bother to lower his voice. "She's just a lookee-lookee. I can always tell. The only way she'll buy that desk is if I practically give it to her. These shoppers come up here from Phoenix, or wherever, all the money in the world, and think they can outsmart the yokels. Of course, I can play the yokel as good as anybody if the occasion demands, but in her case it's a waste of time." The poodle barked shrilly. Wes stroked it fondly. "Hush, darling. I know you share my opinion of that awful woman, but you don't have to be so vocal about it."

Casey had to laugh. "You're terrible, you know that?"

"But of course, darling. It's what I do best," he said smugly.

"I got your message. I had to fly back to LA briefly. Why did you call, Wes?"

"Why, I thought we might do lunch." He twinkled

roguishly at her. "Isn't that the way they put it in Hollywood Land?"

Casey laughed again. "Some do, I suppose. I'd love to have lunch with you, Wes. When?"

"Tomorrow would suit me. L'Auberge. Oneish?"

"That sounds fine."

Now he did lower his voice, with a glance around. "Perhaps we could discuss the meeting you're attending tomorrow night."

Casey tried not to show her astonishment. "You know about that?"

Wes winked. "But of course, darling. This is a small town, after all."

"Well, I hope the whole town doesn't know," she said ruefully. "I'm here on business. People may think I'm a kook, and avoid me if they learn I'm attending a cult meeting."

Wes waved his free hand. "Not to worry. Besides, aren't all Hollywood people considered kooks? And I'm sure you'll enjoy it."

"Wait . . ." She squinted at him. "Don't tell me *you're* a member?"

"Of course, darling. It's loads of fun, and there's not all that much fun to be found in Sedona. I consider myself a people watcher, and what better place to watch people with their hair down? But . . ." He leaned toward her, his voice a conspiratorial whisper. "We'll talk about it over lunch tomorrow. Ta ta!"

Casey left the shop smiling. Wes and his charming bad-boy persona reminded her of Truman Capote. Witty, intelligent, and naughty, he always made her smile. But what if this studied, carefully nurtured personality was only one side of the man? What if he had a dark, dangerous side? No matter how entertaining Wes was, she must not ignore this possibility.

Looking at her watch, she saw that it was still relatively

early, and decided to see if Glenn Cabot was still in his office. He was.

Cabot got to his feet as she entered, his salesman's smile in place. "Ms Rainier! Come in, have a seat."

"Hello, Mr Cabot." She took the chair before his desk. "I've been away for a couple of days: a quick flight to LA for a conference with the producers. I received your message, but I've been sort of busy. I was close by, so I thought I'd drop in and return the call in person."

He bobbed his head. "Considerate of you. It was nothing really important. Just wondering how your location search was coming along." A frown moved across his face like a shadow. "Your movie is still going forward? Not thinking of going to another town, I hope?"

"Oh, no, all concerned are quite happy with Sedona. A couple of questions came up, and it was thought I could handle them better in person, instead of on the phone." Did that lie sound plausible? she wondered; she had told so many that she had trouble discerning what sounded like truth or fiction. "And my search is coming along fine. I've got most of the locations pretty well lined up. One thing I learned on the coast is that at least two new scenes will be required. Script changes." She managed a rueful smile. "Script changes are the norm in this business, but they can be a pain in the rear."

He laughed heartily. "Rena, there are certain aspects in any business or profession that give you a pain in the butt. You should see some of my problems." He leaned forward. "What I really called about was to tender an invitation. Once every two weeks there is a luncheon of the biggies in Sedona." He got a sly twinkle in his eyes. "Some call it a power broker meeting. Others call us the Sedona Mafia. Neither of those names really fit. We talk about important matters concerning our little town, sure, but we have no power to really *do* anything. But many important people attend, and I thought it might be helpful for you to meet some of them. Actually, it's an excuse to have a few belts, share good food, and socialize. How about it, Rena?"

She hesitated, remembering Wes Strom's invitation. She was torn. She wanted to learn what Wes knew about the cult; on the other hand, she might meet someone at the luncheon who could be important to her investigation.

She said slowly, "I have a prior engagement, but I could probably get out of that."

"Would you, Rena? I think the luncheon might be helpful to you. If nothing else, it would be good public relations for your movie. And from what I've heard public relations are always important in the movie business."

After leaving Cabot's office, she found a public telephone and called Wes Strom. "Wes? I just received an invitation from Glenn Cabot to attend a luncheon tomorrow. He says some important people will be there. Could we have lunch another time? How about dinner tomorrow evening, before the cult meeting?"

"The Sedona Mafia? Darling, those lunches are boor–ing."

"You've attended?"

"Of course. But not any oftener than I can help. Those people think themselves Sedona power brokers, but they have little more influence than a fart in a wind tunnel, if you'll pardon my French."

"But it would be good public relations for my company. I think I should attend."

After a brief pause he said, "You're right, darling. You should go." His voice warmed. "And dinner would be better anyway, less rush, less bustle. But if it's to be dinner, I have to bring Robbie along. He would be *so* upset if I didn't."

"I have no objections to that. In fact, I think that's an excellent idea."

After hanging up the receiver, Casey stared at it for a few moments, gnawing on her lower lip. Should she or shouldn't she? She always avoided talking to Bob Wilson as long as possible when she was in the field. Yet she knew that he was steaming by this time, and he just might call her at the hotel.

With a sigh she dialled his number in Phoenix. When he answered, she said, "Hello, Bob."

"Farrel!" he said explosively. "It's about time you called in!"

"I've been busy."

"Yeah, right," he said with heavy sarcasm. "Running off to California, spending the taxpayers' money on a wild goose chase, while the killer's being nailed in Sedona."

"You have such a way with a cliché, Bob," she said serenely. "Vernon Bornfield isn't our killer, Bob."

"It wouldn't be so bad if the task force had received at least *some* credit for it," he said in a snarling voice, "but we didn't. Not one iota."

"Bob, you never listen," she said wearily. "I just told you, the man they arrested isn't our killer."

"Oh, I heard you, but you're probably just saying that because you had nothing to do with it."

"After all this time you should know me better than that."

"I know you're often off the wall. You have any proof this Indian didn't kill those people?"

"The operative phrase is Native American. Indian is a no-no."

"Who gives a damn about that? What proof do you have of his innocence?"

"None that I can spell out yet."

"Then how the hell do you *know*?" He gave a snort of derisive laughter. "Women's intuition, I suppose?"

"You might put it that way. Or maybe just a gut feeling."

"Jesus! Spare me."

"Have I been wrong before?"

"Yeah, you have."

"But not often, you'll have to admit that. Just give me

some time here, okay? In my opinion that's what they're doing by arresting Bornfield, buying time, easing the media pressure."

"That's a pretty serious charge, Farrel."

"Oh, I'm not charging them with anything. My understanding is there was a strong disagreement between the Sedona police and the Yavapai County Sheriff's Department about Bornfield's guilt, and the pros took the day. But I'm right, I know I am, and I'm sure I'm getting close to the truth here."

"You'd better be right, Farrel," he said ominously. "If you're not, your ass is mine."

Chapter Sixteen

There were about twenty people in attendance at the luncheon the next day. The Sedona "Mafia" had a room all to themselves, with a no-host bar, which was where most of the guests were assembled when Casey arrived a few minutes late.

The mood was festive and relaxed, which Casey soon realized was not wholly due to the flowing alcohol. Much of the conversation was about Vernon Bornfield's arrest, and from what she overheard, everyone seemed to believe that Bornfield was guilty as sin. The relief was enormous.

Casey recognized the faces of several people she had met at the Mayor's party. Mayor Caldwell was present; as were Russell Turner, the developer; Vickie Steele; and Glenn Cabot. She also saw some people she recognized from other places, such as Alex Haydon, who was talking with a striking blonde woman that Casey did not recognize.

After Cabot had given Casey the tour and introduced her as Rena Rainier, "The young lady from Hollywood who's going to put Sedona on the map", she said to him, "You say most of these people are important, but I notice that many of them were not at Mayor Caldwell's party. Alex Haydon, for instance."

"Oh, you've met Alex?" Cabot said with a raised eyebrow.

Casey nodded. "Yes, he was fishing in Oak Creek, the day the latest body was discovered in Slide Rock Park. I happened to be there, too, looking for sites."

Cabot studied her intently for a moment, then finally nodded. "Thank God, they finally found the killer. Those killings had to stop. Bad for Sedona's image, bad for tourist business. With each murder tourist trade dropped ten percent, or more."

"Then you think this Native American . . . what's his name, Bornfield, is the guilty party?"

Once again, his keen gaze pinned her. "Certainly. Don't you?"

Uncomfortable under his stare, Casey said quickly, "I really don't have any opinion one way or the other. That's a job for the police. But I've heard talk. Many people seem to think that he's innocent."

"Tree huggers!" he said scornfully. "Sentimentalists. Some of them start screaming racial prejudice when an Indian is arrested for anything, even spitting on the sidewalk. I don't think of myself as prejudiced, but I don't think race is always behind it. We've gone too far in this country. Now we bend over backward when any minority is charged with a crime. But enough of that." He made a dismissive gesture. "Getting back to what you said earlier. When Annie throws a party, she only invites friends, or at least members of her own political party; and Alex has fought her on almost every issue. The same could be said of many of the others here today." He grinned. "As for as this gathering goes, well, the fact is, nobody is *invited* per se. People in town know about these lunches, and come or stay away at their own discretion."

Someone down at the other end of the bar hailed Cabot. He nodded at Casey and walked off.

As Casey wandered around, eavesdropping shamelessly, her annoyance mounted. It was damnably inconvenient that, in her undercover persona, she could not question people directly about the homicides. She was forced to confine her questions to those that showed nothing more than normal curiosity.

Even there she was thwarted to a certain degree. When she talked to people she hadn't met before, they seemed to forget all about the murders, and fired questions at her about Hollywood. Had she ever met Julia Roberts? Sharon Stone? Clint Eastwood? Kevin Costner? To all such questions her answers were evasive. Who was going to star in her movie? She replied that several well-known actors were under consideration and had been sent scripts, but no final decision had been made.

Casey felt a little guilty when she thought about the disappointment that would occur when it became known that no movie was going to be shot in Sedona, at least not by any company Rena Rainier was associated with. But then, since the townsfolk had dealt with movie companies before, they must know how often such deals fell through. At any rate, however she felt about the situation, there wasn't much she could do about it.

She turned to find Alex Haydon at her elbow. With a mental sigh, she managed a smile. Here was another one she had hinted to that her mythical movie company might want to engage his services.

Haydon's weathered face creased in a craggy grin. "Well, have you found out whether or not your bosses will want to use my ranch, or my horses? Purely business interest, you understand. Frankly, I could use the money."

"I can't give you an answer yet, Mr Haydon. I talked to the producer about it, and recommended your ranch as a good location; but he would only say he would think about it. The script is undergoing some revisions, and probably will continue to do so right up until the first camera rolls."

"Hollywood people never seem to have the ability to make a final decision about anything," he said in a grumbling voice. "Movie people are weird. With an exception," he added quickly. "You strike me as perfectly normal. And I'm not just saying that to butter you up, Ms Farrel."

She smiled. "I'm sure you're not, Mr Haydon, and

I thank you." She hated herself for deceiving this nice man.

He was gazing around the room; his face twisted in a grimace of disgust. "Listening to all these people gossip about the murders you'd think they knew what they were talking about."

Casey seized the opportunity he had given her. "By that I assume you don't believe Vernon Bornfield guilty?"

He gazed at her keenly for a moment, but he didn't seem to think the question out of order. "I'm not in the police business, young lady, but I suppose I'd have to say no. I do have some friends in the Sedona Police Department, and in the Sheriff's Office, who think the arrest was rather hasty. Trouble is, a lot of people are quick to believe an Indian is *always* guilty of something."

Casey smiled. "I must say that it's nice to hear a different view. Most of these people seem to have already tried and convicted Bornfield."

He shrugged. "Everyone is anxious for a quick solution, and here's Bornfield, in custody, a likely suspect. They hope he's the killer, because then the thing will be over and done with. It's not entirely prejudice – although there is a lot of that, too. Some people are only too happy to see proof that the 'inferior' races are as bad as they suspect. Personally, I think all that is a waste of good time, and detrimental to the human soul. Unfortunately, the human animal is very tribal, with a built-in propensity toward self-aggrandizement at the expense of any tribe other than their own."

Casey nodded. She felt herself warming toward Haydon. Something about him reminded her of her uncle, Dan Farrel.

"That's a fine attitude, Mr Haydon," she said, "and I commend you for it."

"Aw, shucks, ma'am." Haydon looked down in a pretense of shyness and dug his boot toe into the carpet. "I'm just an old cowhand, ma'am, out of my element here among you city folk. You're liable to get me all flustered."

Casey said dryly, "I doubt there's much danger of that."

Haydon's glance went past her, and he said, "Excuse me, Rena. Someone just came in I need to have a word with."

He went past her. Casey stood looking after him, thinking what a nice man he was. She raised her glass and finished her drink. A hand touched her elbow, and she started, looking around into Russell Turner's flushed face.

His black eyes flashed at her. "You're Rena Rainier, the movie lady, right?"

"And you're Russ Turner, right?"

He got a surprised look. "We've met?"

"Sort of. I was at the Mayor's party the other night."

"Oh, right!" He grinned. "You'll have to forgive me, Miss Rainier. I'd had a hard day, and was a little smashed that night."

She could smell the liquor on his breath, and she concluded that he was a little smashed right now, in the middle of the day. Evidently, Russ Turner was a hard drinker. And now he raised the glass in his hand and drained it.

"How are you coming along with your movie location search?"

"Pretty good. I should have it all nailed down in probably another week."

"The way things work, as I get it, a movie company pays the property owner when they shoot on his property."

"Well, yes, that's usually the case."

"Anything in your movie script calling for filming in a partly finished housing project? Excuse me, *estates*. People hear me call it a project, they'd probably lynch me. No housing *projects* in Sedona." He grinned, running the palm of his free hand over his shining bald head. "I'll be frank with you, Miss Rainier. I'm suffering from cash flow problems right now. Nothing permanent, you understand. But I'm temporarily stalled. I could use a few extra bucks, so if your movie company calls for shooting in half-completed houses, I'm your man."

"Well, there is one scene," she lied. "I'll talk to my producer, maybe it'll work out."

"That'd be great!" he said enthusiastically. "Now that these damned murders are finally solved, maybe things'll settle down. You know, the money people are balking at loaning out development money in the area because of the murders? Says it depresses the market!" He snorted. "Can you believe that?"

Casey said quickly, "Then you believe they've arrested the right man?"

He stared at her, suspicion clouding his eyes. "I have no reason not to. Do you?"

"No, no, it's just that I hear many people here claiming that Bornfield is not the killer."

"Gossip. Gives people something to talk about." He waved a hand airily. "The Indian's the guilty party, no doubt in my mind . . ."

At that moment a rapping sound came from one of the round tables. Casey glanced over and saw Glenn Cabot rapping a water glass on the table, calling for quiet. As silence descended, he said, "All right, people, lunch is being served. Bring your drinks and take your seats."

Turner was already moving toward the bar, clearly intent on refreshing his drink. Before turning away toward her table, Casey looked after him for a moment. The conversation with Turner had given her an idea.

When the lunch was over, two hours later, Casey found a pay phone and called Gabe's motel. He didn't answer. She banged the receiver down in anger. It was damned annoying carrying on an investigation second-hand, as it were. Talking to Russell Turner had given her a line of inquiry that should be pursued, something that should have been done already, but she couldn't do it herself.

It was now the middle of the afternoon, and at the

moment there wasn't much she could do. She was hoping that the cult meeting tonight would open up new lines of investigation; but that meant waiting, and she wasn't very good at waiting.

She drove out to the Enchantment and got into her jogging clothes. She had not jogged in days. Jogging always cleared the cobwebs from her mind, clarified her thinking, and it always vented her anger when she was as irritated as she was at the moment. Also, the meal she had just eaten had been laden with calories. True, she hadn't been forced to eat like a pig, but she had; now she had an opportunity to work off some of the calories.

She ran along the main road down below the hill, past the tennis courts and the golf course, and on up the trail beyond the road. Now it was quiet, the only sounds the rhythmic thud of her footsteps, and soon the whistle of her expelled breath. The air was marvellously clear, scented by pines, and the colourful canyon walls rose on each side of her.

As she ran, she put all thoughts of the case from her mind, making it, in effect, a clean slate, ready to receive any new thoughts that might occur. She laughed at herself. Pretty fanciful image, Farrel, she thought. But she knew from experience that this procedure worked. Often, after a long, exhausting run she found that many knotted problems began to unravel.

She ran for an hour, and she was sweating freely when she got back to the resort; then, instead of returning immediately to her room, she jumped into the rental car and drove up to the 89A and found a telephone. She called Gabe's motel. This time he answered.

"Rena, what's on your mind?"

"Gabe, there's something I need you to do. Should have done it before now, but this undercover business has got me out of sync."

"Whatever you require, boss lady," he said cheerfully.

"Yeah, right. I want you to dig into the financial status of several people involved here. Got a pen and paper?"

"Yep."

"Glenn Cabot; Russell Turner; Alex Haydon; Wesley Strom; Mayor Anne Caldwell; and Vickie Steele."

"You think the killer could be a *woman*?" he said on a note of surprise.

"I doubt it, but I want them checked out anyway. And four people in California, at Camden Industries. Grady Camden, Sam Porter, Martin Smith, and Paul Tate. I want to know their credit rating, their financial worth, what they owe, if any of them are hurting for money. And most of all, I want to know if any of them have paid out or received any large sums of money recently not accounted for by their business or salary."

He said, "You think the motive behind these murders is *money*?"

"At this point I don't have a clue as to the motives, but hopefully this will help us find out. Just get on it, okay?"

"Will do. It's going to take some time, require some digging."

"I'm aware of that, Gabe, but . . ." She laughed. "Somehow, I figure you for a fast worker."

"Now what is *that* supposed to mean?"

Laughing, she hung up without answering.

Casey had made dinner reservations for six o'clock for herself and her guests in the hotel dining room.

When she arrived at ten minutes before six, she found Wes Strom and Rob waiting in the lobby.

"On time, I see."

"Of course, dear lady. I'm always early when I'm dining here. The very best food in Sedona. I always want to get an early start."

"Being on time, or early," Rob said in his high voice, "is a fetish with Wes. In fact, you could say an obsession."

Casey laughed, looking pointedly at Wes's empty arms. "I'm surprised. I see you left Pookie at home."

"I know, it's sad." Wes made a face. "The poor thing was desolated. I've never understood why restaurants won't allow dogs. They're much cleaner, and better behaved, than many people I know."

"Come on, you two." She got between them, linking arms with them. "Let's go eat."

They were shown to a corner table. One whole side and one end of the dining room consisted of walls of glass. It was still daylight outside, and the colours of the buttes were spectacular. From where they sat, Chimney Rock and Capitol Butte could be clearly seen.

Casey sighed. "I could get used to this. It's lovely here, isn't it?"

"But it's rapidly being spoiled," Wes said petulantly. "People always do that, don't they?"

"You're being selfish, Wes," Casey said with a smile. "You should be willing to share all the beauty, not want it kept for just a few."

Rob grinned impishly. "You know what Wes said, many years ago when we first came to Sedona? He said, now I'm here, close the gate and lock it!"

"But you're running a business, Wes," Casey said. "I should think the more people coming through your shop, the better for business."

"True, but I'd just as soon they didn't *move* here permanently. We get enough business from people from Phoenix, Flag, and Prescott."

Casey saw their waiter approaching. "Now order whatever you want, you two. My company is paying. It's a business expense." Casey smiled inwardly, glad her offer wasn't being taped for Bob Wilson's ears; he would hit the ceiling.

"Ah, the life of you movie people," Wes said. "Travelling everywhere, all expenses paid, entertain guests on the company card."

"It can get a little tiring, believe it or not."

After they had ordered a round of drinks, and their dinners, Casey waited until the waiter had left, then leaned forward eagerly. "All right, Wes. You said you'd tell me all about these Children of the Enlightenment."

Wes's face assumed a sly look. "I've had second thoughts. I think it's better you wait and see for yourself. Surprise you."

"That's hardly paying for your supper, Wes. You promised."

He gave her a probing look. "You sure this sudden interest in the Children of the Enlightenment doesn't have to do with your movie?"

"Well, there may be a scene in the movie that involves a cult."

"If you're thinking of exposing the activities of the Cult of the Enlightenment, the Council will be displeased with you, Rena."

Casey pounced. "The Council? Who are they? And what do they do?"

"No one knows who they are. As to what they do, they run the cult. There are thirteen of them."

"Thirteen? They must have a leader."

"Oh, yes, they have a leader. He is simply called the Master."

Casey smiled to herself. Despite Wes's expressed reluctance to discuss the cult, he was quite willing to be interrogated. She said, "It all sounds pretty melodramatic to me."

Rob interjected, "It *is* melodramatic, like something right out of a cheap horror movie!"

Casey looked at him. "I gather you don't approve."

"I certainly do not," Rob said vehemently. "I think it's all bullshit, if you'll pardon the expression. And I think anyone who belongs has mental problems."

Smiling, Wes said, "Rob and I argue about this constantly. We're usually pretty compatible, but not about this."

"Why *do* you belong, Wes?"

"Because, like I already told you, I find it entertaining. I like to watch people at their worst."

"'People at their worst'," she said slowly. "And you, Rob, said something about a cheap horror movie. What goes on at their ceremonies then? Do they have sex orgies? Do they sacrifice animals?"

Wes looked shocked. "God, no! Dear girl, what kind of a person do you think I am? I would never be a party to something like that!"

Casey felt a pang of disappointment. If Wes was telling the truth, tonight was going to be wasted. Still, maybe at the meeting she could learn something about other cults operating in the area. She realized that Rob, wearing a disapproving look, was speaking.

"They *do* sacrifice animals, Wes. You told me about stretching a goat across some kind of altar and cutting its throat. You said they drank the blood!"

"I never drank any blood! Yech!" Wes made a face. Catching Casey's look, he shrugged. "All right, last year on Halloween, shortly after I joined, they killed a goat. But later, they barbecued and ate it. No big harm in that, is there?"

Rob said, "And you also told me about sex orgies." Rob wore a scowl. "That's one reason I never approved. I consider sex private, between two people, not something for public display."

"Oh, honey, you're such a prude." Wes said. But he was smiling, and he reached over to squeeze Rob's hand, then directed his attention back to Casey. "It's true, they do get a little carried away sometimes. The Master preaches freedom in all things. If you feel like doing it, if it makes you feel good, then do it."

Casey said, "You think that's why people join it then, for the thrill of unfettered sex?"

The waiter came with their food, and they were silent until

he left. Wes took a bite and nodded his approval. He looked across the table with a nod. "Yes, that's probably part of it. But they don't have sex orgies every time. The cult preaches against Christian religion, the strict morality of society *and* religion. They teach that you only find contentment within yourself. In my opinion, that's why they attract a following. People desperately long for something to believe in, something that will allow them to indulge in their secret desires, and which will approve, not castigate them for it. Also, they're searching for someone to lead them, guide them, give them a centre to their drab lives. They find all that in the Cult of the Enlightenment."

"They don't worship Satan, petition him for help and guidance?"

A veil seemed to descend over Wes's face, and his gaze dropped to his plate. "That's all I'm going to say. You've already squeezed too much out of me."

Sensing that she had pushed him far enough, Casey dropped it, and devoted her attention to her food.

Shortly after eleven that night, Casey was with Vickie Steele in the other woman's car, bound for an unknown destination. Vickie seemed tense, and not inclined to talk. They were travelling along Highway 79. After they got out of the main park of town, Vickie pulled her vehicle off the road, and turned to Casey.

"I'm sorry, Rena, but I have to blindfold you."

"Blindfold me!"

"I was told to. Since this is your first time, they don't want you to know where the meeting is being held tonight."

Casey felt a chill of fear. What was she getting into here? Had her disguise been penetrated? Would hers be the next body found cold and still by the banks of Oak Creek?

But she couldn't back off now. She had to take her chances. She said resignedly, "Okay, Vickie. If that's the way it has to be."

Chapter Seventeen

Behind the thick pressure of the folded scarf Vickie had tied over her upper face, Casey's eyes shifted under her closed lids. She heard the car start, and felt the movement as it gained speed. Carefully, she made mental notes of directions and times.

After a few minutes they turned onto an unpaved road. Casey's uneasiness mounted.

Trying to keep her voice casual, she said, "Is it much further?"

Vickie replied. "Not much."

"Does your group have very many out of town members?"

"No, almost all of our members are local people."

Casey ached to ask if Barbara Stratton had been one of the out-of-towners, but she held her tongue.

Vickie said in a small voice, "I really am sorry about this, Rena. I know it's humiliating. I argued against it, but the Council ruled against me. *I* trust you, but it's not up to me to say."

Casey laughed lightly. "Well, my feelings are hurt a little, but I'm sure I'll get over it. Do I get to meet the members of this Council tonight?"

"Oh, some of them will be there, but maybe not all. But you won't get to meet any of them personally. They don't mix and mingle with the members. Anything they have to say will be relayed by the Master."

"Doesn't sound very democratic," Casey said dryly. "This Master you mention, does he mingle with the members?"

"Sometimes," Vickie responded hesitantly. "But not often." She cleared her throat. "Before you're accepted as a member, Rena, you'll come before the Council and you'll be questioned. They want to find out how serious you are, if you'll make a good member. They don't want someone who will go around later making light of the whole thing. But even then only the Master will speak to you."

"Do they have a speech impediment?"

She felt Vickie stir. "Now you see, that's the sort of thing . . ."

Casey said hastily, "I'm sorry, Vickie. I shouldn't have said that. I assure you that I take this seriously."

Vickie drove for a moment or two in silence before saying, "I probably shouldn't tell you this, but you'll learn eventually anyway. The Council members are important people in Sedona, and they don't want their identities known."

"But how about this Master?"

"You won't learn who he is, either. They're all masked, you know, and the man we call the Master can change his voice at will. Each time we meet he talks with a different voice."

Casey thought she had asked enough questions; any more and Vickie might become suspicious. They rode in silence for twenty minutes or more. The road became even more rough and bumpy, and Casey sensed they were climbing.

Finally the car slowed, came to a stop, and the motor was shut off. Vickie said, "I'll remove the blindfold in a minute." The sound of rustling and a car door opening. Casey sat quietly, her heart pounding.

When the blindfold came off Casey could see nothing at first; then the lights of an oncoming vehicle popped up over the rise behind her, illuminating the area. She drew back. Beside the car stood a cloaked and hooded figure with the face of a beautiful cat. She relaxed when Vickie's voice came from behind the mask. About twenty other vehicles were parked all around them, and off to the left she could see other cloaked figures struggling up a steep path. Apparently the cult's rites were to take place on another, higher, mesa. Her gaze swept around the area, scanning the license plates of the nearest cars. They were all Arizona plates.

Vickie said, "You ready, Rena?"

"Ready and willing."

Out of the car Casey took a moment to look around. She hadn't the faintest idea where they were. Far off, in what she assumed to be the East, was a scattering of lights, probably Oak Creek. A piece of moon hung in the night sky like a horn, giving off very little light.

As Casey and Vickie started up the steep path, Casey noticed that the stream of cultists had dwindled to a trickle. A glance at her watch told her that it was eleven-thirty. As they neared the top, a flickering yellow glow was visible, and as they crested she saw the reason. Torches were set into the ground at irregular intervals around a large circle outlined by stones. On one side of the circle stood a ring of cloaked figures, wearing smooth, gold-finished masks. She counted them; thirteen in all, apparently identical, but which was the Master?

On the other side of the pentagram, the other cultists were gathered. Like Vickie, they were hidden by full robes and wore animal masks, some quite beautiful. The effect was eerie.

She followed Vickie as the other woman led her to a spot near where the other cultists were gathered. There were about thirty in all. Casey studied the circle, in the centre of which a pentagram had been formed, also of stones. In the centre of the pentagram stood a large, flat rock. She shivered and took a deep breath, attempting to quell her sudden panic.

Placing her mouth close to Vickie's ear, she whispered, "If the members of the Council, and the Master, wish to keep their identities a secret from the members, how do they manage that? They must have cars, surely they don't walk up here. It would be easy to jot down their license numbers and find out who belongs to their vehicles, if anyone was curious enough."

Vickie in turn put her mouth close to Casey's ear. "I don't know. Every time I've attended they're already here. Maybe they *do* walk up. Or they all come together and park somewhere else, but close by. I must warn you, Rena. Don't be too curious, certainly don't let them catch you at it. At the least they'd never accept you into the cult if they found out you're trying to learn who they are."

At the least? Casey wondered what the worst would be, her glance going to the stone altar.

She glanced around at the masked faces, trying to figure out which were men and which women; but it was difficult to tell. She decided that the group was about evenly divided. They spoke quietly, in hushed voices. She felt a chill. If the Children of the Enlightenment was responsible for the murders, some, if not all, of these people must have been present at some of the homicides.

Something occurred to her. Where was Wes Strom? She had just assumed that he would be here. She had told him that Vickie would be bringing her. She studied the cult members again, but saw no figure that she thought could be that of Wes.

She transferred her gaze to the silent Council. Was Wes a member of the Council? That struck her as unlikely. Wes didn't seem to her as a person at all interested in belonging to the power structure of any organization; he was a scoffer, a rebel. She studied each member of the Council carefully, but again did not see a figure that might be that of Wes.

Now one of the Council members – Casey had begun to think of them as the Inner Circle – stepped forward arms raised over its head. A hush fell over the crowd, and Casey assumed that this was the Master.

"Greetings, my children!" the figure intoned in a deep, resonant voice.

Voices rose in reply: "Greetings, O Master!"

"On this night we have cause for celebration."

There was an eerie quality to the voice, like an echo.

The Master continued, "This week, the man who has been so opposed to us, claiming that our ceremonies have destroyed the Indians' ceremonial grounds, has been exposed for the vile murderer that he is! He is now incarcerated for his crimes, and we need no longer be concerned with him. Our prayers for the Great One's intercession on our behalf have been answered. Let us praise Satan!"

The voices rose in unison: "Praise Satan!"

Casey was sorely disappointed. She kept thinking of an old Peggy Lee song, *Is That All There Is?* So far she had seen nothing sinister, not even very exciting. She looked at the people around her. They seemed rapt, intent on the man in the pentagram.

"Praise be thy Name, O Great Satan," the Master cried. "Your children are grateful to you for striking down our enemy. Tonight, we therefore celebrate in thy name, O Great One!" He made a sweeping gesture with one hand, and from somewhere in the darkness a drum began to beat, slowly, hypnotically, then growing, swelling, rising, as first a flute, then a stringed instrument of some kind joined the drum in a rhythm and melody of ever increasing wildness.

Casey watched in surprise as the celebrants began to dance. She turned to look for Vickie, and found her gone; then caught a glimpse of her being whirled away in the arms of a tall person wearing the face of a bison. Another figure, tall, and wearing a lion's face, reached for Casey's hand; but she shook her head, moving back out of reach. The figure reached again, his robe falling open so that Casey could see his sex, engorged and, under the circumstances, threatening. Pushing back his questing hand, she shook her head angrily. He hesitated, and her body tensed; but at last he shrugged and moved away toward another dancer.

Quickly fading into the shadows, she breathed deeply,

waiting for her pulse to slow. She watched in amazement as the rhythm of the music increased, became frenzied. She could feel the drum beat in her bones, and was not immune to its appeal. Under other circumstances . . .

She noticed that the celebrants danced all around the circle of stones, never venturing inside. She also noticed that the Council members didn't join in the dancing, but stood watching silently.

The dancers sang, the words incomprehensible to Casey. And now she became aware that their number had decreased; they were disappearing two by two into the shadows. The torches had burned down now, emitting only a pale wash of light. Vickie and her consort danced past Casey, and Casey watched as the man – she presumed it was a man – dragged Vickie off into the darkness. And then one couple, well within the circle of waning light, fell to the ground and began to copulate, wildly, unashamedly. It was clear that they wore nothing beneath the voluminous robes.

Casey grimaced with distaste. Apparently this was one of the orgies that Rob had mentioned. She would have liked to leave; clearly there was nothing more to be learned here. But obviously she couldn't until Vickie returned.

Her glance went again to the pentagram, and she saw with astonishment that the members of the Council and the Master were gone, faded away into the night, like ghosts.

A hand touched her elbow, and she jumped, startled. Whirling, she looked into Vickie's face. Vickie's lipstick was smeared, her lips set in a loose smile. Her eyes had a dazed look, and Casey had to wonder if she'd taken some drug out there in the darkness, or if she was just dazed from sex. Her cat mask had been pushed up to rest on her head. Her robe was open, exposing most of her full, unfettered breasts, and as she half turned away, gazing off into the dark, Casey saw smears of red dirt on the bottom of her robe.

They stood for a few moments in silence, until Casey finally decided that it was up to her to speak. Her words sounded stilted and awkward: "Vickie, are you ready to leave now?"

Vickie started, turning back. She stared vacantly into Casey's eyes.

Casey had never considered herself a prude, but what had occurred here tonight was not her cup of tea. Was all this just an elaborate excuse for promiscuous sex? She said impatiently, "Well, Vickie?"

"Oh . . . Yes, I'm ready," Vickie said dreamily.

She turned without another word and started toward the head of the trail leading down off the mesa. Casey noticed that the others were heading down as well. They were quiet, with none of their earlier exuberance.

Cars were pulling out of the lot as they reached Vickie's vehicle. As Vickie unlocked her car, Casey said, "Do we have to go through that blindfold nonsense again?"

Vickie looked abashed. "I'm sorry, Rena, but it's necessary, until you become a full member."

As she submitted to the indignity of the blindfold, Casey pondered whether or not she wanted to go to the trouble of joining. From what she had witnessed tonight it could be a waste of time and effort, and yet she had the feeling that it might be worthwhile. What she saw tonight might be a facade, hiding much darker activities. She'd gone this far, she might as well venture a little further.

As they drove away, she asked, "I noticed that the Council members and the Master seemed to fade away when the dancing started. Is that the usual procedure?"

Vickie said uneasily, "Yes. They're all sort of royalty, they don't socialize much with the rest of us."

"Doesn't that bother you?"

"No, why should it? Rena, did you . . . ?" Vickie asked tentatively. "Did you, you know?"

"Nope. I had what I guess was an offer, but I'm not much for having sex with strange men, particularly not in these times."

"It's fun. Try it, you might like it."

Yeah, right, Casey thought. She said, "Don't you worry? I mean with all the stuff that's out there . . .?"

Vickie shook her head. "The Master protects us."

Casey felt a shiver tickle her spine. "And there's something else: this guy came that came up to me, for a moment I thought he might drag me off anyway. Does that ever happen? Some guy takes a woman by force? Rapes her?"

"Oh, no!" Vickie said in horror. "That would never happen. There are rules against that sort of thing." Her voice rose on an indignant note. "What kind of people do you think we are, anyway?"

That's the trouble, Casey thought, I don't know what kind of people you are!

After they bumped along the road for awhile in silence she said, "Vickie, you said a bit ago *when* I became a member. How do I know when that happens?"

"Oh, you'll know. Don't worry, you'll know, Rena."

It was well after one in the morning when Casey got back to the Enchantment. When she opened the door and turned on the light, she saw a small, black envelope that had been shoved under her door.

With a quickening pulse she opened it. Inside the envelope was a sheet of black paper with a terse message typed on it in white letters:

"Rena Rainier; If you wish to become a member of our organization, you must be interviewed so that we may judge your commitment and qualifications. This interview will be conducted tomorrow evening at nine o'clock. If this meets with your approval, contact Vickie Steele. She will escort you to the place of the interview."

Chapter Eighteen

The first thing Casey did the next morning was to call Gabe Stinton and arrange for a meeting. This time they met in Slide Rock Park. Even early as it was, the park was packed with tourists, sunning on the rocks, preparing for picnic lunches, the kids riding the fast water skimming over the rocks.

Casey had some reservations about meeting in such a crowded place, but they couldn't keep meeting in the same places, and she hoped that no locals were present in the park this early in the morning.

She was waiting at a reasonably isolated spot when she saw Gabe approach, looking around casually. He began walking toward her, and she knew he had spotted her. He stopped a couple of times, watching a few of the children in the stream, laughing at their antics.

Good, she thought, he's learning!

He took his time approaching, finally stopping about three feet away, and stood staring at the creek instead of her.

Casey said, "I attended my first meeting of the Children of the Enlightenment last night."

His head jerked around in alarm, and he stared at her, then his gaze returned to the creek. "Wasn't that taking a huge risk?"

"It's a risk I had to take sooner or later if I'm ever to prove my theory about a cult being behind the murders."

"Even if that's true, how do you know it's this particular one?"

She shrugged. "I had to start somewhere. Even if this isn't the one I'm looking for, perhaps through it I can gain access to other groups."

Without willing it, an edge of discouragement coloured her voice. "I must admit, if what I witnessed last night is typical, these people are more or less harmless. Some people might consider what they did sinful, but it was a long way from murder, or even violence. No sacrifices, not even a goat. Just a little extracurricular sex, a few words of praise to Satan, apparently giving him credit for getting Vernon Bornfield out of their hair."

Gabe's voice quickened. "They *are* Satanists then?"

"It would seem so, but that doesn't mean they have human sacrifices. Speaking of Bornfield, what's the latest on him?"

Gabe shrugged. "About the same. He's still in jail, still the chief suspect. Lieutenant Martin did tell me, in confidence, that it's his opinion they're going to have to release Bornfield eventually. All the evidence against him is circumstantial and the only motive they have is the theory that Bornfield killed all those people in order to lay the blame on the cults, hoping in that way to run them off. Martin says the man would have to be crazy to do that, and whatever else he is, the Indian isn't crazy." He was silent for a moment. "So where do you go from here? In regards to the Children of the Enlightenment, I mean?"

"Oh, I'm going to continue. In fact, I'm meeting with the Master and the Council tonight. They're going to interrogate me, see if I qualify for permanent membership." She laughed lightly. "I wonder how it's going to feel, being on the wrong side of an interrogation?"

"You're playing with danger here, uh . . . Rena," he said darkly. "If they're behind all this, they may already be onto you. They may be setting you up."

"I don't think so, Gabe. Why go to such elaborate lengths? If they know I'm investigating them, they'd be more direct.

No, I'm convinced they don't suspect me yet. Besides, how else can I go about it, how can I learn if they're behind the homicides, if I don't get inside the cult, inside their *heads*. It's my job, Gabe, it's what I came here to do."

"I just hope you're right," he said with a sigh. "Just be careful, Rena, damned careful."

"I fully intend to. Now . . . What about the financial status on those names I gave you?"

Gabe laughed. "You're a hard taskmaster, you know that? You only gave me those names yesterday. It's going to take a little time."

"I have a feeling we may not have much of that. I keep waiting for another body to drop, if you'll pardon the black humour."

"Okay, I'll pass on what little I've dug up. The people in California, nothing yet. In Sedona, Wesley Strom has been in the antique business for years. He does a good business, is solid financially, nothing large, but no bad marks." He slanted a sideways look at her. "You *do* know he's gay?"

"Yes, that was pretty obvious from the start."

"His personal relationships have been rocky. He's had several male friends over his years here, but the present one has been around for five years. Apparently Strom has settled down. He was arrested once in Los Angeles six years ago for soliciting. Seems he picked on an undercover vice cop. The case was thrown out of court because the judge ruled entrapment on the part of the cop. As far as I could learn that's his only brush with the law."

"The many relationships are not uncommon among homosexuals," Casey said thoughtfully. "Especially during their younger years. You found nothing indicating any episodes of violence?"

"Nothing like that, no."

"That should eliminate him then. Of course, I never considered him a strong suspect anyway."

Gabe chuckled. "In mystery movies that's the one that always turns out to be the killer."

"This isn't a movie, Mr Stinton, even if I am supposed to be in the movie business. How about the other locals?"

"My run-down on them isn't complete yet. Except for Mayor Caldwell. She has no blots on her record, not even a traffic ticket. And she certainly isn't in any financial difficulty. When her husband died he left her a bundle, and apparently she's a shrewd investor. But you never really seriously considered her either, did you?"

"Not seriously, no. I just can't figure a woman for this. But I need all the background on her you can get, as well as on Vickie Steele."

"I haven't gotten too far yet on the beauty shop lady. I found out she's not getting rich with the shop, barely hanging on, and she's had as much bad luck with men as has Wesley Strom. In the past fifteen years she's gone through three husbands."

"That may account for her belonging to the cult," Casey commented. "She may be hoping to find something there she couldn't find in marriage. What else do you have for me?"

"Well, let's see . . . ." Gabe tilted his head up in thought. "I haven't learned a hell of a lot more. Glenn Cabot seems pretty sound financially, at least his Jeep rental business is doing okay. On the other hand, he has a pretty lavish life style, but I have to dig a little deeper. And that goes for Russell Turner as well. Turner is a wheeler-dealer, and he's cash-poor, from what I've learned so far. I'll have more on both men in a day or so."

"How about Alex Haydon?"

"Not much yet. I have some lines out on Haydon, but nothing interesting yet. And as I told you, the people in California will take a little longer. Mainly, I have to rely there on some California sources, and they haven't gotten back to me yet."

"Light a fire under them, Gabe. I need that information like yesterday."

"You really think the motives behind these killings are financial, Rena? It doesn't strike me as too likely."

"Since a strong motive is missing, I'm fishing here, Gabe. *Anything* in their lives, their backgrounds, may provide a clue. Just keep at it. I'll be in touch tomorrow." She smiled. "Maybe by that time I'll be a member in good standing of the Children of the Enlightenment."

She turned on her heel and left him standing there, heading for her car. From Slide Rock Park she drove directly to Wes's antique shop. She was very curious as to the reason Wes hadn't been at the cult meeting last evening, after telling her he would be there. But Wes wasn't at the shop.

Rob wore a worried frown when he came to greet her. "Good morning, Rena. Wes didn't come in today."

"Is he ill?"

"Says he is. He told me that his stomach was all upset, something he ate last night. I badgered him to see a doctor, but he wouldn't go. Said he'd be all right after a day in bed." Rob shook his head. "Stubborn, stubborn."

"I guess that was the reason he didn't show up at the meeting last night. He told me he'd be there, and I wondered when he didn't show."

Rob nodded. "Yes, he got sick after we left the Enchantment last night. But I don't think . . ." He looked around, lowering his voice. "But you know what I think? I don't think he's sick at all, I think he's faking it."

Casey frowned. "Faking it? But why?"

"Promise not to tell him?"

"Of course."

"I don't think he *wanted* to attend that meeting last night. I think he's sorry he ever joined the Children of the Enlightenment."

"But why? The way he told it to me, he gets a kick out of watching the carryings-on."

Rob nodded. "I know, that's what he *says*. But I think otherwise. Oh, he might have gotten a kick out of it at first. He knows how much I disapprove, so he never tells me very much; but he's let some hints drop about some things they do."

Casey said alertly, "Things? What things?"

He gestured vaguely. "Oh, just things, things he doesn't want to talk about."

"Has he ever said anything about sacrifices? Animals, maybe even human sacrifices?"

Rob wagged his head from side to side. "No, no, nothing like that. Wes would never, ever participate in something like that."

"But he did mention a goat being sacrificed once, which the members later barbecued and ate."

"Oh, that, yeah." Rob made a dismissive gesture. "That was nothing, but humans? No, no, not Wes. Heck, he won't even kill rats or insects in our house, always makes me do it. You know Wes, you think he'd be involved in something like that?"

"I've only known him a few days, Rob. But no, I can't conceive of him being involved in these murders."

Suspicion flared in his eyes. "You sound like a cop, Rena. Why are you so interested in all this? Talking of murders, human sacrifices!"

"I didn't mean to sound like one," she said quickly. "But I'm probably going to become a member, so I certainly would like to know if they're involved in anything bad."

"They worship Satan, they pray to him to give them material things, they praise Satan when good things happen to them, they indulge in sex orgies," he said harshly. "It depends on what you consider bad."

"You seem to know quite a bit about what goes on, Rob, for someone who doesn't belong. How did you learn? You say Wes says very little."

His glance slid away again. "People tell me things."

"People? Cult members, you mean?"

"Well, yes. Mostly, I've overheard some of them in here talking to Wes, when they think I'm not listening."

"Rob, were any of those people members of the Council, or even the Master?"

"How do I know? Nobody knows who they are."

"Not even Wes?"

"Of course not! You heard what he said last night."

"Tell me this then . . . If Wes is sorry that he joined the cult, why doesn't he just drop out?"

"I think he'd like to, but I think he's afraid."

Casey squinted at him. "Afraid of what?"

"When you join you swear an oath you'll never breathe a word of what goes on to a non-member, and you'll be a member of the cult for life."

"I think I heard an 'or' in there. If you drop out, what will happen?" She paused for a moment. "Will they kill you?"

Rob's eyes widened with fear. He looked around and saw a customer examining a lamp in one corner. He said hastily, "There's a customer I have to tend to. Goodbye, Rena." He took a step away, then turned back. "Please don't tell Wes what I've told you, Rena. He'd be . . . well, very upset."

"Of course not, Rob. Not a word."

She stared after him, frustrated. She was convinced that Rob knew more than he was telling, and that he was terrified for Wes. But she was also convinced that he'd told her all he was going to at this time. Maybe if he became more afraid for Wes's welfare, he might open up more.

Vickie Steele was waiting for Casey when she pulled into the parking lot alongside the Steele Magnolia that evening a few minutes before nine.

Getting into Vickie's car, Casey said, "Are you going to blindfold me again?"

Vickie laughed nervously. "Not tonight. We're just going

to an old barn on an abandoned ranch a few miles out of town."

Vickie turned left at the Y and drove toward Cottonwood. Casey tried to keep a conversation going, but Vickie seemed disinclined to chat, keeping her words to a minimum.

Finally, Casey said, "Is something wrong tonight, Vickie? I hope you won't take offense, but usually you talk a mile a minute, but not tonight."

"I'm sorry, Rena." Vickie shook her head from side to side. "It's just that I've never done this before. Oh, I've taken initiates to meetings, like I did you last night, but this is the first time to an interview before the Council and the Master."

"I don't see why it should be all that much different. Is it?"

Casey was watching closely, and saw a shiver pass over Vickie as she replied, "Well, yes. Always before, at the meetings, there are others around. Just members like me, I mean. Tonight, just the Council and the Master. I must confess they always spook me a little. Always so silent, so secretive, so . . . anonymous!"

Casey said slowly, "I can see why that might be intimidating, but have they ever given any reason for you to fear them?"

"No, no, of course not!" Vickie said quickly.

Too quickly, Casey thought.

Vickie turned off a dirt road about three miles out into the country. The road was dusty, bumpy, and no lights could be seen anywhere. About a mile down the road Vickie made another turn to the left. About a hundred yards down this road a dilapidated building loomed up in the headlights. Vickie parked a few yards from the building and shut off the motor, then the headlights. There were no lights on in the building. The quiet was almost eerie, only the crackling sounds of the cooling engine, and the chirpings of night insects.

She said dubiously. "You sure this is the place, Vickie? I don't see any lights."

Vickie gave that same nervous laugh, almost a titter. "Oh, they're in there, don't worry!"

Casey opened the car door and started to get out before she noticed that Vickie hadn't moved. "Aren't you coming in?"

"Oh, no. No one is allowed to be present during an initiate interview except Council members, the Master, and the initiate. I'll wait here for you, Rena."

Casey got out and walked slowly toward the old barn. Was she being set up? Was that the reason for Vickie's nervousness? She could well imagine what Josh would say were he here to see what she was doing.

But she was committed now. She walked on, expecting any second to hear Vickie start her car and roar away, leaving her alone here.

Casey had reached the side door to the barn now. She took a deep breath, and reached out. There was no handle, but the door gaped open a few inches. She took hold of the door edge and pulled. It opened with a screeching sound that sent a shiver of apprehension down her spine.

From the darkness inside a voice said, "Please step inside, Miss Rainier, and close the door behind you."

Chapter Nineteen

As Casey closed the door, a lantern flared brightly. She blinked against the sudden glare. A robed and masked figure stepped toward her, and she took an involuntary step backward.

The figure stopped, and spoke in that distorted voice she recognized from last night on the mesa. "Welcome, Miss Rainier."

Now she saw other robed figures sitting on boxes in a semicircle behind the Master. She counted quickly. Twelve; the Council.

She recalled pictures she had seen of meetings of the Klu Klux Klan. The scene was macabre, and would have been ludicrous in any other circumstances; however, there was nothing even faintly humorous about this. She could easily see why Vickie would feel intimidated by these robed figures.

The Master spoke again. "We understand that you wish to become a member of the Children of the Enlightenment?"

Casey had to swallow a couple of times to ease the dryness of her throat. She finally found her voice. "I am considering it, yes."

"For what reason?"

"Why, I . . . it just seems to be something that I'd be interested in."

"We look with displeasure on those who wish to join us for a frivolous reason." The strange voice was laced with menace.

"I'm quite serious about it, I assure you."

"One thing is rather puzzling to us. You are not a permanent resident of Sedona. You will depart eventually."

"But I will be here for some months, while our movie is being filmed." She said quickly, "And I like Sedona. I'm considering buying a home here, a place where I can come to rest."

The Master was silent for a few moments, pacing back and forth. Finally, he stopped before her. She could see his eyes blazing at her through the eyeholes of the mask, but she couldn't make out the colour.

"You said you'd like to join because it sounds 'interesting'. Could you explain that for our benefit, Miss Rainier?"

"The name, Enlightenment, should explain my interest. Many people, like your members, are searching for enlightenment. I'm looking for a focus in my life, a centre, something that I can truly believe in. In that way, I can find my true self." Casey was quite pleased with the explanation she had formulated on the spur of the moment.

"I see," the Master said slowly, seeming to relax slightly. "You're not satisfied with your life as it is, is that what you're saying?"

"In essence, yes."

"Do you belong to any church, Miss Rainier? Perhaps you know, or will certainly find out, that we do not follow Christian concepts, and all Christian religions arc considered by us to be the enemy."

She said steadily, "I have no belief in organized religion as such. I have never found what I'm searching for there."

He gave a short nod, then resumed pacing again. Casey was still tense and wished she could sit down, but apparently she wasn't going to be given permission to do so. And were the Council members going to ask questions? All the while she had been standing there not a one had spoken a single word; they remained as silent and unmoving as statues.

The Master wheeled about, those glittering eyes fixed on

her. "It has come to my attention that you attended our services last night. Then you must know that Satan is our true Master. We worship him without reservation, and obey him without hesitation. In so doing, we receive many things that we ask for. And also in doing so, our members are often asked to do things not approved of by society. We believe in doing what makes us feel good, and that is the only law we follow. Do you fully understand these concepts?"

"Yes, I think so." This time her voice was a little shaky. What was she getting into here?

"And do you agree, without reservation whatsoever, to follow our laws? Do you swear complete and eternal allegiance to our Lord of Darkness, Great Satan?"

"I agree to follow your laws, and I do swear allegiance to," she swallowed dryly, "to the Lord of Darkness."

The Master gave a curt nod of approval. He turned around to face the silent Council. "Is it agreed that we now accept Rena Rainier as one of us?"

One by one, like puppets, all twelve heads nodded assent.

The Master faced Casey again. "Welcome to the Children of the Enlightenment, Rena Rainier. One final word of caution, however. Should you ever violate our rules, the penalty will be severe."

"I understand."

"Good!" The Master raised his hands over his head. "We ask your blessing on your new initiate, O Great Satan! May all the things she is seeking be found in your service, O Lord!"

He fell silent for a few moments, hand still upraised. The old barn was quiet as a tomb. Casey scarcely dared take a breath, afraid that she would inhale the stench of brimstone. She scolded herself for letting her imagination run wild.

The arm came down, and that burning glare pinned her. "There is a meeting on Thursday night, two nights from now, during which you will initiated, Rena Rainier. You will be contacted and escorted to our meeting place." He motioned imperiously. "You may leave us now."

Casey turned and walked out on suddenly weak legs. She realized for the first time that she had been truly frightened. The lantern was turned off as she closed the door behind her. She half expected Vickie's car to be gone, but it still sat there, dark and quiet, except for the firefly glow of Vickie's cigarette through the windshield.

Where were the vehicles of the other thirteen? The only one in sight was Vickie's. Had they walked here; or were their vehicles parked out of sight?

Casey had barely closed the door before Vickie said eagerly, "Well, Rena? What happened?"

Casey laughed shakily. "I'm not quite sure. But I've been accepted as a member, that much I can tell you."

"Great!" Vickie said happily. "You'll never regret it."

She started the car and swung back the other way, heading toward the highway.

Casey said, "Thursday, I'm supposed to attend a meeting and I'll be initiated. Will you be there, Vickie?"

Vickie shook her head, no, and Casey felt her pulse flutter. Why wouldn't Vickie be present? She started to ask, then kept quiet. Maybe all the cultists weren't always present at the initiation of a new member.

Vickie was unusually quiet again on the ride back into town. Finally, Casey asked, "I'm curious about something, Vickie. No one has mentioned any dues. It wasn't mentioned tonight, either, and frankly I was too intimidated to ask."

"Oh, there are no dues," Vickie said quickly. "The Master isn't in it to make money."

"Seems a little strange. Any organization I've ever heard of charges its members *something*, even the non-profit ones. Of course," she laughed, "I don't suppose a cult like this could very well file with the IRS as a non-profit group. But there must be some expenses, even if nominal. Who takes care of that?"

"I don't know," Vickie responded with a shrug. "The Master, I suppose."

"Must be some rich guy, then."

Vickie said nothing, and Casey also fell quiet. Back on the lot where Casey had left her rental car, she said, "Thank you, Vickie, for introducing me to the cult, and for taking the trouble to chauffeur me around."

"It was no trouble, Rena. We take turns doing that for new, prospective members."

After an exchange of goodbyes, Vickie drove off, and Casey got into the rental. She sat for a moment. She was elated by what had transpired tonight, more convinced than ever that the cult was involved in the homicides. She was finally getting a handle on the case!

She would have liked to share her news with someone, but it was too late to try and arrange a rendezvous with Gabe. Maybe Josh would be home. If he was, he would still be up. Josh was an old movie addict; it was his favourite way of relaxing from a hard day on the streets. How many times had she caught him asleep late at night before the TV?

She drove until she found a pay phone relatively isolated, and punched out his home number. He answered on the second ring.

"Hello, Detective."

"Casey! I was just sitting here thinking of you."

"Yeah, sure. Probably watching some old movie."

"That's right, I am. But the movie is *Laura*, and she reminds me of you."

She laughed. "Come on, Detective! You're full of it."

"She does, I swear." His voice lowered, taking on an intimate note. "I miss you, babe."

"Same here. And maybe I'll be back in Phoenix sooner than either one of us thought."

His voice quickened. "You're about to solve the case?"

"I won't go quite that far, but I made some progress. I was just interviewed for membership in the Children of the Enlightenment. It was quite a scene, Josh, real spooky. Thirteen guys, including the Master, all robed and masked, gathered in an old barn, with just a Coleman lantern for light. The only one who said a word was the Master, the others were silent as the grave."

"You just be damned sure you weren't auditioning for a grave," he said roughly. "As I think I've mentioned a time or two, some of these cults are not safe to screw around with. Especially if this one is involved in these murders."

"And as I've mentioned a time or two, Detective," she retorted, "certain risks go with the job." She laughed. "As the saying goes, danger is my business."

"Don't be flippant, Casey. Not about something like this."

"Would you let risk deter you on a case?"

"Most of the time when I put myself in danger, I have some backup."

"And just who would I get to back me up? If I used Gabe, it would blow my cover, let the whole world know I'm not here scouting for a movie location, but sniffing around for a killer."

"If you *are* in danger, your cover is already blown. They know who you are. Did you ever think of that?"

"Of course I have. But I don't think anybody does know."

"Your famous 'feeling', I suppose?"

"Something like that, yes."

His exasperated sigh came over the line. "Damned stubborn female. I could talk until I'm hoarse, and all to no purpose."

"You've got that right." She softened her voice. "I appreciate your concern, Josh, but a woman's gotta do what a woman's gotta do. But I'll be careful, I promise. You're a good man, Josh Whitney, and I love you for it. Goodbye for now."

"Wait, wait! What did you say?"

But she was already hanging up. She stood for a few

moments with her hand on the receiver, a musing smile on her lips. She did love the big hunk, but she rarely ever told him so. She turned away from the phone, thinking, Someday I'm going to have to make a decision. Otherwise, there was a strong chance she'd lose him, and she didn't want that to happen.

She met Gabe the next morning at the Sinagua Plaza. It was after ten, the shops were all open, and the Plaza was already crowded. Casey figured they would be safe among the crowd. Gabe was already waiting, sitting alone on a bench, ostensibly reading a paper. Casey sat down on the other end of the bench.

"You have anything for me, Gabe?"

"A few items. Russell Turner is in deep shit, financially speaking. He's overextended credit wise. From what I can dig up on him, he operates close to the edge, has been close to bankruptcy a number of times, but always seems able to pull out of the hole somehow."

Casey asked, "Any indications of large sums of money coming into his bank accounts from unusual sources?"

Gabe hesitated. "Not that I've been able to find so far. Sure, there have been large deposits, but they all seem to have come from banks, investors, places like that. I'll keep digging, of course. Why do you ask that?"

"There's a reason, but I don't have anything concrete to go on. Is there anything along that line on any of the others?"

"Not that I've been able to find. Cabot's account shows only deposits from his business. The same goes for Alex Haydon, but his business seems on more solid ground that Cabot's, certainly in better shape than Turner's."

"How about numbered accounts? In Switzerland, the Bahamas, whatever?"

"That's not all that easy to do, uh . . . Rena. Banks with numbered accounts are pretty damned secretive about their depositors."

She smiled quickly. "You can do it, Gabe. I have full confidence in you."

"Oh, now that's the steel fist in the velvet glove if I ever heard it." He heaved a sigh. "I'm working on that, but the impossible takes a little time."

"How about the California contingent?"

"I'm working on that, too. The president of Camden, Grady Camden, is one well-off sucker, worth a conservative ten million, and that's not taking in account the company, which is worth another twenty mil. The past two years their stock has been climbing like Jack up the Beanstalk."

"I don't really consider him a suspect, anyway. How about the other three VPs?"

"Nothing of much interest so far. All are well off, with homes in the million-dollar range in and around Beverly Hills. They draw good salaries, with stock options. Credit ratings are all excellent. One thing interesting . . ." He hesitated.

Casey pounced. "What?"

"I'm not sure," he said slowly. "I haven't been able to pin it down yet. It may be nothing. But about a month ago a large block of Camden stock was unloaded on the market. At the price the stock is selling for, the seller pocketed around a hundred thou. But I'm finding it hard to dig up the name of the seller."

Casey swallowed her disappointment. "Go in through the back door. Find out how much stock each VP owned before, then find out how much they own now."

"I'm doing that, but it takes time," he said tartly. "I don't suppose you'd care to let me in on your thinking here? Why all this interest in their financial conditions?"

"Not right now, Gabe. It's just a hunch, and I may be way off base. When I'm more sure of my ground, I'll share it with you. Just keep digging, you're doing a fine job, Gabe," she said warmly.

"Why, thank you, ma'am," he said in a dry voice.

"One thing you haven't mentioned," she said, "is a rap sheet on any of these people, except for Wes, Wesley Strom."

"There's a damned good reason for that. There isn't any. That's the first thing any investigator worth his salt checks for."

Casey clucked in disappointment. "Nothing? Not even traffic tickets?"

"Clean as new snow. Oh, I found a few traffic tickets here and there. I doubt that anyone who drives a vehicle doesn't get a traffic ticket now and then. But I found nothing beyond that. Nothing of a felony nature, not even misdemeanours. After all, Rena, these people are respected, hard-working citizens. I know that any cop who's been at it awhile thinks the worst of anybody they come across in the course of an investigation. But let's face it, the majority of citizens never commit any real crimes."

"You're right, of course," she said with a sigh. "And it's not at all unusual for a killer to have never stepped over the line before."

"There you go," he said, spreading his hands.

"Okay, Gabe," she said abruptly. "You leave now. I'll wait here for a bit."

She sat for a while, watching the tall, gangling figure of Gabe Stratton walk away, until he disappeared in the crowd. Gabe was a good investigator, yet he was still relatively inexperienced. She found it especially aggravating in this undercover assignment that it wasn't feasible for her to do all the investigating herself. She was convinced that Gabe was missing a few things of importance, things she could have uncovered if she had a finger on it herself. Of course, that could be her ego speaking . . .

She laughed wryly at herself, got up from the bench, and went in search of a pay phone. Finding one, she punched out a number, hoping that her uncle, Claude Pentiwa, was in his gift shop today. He opened and closed it whenever it suited him; he could as easily be out hunting on the mesa today.

To her relief he answered on the third ring.

"Hello, Uncle."

"Oh–ee–e! *Nessehongneum!*" Claude Pentiwa said, his resonant voice warm with pleasure. "I have been expecting you to call."

Casey held the receiver away from her ear for a moment, staring at it in puzzlement. "Why is that, Uncle? Are you becoming psychic in your older years?"

"I have read about the many killings in Sedona, and I know that when white people are killed in a sensational manner, it is often your chore to track down the killer. Of course," his hoarse chuckle sounded, "the more white people who . . ."

"I know," she chimed in. "The more white people who kill each other the better it is for the Hopi."

"Oh–ee–e! I am surprised, *Nessehongneum*! You are coming to think like a Hopi."

"Uncle, you know better than that. Why must we always go through this? It is my job to catch murderers, no matter what race their victims may be."

"Then why is it that you have never tracked down the killer of a Hopi, niece?"

"I wouldn't hesitate for a second, Uncle, if it ever came up. Besides, you very well know that the murder of a Hopi comes under federal jurisdiction, not state."

He made a dismissive sound. "Only if it happens on the reservation."

Casey sighed. She loved Claude Pentiwa, but he was being particularly obstreperous today. She said, "A Yavapai, Vernon Bornfield, has been arrested for the murders. I'm convinced he's innocent, and I intend to prove it."

"Why was he arrested?"

"There was some circumstantial evidence, but I think the chief factor was the fact that he had been speaking out against the Children of the Enlightenment, claiming that they were desecrating the Yavapai ceremonial grounds." She thought it better not to mention that it was possible that Bornfield was arrested to take the heat off the investigators.

Claude Pentiwa grunted. "I doubt that a Yavapai has the stomach to slay a white man. They are a meek tribe. They should do as we Hopi have done. We have forbidden any whites from attending our sacred rites. In fact, there has been much talk among the elders to close all the mesas to whites."

"Surely you don't agree with that, Uncle. If that happens you would have to close your shop, and lose your livelihood. The other shop owners on Second Mesa would suffer as well."

He said, "That might not be such a bad thing. We could return to hunting and farming, as we have done since ancient times, before we became soft and adopted the white man's ways." He cleared his throat, and abruptly changed the subject. "You are having a problem with your investigation, *Nessehongneum*?"

Casey wasn't startled by his question; she often called him when she was having trouble with a case. Talking to him not only clarified her thinking, but he often went right to the heart of the matter, providing an invaluable insight.

"Yes, Uncle, I am. I haven't been able to isolate a motive for the homicides. I'm pretty convinced now that the cult is somehow behind them, but why? At first I thought the murders might be some kind of sacrificial rites, but I've discarded that theory."

"You once told me of the reasons why the white man killed other white men. Do you recall?"

"Well, there are several. But the three most common are sex, money, and fear."

"I think you have forgotten something."

"Oh, what?"

"That in the society of the white man, all men want to be Chief."

Another of Claude's cryptic sayings, Casey thought. She said dutifully: "I'll remember that, Uncle."

"How is the boy?" he said gruffly.

"Donnie is fine, Uncle."

"It has been almost a year since I have seen him."

"Donnie is in Prescott, Uncle, at the moment, visiting with the Farrels. He's on summer vacation. If I wrap this up soon, and I think I will, we'll drive up to Second Mesa to visit with you."

"I would like that very much. Goodbye, *Nessehongneum*," he said and hung up abruptly, as was his habit.

Chapter Twenty

The next morning Casey drove out to Wesley Strom's antique store. She was still curious as to why Vicki Steele was not going to attend the cult gathering that evening. She sensed that Vicki either didn't know or wasn't about to tell her, so she decided to ask Wes if *he* was attending.

When she entered the shop she didn't see Wes anywhere. Rob saw her and came hurrying over.

"If you're looking for Wes, he's not in today, either." His face was creased with worry, and he was practically wringing his hands.

"You mean he's still sick? Have you found out what's wrong with him?"

"I don't know, Rena. He just remains in bed most of the time. The only time he's gone out is to walk Pookie."

"Then he should certainly see a doctor."

"He won't go. I nagged and nagged, but he refuses to go." Rob leaned toward her, lowering his voice. "I still don't think he's really sick. I wanted to stay home with him today, not open the shop at all, but he wouldn't have it. I've never seen him like this, Rena!"

"But I don't understand, Rob," Casey said, frowning. "If he isn't sick, what's wrong with him?"

"It's like I told you yesterday." Now Rob's voice was little more than a whisper. "I think it has to do with this rotten cult! I think that's what is bothering him. I think something has happened that's frightened him. I faced him with that just this morning. But he just went pale, turned over in bed, and refused to discuss it."

Casey worried her lower lip. "That is strange. I wonder if he'd talk to me about it?"

"I doubt it, but you might try. I would suggest that you don't call first. If you do, he might refuse to see you. The mood he's in, he might even panic, and leave town. Why don't you drop in on him unexpectedly? Our house is only a few minutes drive from here, just off Bell Rock Boulevard."

The house where Wes and Rob lived was located in a small cul-de-sac, partially hidden behind flowering shrubbery. It was a small, redwood house, bordered with a narrow lawn and a bed of brilliant flowers. Everything was neat and well tended.

She went up three steps and pressed the bell. As it rang inside, she heard the yip-yip of Pookie. She waited a full minute, then rang the bell again, and didn't take her thumb off until she heard the shuffle of footsteps inside. Wes probably didn't want to see her, but she didn't intend to give up.

The door opened a crack, and Wes put one eye to the crack. She caught a whiff of alcohol.

"Oh, it's you, Rena. I'm sorry, I'm not up to company. I'm not feeling at all well."

"Rob told me. Talking a bit won't make you any sicker, Wes. You might as well let me in. I'm not about to go away."

"Oh, all right," he said petulantly. He opened the door and stepped back, Pookie cradled in one arm. "I suppose that damned Rob told you I was home. I practically had to throw him out of the house this morning."

"You know he was only concerned about you."

"Sometimes he can be annoying, clucking around me like an old hen," he said in a grumbling voice. "Well, you're in, you might as well come on back." He turned away with a gesture.

She followed him back to the Arizona room overlooking a backyard pool. At least he must have gotten out of bed this morning, since he was wearing a pair of faded shorts, a brightly flowered, short-sleeved shirt, and flip-flops.

The Arizona room was filled with flowering plants, which scented the room rather heavily. A TV set was on a stand in one corner, tuned to a soap opera. Wes hurried over to switch it off.

He faced her with a somewhat sheepish look, but spoke with some of his customary cheeriness. "I admit it, I'm a shameless soap watcher when I'm home during the day. I don't know who writes those things, but they dream up such complicated lives for the characters that I find myself fascinated."

He flopped down into a rocking chair and gestured to the couch. Casey studied him as she sat down. His eyes were red, his face wan and unshaven. Although there was no grey in his hair, his beard was stubbled with it. She was shocked at his appearance; he seemed to have aged several years since the night of their dinner.

She asked, "Rob says you refuse to see a doctor, Wes. If you're really sick, maybe you should."

He waved a hand. "No, no, it's nothing serious. Must be something I ate." He tried a confident smile, but it slid off his face at once. "What did you want to see me about, Rena? I'm not very good company when I feel like this."

"Well, I was concerned about you after what Rob said. And I was curious about why you didn't attend the meeting of the cult the other night. You said nothing at dinner, so I just assumed you were going to be there."

His gaze slid away. "I got sick right after leaving the Enchantment. Must have been something in the food."

"Wes . . . I don't think you're telling the truth. I don't think you're sick at all. Not physically, anyway. I think you saw or heard something about the cult that upset you."

"Why would I lie? I'm not feeling well, I tell you," he mumbled, still not meeting her gaze.

"Wes, you're being evasive. I'm one of you now, you know. I was interviewed by the Council and the Master. I'm now a member. I'm to be initiated tonight!"

His head swivelled to meet her gaze. "No, Rena, don't! It would be a mistake. Walk away from it. Don't become a member."

She peered at him in astonishment. "But why? You've never warned me away before. You seemed to think it'd be something I would be interested in."

"I was wrong," he muttered. "Don't do it, Rena. If you want to join a cult, there are others. Besides, you'll be leaving Sedona when your movie is done. There are similar groups in Los Angeles."

She used the lie she had concocted for her question and answer session with the Master. "But I'm thinking of buying a home here, and spending several months a year in Sedona." She leaned toward him. "You're frightened of something, Wes. What is it?"

"I'm frightened for you, Rena." He squeezed Pookie in his arms until the dog yelped and squirmed free. The animal stopped a few feet away and looked at Wes accusingly; Wes ignored him.

"But why, Wes?" she demanded. "You must have a reason, for heaven's sake!"

"I can't tell you," he said sullenly. "You'll just have to take my word for it."

"I think you owe me an explanation, Wes."

"I don't owe you anything. We just met a few days ago."

She sat back, assuming a hurt look. "I thought we were friends, Wes. Apparently I was mistaken."

"We *are* friends, Rena. If we weren't, I wouldn't be telling you this much," he said, agonized. "Can't you understand? I'm afraid for you, as well as . . ." He stopped abruptly, his glance sliding away.

"No, I don't understand." A chill ran down her spine. "You mean, I may be in danger? Is that what you're trying to tell me? What's happened to make you think that? You certainly didn't seem to think so the last time we talked."

"That's all I can say. If you can't take my word for it, then whatever happens is on your own head." He got to his feet. "I think you'd better leave now."

He picked up Pookie, stroking the dog's head, as he walked over to the window. He stood with his back to her, staring out at the pool, murmuring, "I'm sorry, Pookie, for being mean to you."

Casey stared at his back for a few moments, then turned slowly, and left the room.

A telephone call to her room in the Enchantment came at ten that evening. A husky male voice instructed her to be parked in the southeast corner of the Bashas Shopping Centre at a quarter to eleven. She had been pacing the room nervously for two hours, awaiting the call, dressed and ready. She was wearing dark slacks, a loose black, long-sleeved T-shirt, and ankle-length boots.

Ten minutes after the call she was out of the room. She arrived at the rendezvous point with time to spare. There were no other cars parked in the corner, and she noticed that the light on the pole was burned out. Or had it been put out for the occasion?

She settled down to wait. Despite her apprehension over the coming meeting, she dozed slightly. She hadn't slept well last night. She awoke with a start to a rap on the window by her ear. A quick glance at her watch told her that it was precisely nine o'clock. She looked through the car window and saw the bulk of a male figure in the dim light.

Casey slid quickly out of the car. A hand seized her arm

in a rough grip and guided her to a dusty pick-up in the adjoining parking slot. The man did not speak, and his face was shadowed by a black cowboy hat. Casey had hoped for a look at the rear license plate on the pick-up, but she wasn't given a chance. She was ushered into the pick-up seat, the door closed firmly after her, and the man went around to get into the driver's seat. Well, at least he wasn't hidden by a robe, so she should get a good look at his face. Whether it would be someone she knew and recognized was another matter.

The driver, the hat still shading his face, drove out of the lot, turning left. At the Y he turned right into 179, and Casey had to wonder if their destination was the same mesa where Vickie had taken her for that first meeting. As they drove under a street light the driver's face was illuminated briefly, and Casey thought it looked familiar, but she couldn't quite put a name to it.

Then, as they drove around a curve, bright lights from an oncoming car lit up the driver's face clearly. Casey laughed aloud.

The driver turned his face toward her, and she clearly saw a familiar face, that of Jack Nicholson!

"Hi, Jack," she said, choking back another laugh.

The driver merely grunted behind the close-fitting mask, and returned his attention to his driving.

Casey subsided and relaxed, still smiling. It seemed that every time she began to feel truly apprehensive about the Children of the Enlightenment, one, or more, of the cult members did something ridiculous that brought laughter. On the other hand, she thought, suddenly sobered, their penchant for going to almost any lengths to conceal their true identities was chilling. It could only mean that they had something bad to hide.

A few miles up Highway 179 the pick-up turned to the left, onto a dirt road that was bumpy as hell, and Casey was fairly certain now that they were headed for the same mesa.

And such proved to be the case. But this time, there were only a few cars parked down at the foot of the mesa, and there was no press of people going up the trail to the top. In fact, there was not another person in sight. The driver parked the pick-up and motioned for her to get out. Casey got out quickly and crossed behind the back of the pick-up for a look at the license plate. All to no avail. Mud had been smeared over the plate, completely obscuring the numbers.

The man wearing the Nicholson mask hurried around to her, giving her a sharp, suspicious glance through the eyeholes. In the dark she couldn't even gauge the colour of his eyes. He took her arm in a firm grip and hustled her toward the trail.

Casey went along willingly enough as they toiled up to the mesa. After all, she'd gone this far, it would hardly do to back out now, even if she could. But the nearer they got to the top of the path, the more uneasy she became.

And when they topped the path her fears increased. The pentagram was there, as were the flickering torches, and the masked and robed figures of the Council. The only difference was the number of worshippers: this time they were only six, probably all men, by their height.

The Master spoke in that eerie, distorted voice. "Welcome, Rena Rainier. Are you prepared to become a full member of the Children of the Enlightenment?"

Casey swallowed and then managed to speak. "Yes. I am."

The Master gestured curtly, and one figure separated from the group, and approached. Before Casey knew what was happening, it had seized her free arm in a vice-like grip.

"Hey!" She began to struggle. "What is this?"

The Master said, "We have to be careful until you are an accepted member, Miss Rainier. Search her!"

Another figure stepped forward, and tore her purse from her grasp and rifled through it, then said "Nothing" in a masculine voice, and tossed it onto the ground. Quick, rough hands ran over her torso, lingering on her breasts, then on down to her waist, patting the pockets of her trousers. Casey decided it was useless to struggle, and stood quietly. Past the man who was patting her down, she saw two other men approaching, each carrying a pitcher. Each member of the Council produced a shiny, metal cup, and held them out as the two men poured liquid into each cup. The Master's was the last cup filled. The man who had conducted the search of Casey's person now stepped back. "She's clean, Master!"

One of the men approached Casey with a pitcher and yet another metal cup. He poured liquid into it, and held it to her lips. She turned her head aside, refusing to drink.

"Drink, Miss Rainier!" the Master said sternly. "It is required. It is part of the ritual."

He raised his own cup high, as did all the members of the Council. "It is harmless. See?"

He drank deeply from the cup, as did the Council members. "The drinks puts you, as well as all of us, in the proper frame of mind, for the initiation ritual."

Casey allowed the cup to be placed to her lips. The liquid was biting and bitter. She filled her mouth full, but didn't swallow. Calculating correctly that the two men holding her had relaxed somewhat since she had been so docile, she squirmed in their grip, partially freeing herself, and half turned away. She coughed and bent, letting most of the drink dribble unseen out of her mouth.

The Master laughed scornfully. "Come now, Miss Rainier. The taste is not all that terrible. You will come to like it, I promise you." He raised his cup high again. "We drink this toast to you, O Lord of the Darkness. And we ask your blessing on this woman, your new and faithful disciple."

He raised the cup and again drank. The others followed suit. Casey was once again firmly in the grasp of her captors, and she waited, somewhat fearfully, for what was to happen next.

* * *

She was almost certain that the cup had contained some kind of drug, probably some potion to render her helpless. Time to perform an acting job. She relaxed in the grip of her captors, letting her head wobble slightly. If she was wrong, they would probably think her actions strange . . .

"Good! Bring the woman into the house of our Lord," the Master said, his eerie voice holding a note of satisfaction.

The two men picked her up easily and carried her inside the pentagram. Casey opened one eye just a slit as they stretched her out on her back on the flat rock used as an altar. One man stood at her head, hands holding her shoulders down. The other stood at the foot, holding her ankles. Casey choked back a pulse of panic. She may have let things go too far!

Through her lashes she could see the Master standing beside her, his arms raised to the night sky. "O Great Lord of Darkness, we offer up this woman as a sacrifice. But she is not a worthy sacrifice. She is a foe, believing not in your powers and your greatness. In truth, she is a foe, like the last one, the man. So tonight you shall receive into your keeping one who is here under false pretenses." His head came down, and light from the flickering torches reflected off the fierce glare of the eyes partially hidden by the cowl. "Do you think us stupid, Casey Farrel? Do you not think we know your true identity? That we do not know you came here investigating us, that you wish to expose our secret and sacred rites to the world? Tonight, you pay with your life for that ultimate sacrilege!"

From under his robe he drew a long, curved dagger; and raised it high. Light glinted evilly off the blade. In a voice that seemed to Casey to hold all the evil in the world, he said: "Can you hear me, Casey Farrel? You will now pay with your life for your perfidy!"

Casey knew she had to act. Tensing herself, she gathered all of her strength and tore free of the grip of the two men. Desperately she rolled to her right and off the altar. The fall to the ground knocked the breath from her.

The Master shouted, "Seize her, you idiots! You didn't watch to see that she swallowed the potion! Let her get away and you will pay dearly!"

Casey heard the two men cursing and scrambling toward her. She rolled twice, doubling up as she rolled, frantically fumbling for the pistol in the ankle holster she had strapped on before leaving her room, hoping that they would be so confident of their superiority that they would not search her too thoroughly. Wes's strange behaviour earlier today had triggered warning bells in her mind.

Just before the first man reached her, her fingers closed around the gun. She yanked it out of the the holster, rolled again, and scrambled to her feet. Holding the gun in both hands, she aimed it at the Master across the altar. The others froze in their tracks.

She said steadily, "Everybody stay right where you are. I know how to use this and don't think I won't!"

There wasn't a sound from anyone, not a twitch of movement. The silence stretched and her tension mounted; then the Master spoke, quietly this time. "There are many of us, and she is only one. She cannot shoot all of us. Take her!" Suddenly the frustration of the past few days and the fear that she had experienced here tonight turned into rage, boiling over until Casey's hands, and the pistol, began to shake.

"I may not be able to get all of you, true," she shouted, "but I can damned well kill your Master, and another one or two before you can stop me! I am a good shot, and this gun is aimed dead centre on him. He dies if one of you makes a move toward me. So either make your move, or back off."

Past the Master, Casey saw that the few men outside the pentagram were already drifting away, dropping off the edge of the mesa. Casey was still on a fear and adrenaline high, and she calculated her chances on arresting the bastard.

Now the Master gestured, and the two men who had been about to move in on Casey began backing away, then broke into a trot toward the head of the trail leading down. Could she force the Master to go with her?

Even as these thoughts raced through her mind the Master spoke again. "It seems, Miss Farrel, that we have reached a stalemate. For the moment. But we are not finished."

His head tilted, and the moving torchlight flickered across the golden features of his mask. The torches were burning down now, and soon the darkness would be complete.

Casey's mind was going a mile a minute. What was she going to do? She had the Master in her gun sights, but there were other men somewhere out there in the darkness, doing what?

The golden mask nodded. "If you should be foolish enough to shoot me, Miss Farrell, you will never leave this Mesa. My followers are *very* loyal. And if you think you can arrest me, take me with you, the same caveat applies. I suppose, when it comes right down to it, we must compromise, and let each other go."

Two emotions surged through Casey, leaving her weak with relief, and hot with disappointment.

She nodded, swallowing to clear her throat and gather her voice. She mustn't let him see how terrified she was. When she spoke her voice was clear and steady.

"I hate to agree with you, but you're right. There is just one thing. Would you call the others back? I'd feel better knowing where all of them are."

He nodded slowly, and she felt certain that behind the cold metal of his mask, he was smiling.

"Why, of course, Ms Farrel. I wouldn't want you to feel nervous." A mechanical chuckle came from the mouth of the mask, and the hair along Casey's spine lifted. He whistled, and the sound pierced the darkness.

Immediately the others began to reappear, and Casey was glad that she had not attempted anything foolish.

When they all stood within the range of the waning torchlight, she counted them. When she was certain that they all stood within her sight, she began to back away toward the trail head.

She stopped as her heel encountered one of the stones. The Master said, "Leave with this thought, Miss Farrel. Your death sentence has been passed, and it will be carried out, if a little delayed. And remember this. We are many, while you are only one."

Casey didn't reply. She carefully backed toward the path. One of the two torches went out, and by the time she reached the trail and started down, she could barely discern the Master and his Council.

She turned then and began to hurry down the steep trail, anticipating a bullet with every step.

She reached the bottom of the trail safely. The pick-up of the man who had driven her here was gone. She began to walk quickly along the edge of the dirt road. She recalled seeing a few lights off the road as they came in. She should be able to arouse someone so she could use their phone to call the Sedona police. Of course, by that time all the people she had left behind on the mesa would be long gone.

Even as she had this thought, she heard the faint sound of hoofbeats on the other side of the mesa. She paused, head cocked as she listened. Had they gotten here on horseback? Was that why Vickie Steele had never seen any vehicles belonging to the ruling members of the cult?

Then she heard motors roaring into life. There must be another approach to the mesa, and a spot where the Master and Council members could park.

There was one good thing resulting from this night that had otherwise been a disaster: she was out of the closet now. Her cover blown, she could now operate openly as Casey

Farrel. Whether or not that was something she could use to her advantage remained to be seen.

She began walking again, striding along as briskly as she could, given the dark night.

Chapter Twenty-One

Lieutenant Martin was coldly furious. "So you're Casey Farrel, not Rena Rainier. Instead of being in Sedona scouting movie locations, you're here snooping around in *our* case."

"That's right, Lieutenant," Casey said with a sigh. They were in the lieutenant's vehicle parked at the base of the mesa. It was now one o'clock in the morning. They had just spent an hour, with other detectives, scouring the mesa. There was nothing there, of course. Casey was tired to the bone, disgruntled, and still shaken by her encounter on the mesa. Most of all, she was still unnerved by her close call. She was certainly in no mood to be scolded by Lieutenant Martin, although she supposed he had some reason to be angry.

"Why couldn't you have come to us, confided in us? I'm sure you know that it's considered common courtesy to notify locals when you invade their turf. Why didn't you?" He thrust his face close to hers, his breath hot on her face. "Didn't you trust us? Did you think one of us would let leak the fact that you were an undercover investigator from the Governor's task force? Is that it, *Ms* Farrel?"

"No, Lieutenant, that isn't it. At least not so far as I'm concerned," she said wearily. "The order came from higher up. From the Governor himself, as a matter of fact."

Martin sat back behind the wheel, staring through the windshield. "So even the Governor doesn't trust us to handle this case."

"I don't think that's it, Lieutenant." She reached out to touch his rigid hand on the wheel. "I'm guessing here, but he was probably thinking that something different had to be done. He was getting a lot of heat. The homicides were scaring away tourist trade, et cetera. You'll have to admit that you weren't getting anywhere, neither the Sedona police, nor the investigators from *two* sheriff's departments."

"But this other task force investigator, Gabe Stratton, got in touch with me. Good man, by the way."

"Yes, he is," Casey agreed. "I needed someone else up here, as a sort of liaison, and someone who could investigate openly, in areas that I couldn't."

"What you're saying is," Martin said bitterly, "he was to get close to me, pump me for what he could, then run to you with it?"

"Something like that, yes," she admitted. "It was necessary."

He was silent for a few beats. "You could have been killed up on that mesa tonight. You realize that?"

"Oh, yes. Yes, indeed," she said with a shaky laugh. "But at least now we know that the Children of the Enlightenment is directly involved with the murders, something we didn't know before."

"*We* don't know anything of the sort."

She twisted toward him. "If they're not involved, why try to kill me? And it proves something else . . . If I hadn't been undercover, they would have been after me sooner." She fell silent for a moment, then said slowly, "The question now is, how did they find out who I was?"

"At least you can't blame us," the lieutenant said with a curt laugh, "since none of us knew about you."

Casey gnawed thoughtfully on her lower lip. "I must have been stepping on somebody's toes, and they gave me a close look, found out who I really was. It wouldn't be too hard, if someone really took the time and effort."

"You realize that this so-called Master wasn't kidding with his threat. They're going to be after you. Maybe it'd be best if you just quietly fade away, leave it up to us now. Don't misunderstand me, Casey," he added hastily, "what you've uncovered has been an enormous help."

"Thanks a whole bunch, Lieutenant," she said dryly, "but I haven't come this far to give up. I'll be in it until the end. It's my job, and I've been threatened before. That hasn't stopped me."

He looked over at her, smiling faintly. "Pretty macho, aren't we?"

She said tartly, "You mean, for a woman? Could be, but you're not getting rid of me that easily."

There was a rap on the driver's side window. Casey looked past Martin and saw a man in a sheriff's uniform. Martin rolled down the window.

The sheriff's man bent down to peer in. "There is another place to park around the side of the mesa, Lieutenant. We checked it out thoroughly, but found nothing important. Several vehicles had been parked there, but it's all a confusion of tire tracks. We'll come back tomorrow in daylight and take a few tire impressions, but I don't think it'll be much help. Of course, if we can pinpoint a suspect, we might match a tire print to his vehicle."

Casey spoke past the lieutenant. "I'm sure I heard a horse, hoofbeats riding off. I don't know if the horse belonged to any of the cultists up there, but it would seem a coincidence if it wasn't."

The sheriff's officer shook his head. "Didn't see anything like that, Ms Farrel. We'll look again tomorrow, but I doubt we'll find anything. If there were any hoofprints, they'll likely be covered up by the vehicle tracks. The same goes for the dirt road out of there. We'll leave a man here all night, Lieutenant, to secure the scene until we can get back."

Martin nodded. "Thanks, Mac."

The man left, and Martin turned to Casey. "Have we about covered everything, Casey?"

"Pretty much." She hadn't told him about Wesley Strom and his strange behaviour; she wanted to talk to Wes herself first. "How about Vickie Steele? Are you going to talk to her tonight?"

"It can wait until morning. She's not going anywhere. You don't see her as our killer, do you?"

"No way. She's into the cult, of course, but I'm convinced she isn't connected with the homicides. I doubt she even knows about them."

"We'll wait until the morning then. I suppose you want to sit in?"

"Depend on it, Lieutenant."

Martin started the car. "We'd better get you back to your car, and call it a night. We're not going to get much sleep as it is. You want to drop in at the station at eight in the morning, Casey?"

"I'll be there."

Despite the lateness of the hour, Casey didn't return to the Enchantment after Lieutenant Martin dropped her off at her car. Instead, she drove immediately to the home of Wesley Strom. As she parked, she could see a faint glow of light from the pool area at the back. Instead of ringing the doorbell she went down the side of the house to the gate, which was unlocked. She opened it and walked toward the pool. She could see someone lying prone in a deck chair. Her footsteps muffled by the grass, she approached the chair. Just before she reached it, Pookie reared up from where he had been resting on a naked male chest, and began yipping. Wes Strom, wearing only swimming trunks, bolted upright, his eyes wide in fright.

"Hello, Wes," Casey said quietly.

His gaze found her. "Rena! You scared the shit out of me!" He held his wristwatch up to where he could see it. "It's after two o'clock in the morning! What in the world . . .?"

Casey pulled a chair up facing him. "I have some urgent questions, Wes."

His eyes searched her face closely, and she could see a look of relief cross his face. There was a bottle of brandy and a glass on the table by his chair, and she could smell the liquor strongly.

He said tentatively, "Are you all right, Rena?"

"I'm fine, no thanks to you. And it's Casey, not Rena. Casey Farrel. The masquerade is over, Wes, at least on my part."

His eyes bulged, seemed on the verge of popping out of his skull. "Masquerade? Casey . . .? What are saying?"

"I'm saying that my real name is Casey Farrel. I'm an investigator for the Governor's Task Force on Crime. I was sent up here to look into the homicides, Wes."

His effort to grapple with this was apparent. "You mean all that about working for a movie company is . . .?" He leaned toward her, alcohol fumes coming at her in waves. "You're a *cop*?"

"That's right," she said laconically.

He sank back with a whoosh. "I don't believe this!"

"Believe it."

He squinted at her. "What did you mean about a masquerade? I mean, about it ending on your part?"

"I mean, Wes, that you've been hiding something from me the last couple of days. You've been terrified of something, something you haven't told me. I learned, definitely, last night that the Children of the Enlightenment is behind all these killings. Maybe you didn't know that before, I'm willing to accept that. I think you learned about it, Wes. And I'm not leaving here until you come clean."

"You went up there last night, Re . . . uh, Casey? I tried to warn you."

"You didn't try hard enough. Yes, I went, and I came this

close to becoming another sacrifice." She held up thumb and forefinger a half-inch apart.

"Dear God!" he said in a whisper. His eyes closed. "I didn't know for sure, but I was afraid . . ."

"Afraid of what? That I'd be killed? Come on, Wes, talk to me!"

Goaded, he shouted, "Yes! I was afraid you'd become another sacrifice."

Casey said softly, "How long have you known, Wes?"

His glance skipped away. "The night we had dinner. Right after that, one of the Council members called me. He let something slip."

"Why? Why were they killing people?"

"I don't know! I suppose . . . Well, I guess they graduated from sacrificing goats to humans."

"Did you ever witness a sacrifice, Wes?"

"No, no, I swear!" He wagged his head violently from side to side. "Do you think I would still be a member if I had? It's sick, sick."

"But last night, on the mesa, there were others present beside the Council and the Master. Not many, true, but some. So there must have been cult members present at the other killings."

"If there were, I wasn't one of them," he muttered. "They must be a select group, picked just for the sacrifices."

"Who was the Council member who talked to you?"

"I don't know."

"But you talked to him on the phone. What's his phone number?"

"I don't know, I tell you! He called me, I didn't call him!"

Casey sighed in frustration. "In all the time you've been a cult member, you must have identified one or another of the Council, a clue, something."

"No, I swear, Casey!" Despite the warm night Wes was sweating heavily. "If I knew anything, I'd tell you. Now that I know . . . I wouldn't want to see them get away with murder! They go to great pains to conceal who they are."

"Wes, you'd better be levelling with me. If I find out you're lying to me, I'll see to it that Lieutenant Martin throws an obstructing justice charge on you! I promise you that."

Wes leaned toward her. It was all she could do to keep from recoiling from the combined odours of alcohol and sweat.

"I'm telling you everything I know, Casey. If the cult is behind the murders, if you're right about that, I'd do anything in my power to put a stop to it!"

"Oh, I'm right, I'm convinced of that . . ." She broke off at the sound of footsteps on the walk leading to the back door.

She glanced around to see Rob coming toward them, wearing a robe and slippers.

"I thought I heard voices out here, and thought Wes was talking to himself . . ." His glance took in Casey. "Rena, what on earth are *you* doing here at three o'clock in the morning?"

"Not Rena, she came around under false pretences," Wes said grumpily. "Name's Casey Farrel. She's here investigating the murders." He reached down and plucked Pookie off the ground. The dog yipped a couple of times, struggled to get free, then subsided as Wes began to stroke her.

Rob gaped at Casey. "You're a cop?"

"That's right, Rob." Casey got to her feet. "Sorry for lying to you guys. But it was necessary." She pinned Wes with a stern gaze. "I'm going to have to tell Lieutenant Martin about your connection with the cult, Wes. I can't keep things from him any longer. He's going to be pissed as it is. He's going to come after you."

"Let him come. I'll tell him what I told you, everything I know."

"It'd better be all you know, Wes. If I find out . . ." She

nodded to Rob. "Good night, Rob. And see that he gets some rest before he unravels."

"I will, uh, Casey, if I have to tie him to the bed."

Casey drove to the hotel. She was exhausted, but at least she'd be able to get four hours or so of sleep before she was due at Martin's office at eight in the morning.

Casey arrived at Lieutenant Martin's office a few minutes before eight the next morning; the lieutenant was already at his desk. Casey was groggy from too little sleep, and felt frazzled and unkempt. There had been a message from Gabe when she got back to the room last night, but she hadn't returned the call. She felt guilty about that; she hadn't yet called and let him know what happened last night, and he might have important information, but her mind wasn't functioning at full capacity yet. She decided a call to him could wait until after the interview with Vickie Steele.

"Good morning, Casey," Martin said. "You look a little frazzled around the edges. Get any sleep?"

"Not a hell of a lot. After you let me off, I detoured by to see Wes Strom. I told you about him?"

Martin leaned back, staring at her with slitted eyes. "Yeah, but why do I have the feeling you didn't lay it all out?"

"You're right, I didn't, Lieutenant." She grinned wryly. "Still caught in the undercover syndrome, I guess. Besides, I felt I owed Wes an explanation before I turned you loose on him, and I had some questions I needed answers to at once. He's not going anywhere. He's expecting you to call on him."

He grimaced. "I hope you're about to tell me what you learned."

"Yeah. I'm afraid it isn't very much."

Succinctly, she related what little Wes had revealed.

"You think he told you all he knows?"

"I believe so, yes, but who can be a hundred percent sure?

I never did suspect him of having anything to do with the murders. He joined the cult for the fun of it."

"Some fun it's turned out to be." Martin glanced at his watch. "I thought it'd be better to interrogate Vickie Steele here, instead of at her shop or home. Always more intimidating. I sent a car for her. Should be . . ." He looked out the window. "There's the car now."

A few minutes later Vickie Steele was ushered into the small office by a uniformed officer, who then closed the door, leaving them alone.

Vickie's eyes went wide at the sight of Casey. "Rena! What are you doing here?"

Casey went quickly through the explanation about her undercover role, now discarded. Vickie seemed slightly stunned by this revelation, and every few moments as they talked her glance would move to Casey, as if she still didn't quite grasp the fact that Casey was an investigator.

Lieutenant Martin began the interrogation. "Ms Steele, Casey tells me that you are a member of the Children of the Enlightenment, that you drove her to the site where she was questioned about her own possible membership. Is that substantially correct?"

Vickie bobbed her head. "Well, yes. Rena . . . uh, Ms Farrel said she wanted to become a member."

Casey intervened, "You didn't know I was an investigator at the time, did you, Vickie?"

Vickie stiffened. "Of course I didn't! If I had, I would never have . . ."

"No one has called since that night you drove me to the old barn, asking questions about me, about whether I was an investigator?"

"Of course not! I just said I had no idea!"

"They learned somehow, Vickie," Casey said. "I found that out up on the mesa last night."

"Well, they didn't learn it from me."

"They tried to kill me."

Vickie gasped, hand going to her mouth. "I don't believe you!"

Lieutenant Martin said, "It seems to be true, Ms Steele. And it confirms Casey's theory that the cult is responsible for the series of homicides."

Vickie wagged her head from side to side. "I can't believe they would kill people! I certainly knew nothing about it."

"Ms Steele, if you're lying to us," Martin said grimly, "and we find out, you could face criminal charges: accessory to murder."

"I knew nothing, I swear!" Her eyes swung from the lieutenant to Casey, back and forth twice. "Casey . . . You know me. You know I wouldn't have gone along. I would have left the cult long ago. I would have reported it to the police!" Her voice was pleading, and tears misted her eyes.

"I would like to believe that, Vickie," Casey said gently. "But you must admit that it's hard to believe that they have killed four people and you remained ignorant of it."

Vickie reached out to seize Casey's hand. "I never! You have to believe me!"

Casey glanced at the lieutenant, who nodded slightly, giving her permission to continue.

She said, "You told me that you didn't know who the Master is, nor did you know the identities of any of the members of the Council. Do you still hold to that? I find that really hard to accept."

Vickie hesitated, looking away.

Casey pressed, "You *do* know. You must tell us, Vickie!"

Vickie sighed. "If I tell you, will you keep it a secret? If what you say is true, they'll kill me if they find out I snitched."

Casey hid a smile. Apparently, Vickie had been watching too many cop shows. She said, "It'll go no further, Vickie. I promise. But we need to know. If we can question one of them, it might be the key to this whole thing."

"All right, Russell Turner is a member of the Council," she said in a rush.

"Are you sure?" Casey asked. "How did you find out?"

"He told me one night last week. There was this cocktail party. I was there. Russ was bombed. He knew, of course, that I belonged. He told me that belonging to the cult was the best thing that ever happened to him. He said that he had asked the Master to bless his business. He was about to go bankrupt, and then, like a miracle, he found someone who was willing to loan him a large sum of money, enough to bail him out. He gave the cult credit for that."

"He said nothing about the cult committing the murders?"

"No! I told you, Casey, I didn't know about that. If he had told me that, do you think I would have kept quiet?"

Casey sat back, looking across the desk at the lieutenant. Martin was already on the phone. He turned his chair around while he talked briefly. Disappointment was mirrored on his face as he hung up. "His office claims Turner is out of town until Monday. They claim they don't know how to contact him."

"Do you think what happened last night on the mesa spooked him?" Casey asked. "He might have run?"

"There's no way of knowing. It's possible."

Casey said thoughtfully, "If he hasn't run, and you put out an APB on him, it might tip him off."

Martin nodded meagrely. "There is that. But I don't have too much choice. I'll have a check made on all airlines, put his license plate on the hot sheet, keep it as quiet as possible." He transferred his gaze to Vickie. "You may go now, Ms Steele. But I must warn you to keep quiet about what was said here today. And keep yourself available for further questioning. If you think of anything else, contact me immediately." He looked at Casey, a faint smile curving his lips. "Or Casey."

As the door closed behind Vickie, Casey said, "Thank you

for that. I suppose I really shouldn't expect such cooperation. Many officers would have closed me off completely."

"What the hell." Martin spread his hands. "I'm interested in catching our killer. And if cooperating with you helps to do that, I'm more than happy to oblige."

After leaving Lieutenant Martin's office, Casey drove directly to Gabe Stinton's motel. The time was just short of nine, and she found Gabe in the coffee shop having breakfast. As she approached his table, he looked up at her, gaping at her in shock.

Gazing furtively around the room, he whispered, "Rena, what are you doing here?"

She batted a hand at him. "Relax, Gabe, it's okay." She slid into the booth across from him. "And you can call me Casey right out in public. I'm out of the closet now." She wondered how many more people she would have to tell before it became common knowledge.

Gabe leaned across the table. "I don't understand. What happened?"

Casey saw a waitress approaching, and motioned him silent. She realized she was ravenous, and ordered a big breakfast. After the waitress had taken her order and poured her a cup of coffee, Casey waited until she left before saying, "Last night happened, Gabe. The ruling order of the cult has found out who I am."

"What happened last night?"

"They tried to kill me."

"What?" He reared back.

"But they didn't succeed, as you can see. Relax, and I'll fill you in."

For the next quarter hour she talked and Gabe listened as she related the events of last night. During that time her breakfast arrived, and she talked between bites.

When she had finished Gabe shook his head in wonder. "You could have been killed!"

Casey grinned. "Must you state the obvious, Gabe? The point is, I wasn't. And more important, we now know for certain sure that the Children of the Enlightenment is our perp, either collectively or individually."

"What do you mean, individually? They're all equally guilty, if you're right."

"If you want to be technical, you're right. But I think the main guy, the Master, so-called, is the real killer, the others just sheep following the leader. He's the one I want to nail."

"But even after last night, you're not any closer to knowing who he is."

"Oh, I think I'm a little closer, but if you mean can I identify him, no, I can't," she admitted. "And it's damned frustrating!" She slammed her palm down on the table. "I was practically within arm's reach of him, and I had to walk away without learning who he was."

"Maybe that should be a lesson to you. If you'd let me in on what you planned and brought me along as backup, we might have him behind bars now."

"Don't lecture me, okay?" she snapped. Then she relented. "You're right, Gabe. That would have been the right thing to do. This case is getting to me. I don't always do the right thing."

She took the last bites of her breakfast while Gabe contemplated her in silence. Leaning back with a satisfied sigh, she said, "What did you call about, Gabe?"

"Huh?" he said blankly. "Oh! I almost forgot, hearing what you had to say." He leaned toward her, wearing a look of satisfaction. "I finally got some solid results on the California people." He paused, waiting for her reaction.

"Well? Tell me!" she demanded.

"I found out who the Camden executive was who sold his company shares. Fifty thousand dollars worth two days before Barbara Stratton was killed!" He gazed at her in triumph.

Casey leaned forward eagerly. "Who? Who was it?"

Chapter Twenty-Two

Casey smiled to herself. Once again she was flying into Los Angeles; twice within a week, and she had once sworn she would never return. At least this time it wasn't just a fishing expedition; she had a definite target in mind.

Before leaving Sedona she had made a quick call to the Beverly Hills Police and talked to a Lieutenant Breck Mackay, and outlined her purpose, being as brief as possible. This time she didn't want to invade their turf without alerting the locals, and she was going to need their assistance.

Her plane was due to arrive at LAX around three in the afternoon, which would give her just enough time to make it to Camden Industries before closing time. Lieutenant Mackay had promised to meet her at the airport.

The lieutenant didn't look much like a cop. He was slender, wiry, quick-moving with a narrow, darkly handsome face. His eyes were brown, keenly intelligent. He had the look of an affluent executive. But then, Casey reflected, this was Beverly Hills, not the mean streets of Los Angeles, and it was common knowledge that Beverly Hills was different.

He didn't speak much until they were out of the airport and on a surface street. He drove fast, but expertly, and as they talked, he rarely looked at her, but kept his attention on the heavy traffic.

"Now, Ms Farrel, why don't you fill me in? I gather from what little you told me on the phone that this is in connection with the series of homicides in Sedona. How are we hooked in here?"

Casey was silent for a moment, sorting out her thoughts. "Well, I suppose you know that two of the victims, the last two, worked in Beverly Hills? Barbara Stratton and Leo Thornesburg?"

"Yeah, I knew that," he said with a nod. "They worked at Camden Industries."

"That's correct. And since they worked together, I thought that there might be a connection. Now it seems I was right. And before you explode," she held up a hand, "I'll admit I committed a no-no. I came out here a few days ago, nosing around. I am well aware that I should have contacted you guys first. But at the time I was here, I thought it might be a waste of time, mine as well as yours. So I thought, why bother you?"

"Hardly a bother, since it's our job," he said coolly. "But that's water under that well-known bridge. Suppose you just tell me about it, so I'll know what the hell's going on before we barge into Camden. They're pretty strong in Beverly Hills."

Succinctly, Casey outlined the bare facts of the case.

When she had finished, he nodded thoughtfully. "From what you tell me, you were operating off the top of your head, on a wild-hair theory, when you came over here the first time."

She laughed lightly. "That pretty much says it, yes."

"So if you'd come to us first, we probably wouldn't have given you much cooperation, anyway."

"That's what I was afraid of."

"So we'll just keep your first trip between us. At least this time you have a legitimate reason for being here. Now let me see if I have this straight. You've discovered some strong evidence that this cult in Sedona is behind the murders, and you think someone at Camden paid to have Barbara Stratton killed?"

"That's what I think, yes."

He shook his head. "Pretty far-out. Sounds like a Hollywood script. Why on earth would this person go to all the trouble of paying a cultist to murder Stratton, and in front of the cult members?"

"For one thing, unless you're a member of the underworld, it's not that easy to find a killer for hire."

"That's true. So how did this guy get onto the killer cultist?"

"I don't know the answer to that. Maybe it was by word of mouth. As to why he kills the victims before witnesses, I figure it's a cover-up. If the police connect the crimes to the cult, the killings will be tagged as sacrifices to their gods, the doings of a Satanist cult, the murder-for-hire motive never uncovered."

"And the witnesses, the cult members, know nothing of this hidden agenda."

"Right. As far as they know, this is simply a ritual sacrifice. From all accounts, the Master is the one who performs the actual killing, and I believe he's our hit man!"

Mackay made a clucking sound. "On second thought, this thing is too wild, off-the-wall, for a Hollywood script."

They were into Beverly Hills now, only a few minutes from Camden Industries. Casey said, "I well realize that, but it's *my* script and I'm stuck with it."

"This Camden executive, he sold his Camden stock, and sent the money to Sedona?"

"He sold the stock, that we know. As for sending it to someone in Sedona, that I'm assuming. That's why I'm here, I'm hoping he'll tell me."

Mackay looked at her askance. "You figure he'll just give you that information? I don't think so; but we'll soon find out. We're here." He drove into the Camden parking lot. "If you want my fix on the situation, I very much doubt he's going to be all that cooperative. A man doesn't become an executive with a company like Camden by being stupid."

Casey got out of the car and walked around to join him. As they walked into the building, she said, "I'm going to ask him what he did with the money. It didn't show up in his bank account."

Mackay shook his head. "He'll no doubt tell you to mind your own business, or else he'll have a good story."

"No doubt. Our job will be to prove he's lying."

"If he *is* lying."

At the reception desk Casey took the lead. "We'd like to see Paul Tate, please."

The receptionist eyed her dubiously. "Do you have an appointment?"

"No, but I'm sure he'll see us. I'm Casey Farrel, from Arizona. I'm an investigator with the Governor's Task Force on Crime for the state of Arizona. And this is Lieutenant Breck Mackay, with the Beverly Hills police."

The receptionist's eyes went wide, and she caught her breath. "Just a moment, please."

She picked up a receiver, punched a button, and half turned away, speaking into the receiver in a low voice. Shortly, she hung up, looking up at Casey in apprehension. "Mr Tate said he'll see you. His office is . . ."

"I know where his office is. Come on, Lieutenant."

Casey led the way to the stairs, up to the second floor, and then down the corridor. When they were two doors away, a muffled gunshot sounded behind Tate's office door. Casey and the lieutenant exchanged startled looks, then broke into a run. Mackay seized the doorknob and tried to turn it.

"Locked! Stand back, Casey!"

Mackay threw his shoulder against the door; it didn't yield. He took two steps back, then threw himself at the door again. It splintered open, and Mackay, off balance, staggered inside, Casey right on his heels.

The room smelled strongly of cordite. Paul Tate was sprawled across his desk, one cheek resting on it. His right arm was flung wide, a pistol resting loosely in it. A blackened hole oozing blood was in his right temple.

Lieutenant Mackay was across the room in a few strides. He bent over Tate, feeling for a pulse. He straightened up, and said tersely, "He's dead."

At a sound behind them, Casey whirled. Several people were crowded in the doorway, peering in with shocked faces. Casey snapped, "Don't anybody come in!"

Mackay was at her side, hand on her elbow, guiding her toward the door. In her ear he said, "It's suicide, almost a certainty, but I have to get our people in here. I need to call in, but I don't want to use his phone. You guard the door, Casey. I don't have to tell you not to let anyone inside."

Mackay closed the shattered door as best he could, and raised his voice. "Why don't you all go back to your desks? There's nothing you can do here. And I need to use a phone."

Grady Camden, face grey with shock, stepped forward. In a hushed voice he said, "Is Paul dead?"

Casey said, "I'm afraid so, Mr Camden. This is Lieutenant Mackay. He needs a telephone."

Camden shook his head sharply. "Of course. You can use mine, Lieutenant."

Mackay followed Camden down the hall. The others, talking in hushed voices, began to disperse. Casey, finally alone, leaned against the wall, battling with her own shock, trying to make sense of this new development.

A few minutes later Mackay returned. "My people will be here shortly." He scrubbed a hand across his chin. "Why in hell would Tate do something like this? It doesn't make sense."

"It had to be something more than just us arriving on his doorstep." She was over the shock now, and felt a sense of urgency. "Something happened, Lieutenant, something spooked him, and the announcement that we were here to interrogate him pushed him over the edge. We have to talk to his wife."

He nodded sombrely. "I agree. As soon as someone arrives to take charge here, we'll pay her a visit."

The Tate residence was located on the edge of Beverly Hills, a few blocks off Pico, Tudor style; Casey judged it to be in the million-dollar range.

As Mackay parked the car, he said resignedly, "I always hate doing this, notifying the survivors, and it gets worse every year. It's the questioning that's probably the worse. How do you explain to a wife or a husband or a parent that you must intrude on fresh shock and grief to ask questions?"

"But it's necessary," Casey said, "and usually urgent. In this instance, probably more than most."

"I know, I know," Mackay responded. He opened his door. "So let's get to it."

The doorbell was answered by a pretty brunette of thirty-some years. She was carrying a baby in her arms, and Casey remembered for the first time that she had recently given birth.

Mackay said formally, "Mrs Paul Tate?"

"Yes, I'm Connie Tate."

"I'm Lieutenant Mackay, with the Beverly Hills Police, and this is Casey Farrel, an investigator from Arizona."

Fear leaped like a live thing into the woman's eyes. "Has something happened to Paul?"

"I'm afraid so," Mackay said in a grave voice. "May we come in?"

"Oh . . . certainly." Connie Tate stepped back.

Casey and the lieutenant entered and closed the door. They were in a small foyer. Casey said gently, "Perhaps we could all sit down?"

Connie nodded mutely and crossed the foyer, leading the way into a large, exquisitely furnished living room.

In an unsteady voice Connie Tate called, "Bertha, would come here, please?"

In a few moments a large middle-aged woman came into the room, drying her hands on a kitchen towel. "Bertha, would you mind little Daniel for a bit, please?"

She held out the baby, and Bertha took the child, smiling down tenderly. She left the room quickly, and Mrs Tate gestured to chairs grouped around a large, square coffee table. Casey and Mackay sat side by side, and the other woman sat across from them. Her hands gripped together tightly in her lap, she leaned forward, waiting tensely.

Mackay said, "There's no easy way to put this, Mrs Tate. Your husband is dead. I'm sorry."

Connie's eyes clenched shut, and she swayed back and forth. Casey saw tears ooze out from beneath the closed eyelids. After a moment Connie opened her eyes and spoke in a choked voice, "How did it happen? An accident?"

Mackay cleared his throat. "No, Mrs Tate. To all indications Mr Tate shot himself."

"Suicide?" Connie's hands flew to her face. "Paul would never do that."

"I'm afraid there's no other conclusion to be reached."

"But why? There is no reason." Her words were a plea for understanding. "We were happy, Paul was doing well at work, very well, he was expecting to become president of the company. And we just had a baby, something we've been praying for. Why would he kill himself?"

Casey touched Mackay's arm, signalling she would take over. "That's what we're hoping to find out, Mrs Tate. We realize this is an inopportune time, but we have a few questions. Are you up to it?"

"If it'll help, of course I am." The tears were flowing freely now, but Mrs Tate stared at Casey through them.

"You just said your husband was expecting to be promoted to president of Camden. Why would he expect that?"

"Why, he told me that he was the logical choice, now that Barbara Stratton was dead. He was expecting the news any day."

"Your husband was ambitious then? This was something he wanted very much?"

Mrs Tate looked confused. "Of course, he wanted it! He had been looking forward to it. Wouldn't anybody?"

"Just how far would he go to attain this goal?"

Connie blinked. "I don't understand. He threw himself into that job, body and soul. What else could he do?"

"I see," Casey said thoughtfully. "You said you were happy, that you both were happy, that he had no reason to kill himself. Was your husband open with you?"

"What do you mean?"

"Did he confide everything to you?"

"Of course he did! What are you getting at?"

Casey doubted very much that this woman knew anything about Tate's possible involvement in the death of Barbara Stratton, and decided to abandon that line of questioning. She said, "Did anything unusual happen the past twenty-four hours, anything out of the ordinary?"

"Nothing that I . . ." She broke off, frowning. "There *was* something last night, but I don't see what that has to do with anything."

"You never know, Mrs Tate." Casey leaned forward eagerly. "What was it?"

"Well, there was a phone call last night, waking us up out of a sound sleep. I remember I was annoyed, because it woke the baby up, and I'd only gotten him asleep."

"What time was the call, Mrs Tate?"

"Oh . . . it must have been around two in the morning, somewhere around that time."

Casey calculated swiftly. Arizona didn't recognize Daylight Saving Time, so the time there was the same as California time, which would mean that the call was placed after the episode on the mesa, plenty of time for the caller to get down off the mesa and to a phone.

"Do you know who the caller was, or where it came from?"

Connie wagged her head from side to side. "No, Paul didn't say, said it wasn't important."

"Did you overhear what he said?"

Again, the woman shook her head. "No, I went into the nursery to try and quiet the baby."

Casey turned. "Lieutenant?"

"Yes, I know." Mackay got to his feet. "Mrs Tate, may I use your phone?"

"Of course. There's one in Paul's study." She gestured. "It's just down the hall, first door on the left."

As Mackay left the room, Casey said, "Mrs Tate, this is a rather delicate question, but I must ask it. Could it have been a woman who called your husband?"

The woman recoiled as if she'd been slapped. "You mean, like a girlfriend?"

"Well, yes."

"No, no, Paul never played around," she said vehemently. She added on a note of triumph, "Besides, I answered the phone. It was a man, asking for Paul!"

Casey remembered Paul Tate admitting to an affair with Barbara Stratton, but saw no purpose in revealing this. She said, "I don't suppose you recognized the voice?"

"I'd never heard it before."

"How did the voice sound? Deep, high, anything like that?"

"Well, he only spoke two words to me, 'Paul Tate'." Connie Tate frowned. "But now that I think of it, the voice did sound a little strange. Weird, distorted."

The cult Master, of course. "Another difficult question, Mrs Tate. We have information that your husband sold fifty thousand dollars of his Camden stock several days ago. Do you know anything about that?"

Connie Tate got a startled look. "Fifty thousand? Good heavens, why would he do that?"

"That's why I'm asking you."

"I have no idea. Unless it was some kind of an investment he was making."

"Would he have been likely to discuss that with you?"

"Oh, no. I have no head for finances." Connie laughed with a helpless little gesture. "Paul set up a separate checking account for me. Household bills, shopping, little things like that."

"Then you have no idea why he withdrew the money?"

"None whatsoever. I can't even imagine. You sure there hasn't been some mistake?"

"No mistake, Mrs Tate. We're sure of our facts here."

Lieutenant Mackay returned in that moment. "You finished, Casey?"

Casey got to her feet. "I have no more questions. Unless you can think of something."

Mackay shook his head.

Casey got to her feet. "Thank you, Mrs Tate, for being patient with us at this difficult time for you. And you have our sympathy."

Outside, in Mackay's vehicle, the lieutenant said, "As I'm sure you've already surmised, the phone call last night did come from Sedona."

"And?"

Mackay shrugged. "And it was made from a pay phone."

Casey's shoulders sagged. "Why did I expect anything else? But at least we found out something that helps tie it together." She told him what Mrs Tate said about the voice on the phone. "And that's exactly how the Master sounds in person. He uses some gadget to distort, disguise his voice."

"I made another call in there. I called Tate's bank; I just caught the manager before he left for the day. It took a little persuasion, but he finally checked and learned that Tate bought no certified cheque, nothing on paper."

Casey said slowly, "Then I suppose Tate sent the money to Sedona in cash. He certainly didn't deliver it in person. The question is, how was it sent, and who to? Seems a little risky sending that much money by mail."

"I would think so. There's UP, Federal Express, even a courier service."

Casey felt a faint pulse of excitement. "Then we should be able to run that down."

"Probably, but want to bet it was sent to a fictitious name and address?"

"Or maybe, if we're lucky, to a second party, one of the cultists, to deliver to the Master." Then she shook her head in despair. "But if that's the way it was done, this second party would have delivered it to the Master *as* the Master in full regalia, which means shit as far as identification goes."

"I think you have it figured out pretty good, Casey." He risked a quick glance at her. "You flying back to Arizona tonight?"

Casey shook her head. "No, I reserved a motel room. Flying back to Phoenix this late, I wouldn't be able to make a connection to Sedona."

"How about having dinner at my place? Sharon, my wife, never minds an unexpected guest for dinner."

"No, thanks, Lieutenant. I've had a long day. I'm going to make do with room service, then curl up with my bleak thoughts." She added bitterly, "You know what ticks me off? I came all the way over here, sure I'd find what I needed to break the case, but I'm no further along that I was!"

"That's police work for you. You take what you think is a step forward, only it turns out to be a step backward."

She gave him a quick smile. "You sound like a friend of mine in Phoenix."

"Another cop?"

"Of course. What else?"

Chapter Twenty-Three

Casey arrived back in Sedona shortly past noon the next day. She drove directly to Gabe's motel, hoping to catch him in; and found him swimming laps in the pool. She stood on the edge of the pool, waiting for him to reach her. He swam with powerful strokes, arms cutting the water easily.

He gripped the edge of the pool, pushed his hair out of his eyes, and then glanced up and saw her. "Casey! Hi."

"Hi, yourself. Some people have it pretty easy."

He grinned. "It's Saturday, after all. Aren't I entitled to a day off?"

He braced on his hands on the edge, and climbed out to stand beside her. He shook himself, and droplets of water splattered her. "Sorry about that," he said with a laugh. He strode to a nearby deck chair where he sat down and picked up a large towel and began drying himself. She drew up another deck chair next to his. "Coke? Something?"

"Not right now, thanks."

"What did you find out in California?"

She told him what she had learned.

He said thoughtfully, "So you've pretty well proved out your theory that this Tate paid someone here to kill Barbara Stratton."

"But I didn't get very far finding out who the actual killer is."

Gabe squinted at her. "And you're thinking that the first two murders were paid killings also? That some executive thought that eliminating a fellow executive would result in promotion?" He grinned faintly. "Sort of die, you sucker, get out of my way?"

"I'd bet on it," she said vehemently. "Except for Thornesburg. He was killed, I'm sure, because he somehow learned the real story behind Stratton's death and came here to nose around."

"How about the companies where the other two executives worked?"

"I may have to visit them." She sighed. "But I was hoping to avoid that; it would mean a lot of travelling and might be a waste of time. It's the weekend. If nothing turns up by Monday, I may have to take that route. I don't suppose you found out anything more about our suspects here since we talked last?"

"I told you that I learned that Vickie Steele isn't doing all that well with her beauty salon. She's hanging on by her fingernails. Probably spending too much time with this cult business, instead of her own business. And Alex Haydon was in some financial difficulty a year or so back, but he pulled out of it okay. Originally he had a working ranch, horses, some cattle. Then he turned it into a half-assed dude ranch, and he was soon out of the red. And Cabot seems to be doing okay. Russell Turner is the only one really in big trouble financially, and it looks like he got a money transfusion recently."

"Oh, I forgot to tell you. Lieutenant Martin and I learned that Turner is a member of the Council. But he's disappeared, at least temporarily. The lieutenant is looking for him."

Gabe sat up, his eyes flaring. "Then maybe he's our guy!"

"I'd like to think so, but I've got a feeling that would be too easy. The Master, whoever he is, is too devious to be so obvious."

"But it could be," Gabe said stubbornly. "He's a Council

member, he just came into a large sum of money, and he's disappeared!"

Casey shook her head. "Well, we can hope, but I still don't think so."

Gabe drained the Coke. "So then, what's next on the agenda?"

"I'm going to drop in on Lieutenant Martin, see what, if anything, has developed with him. If he's in the office today."

"Oh, I'm sure he's in. He's been working long hours, seven days a week, trying to break this case."

"I need him to go with me to check out all the delivery services, see if we can learn which one delivered Paul Tate's fifty thousand dollars."

"Why can't we do that together?"

"No, Gabe. Some of them may not want to cooperate without a court order. Martin, being the local law, will have more clout. Besides, I wouldn't want to disturb your leisurely Saturday," she said with a laugh, getting to her feet. "You going to be around the motel all day?"

"Plan to."

"Then I may drop back later, if I've learned anything."

Lieutenant Martin was in his office. He jumped up when she came in. "Casey! I've called you several times and left messages."

"I've been in California, you knew that."

He nodded. "Yeah, I knew that, but I . . . Never mind." He waved a hand. "Russell Turner showed up yesterday, on his own. When he heard I wanted to talk to him, he came in voluntarily. He claimed he was up in Flag on business, had just neglected to tell his office people."

"What did he have to say for himself?"

"We questioned him extensively, both the sheriff's people and myself. He finally broke down and admitted that, as a member of the Council, he was present when all the homicides were committed. He said they were all done as cult sacrifices to Satan in supplication and repayment for past favours granted and future favours to come."

Casey grimaced. "You think he really believes that, Lieutenant?"

"After wearing myself out talking to him, I do, yes. Weird as it may sound, Turner truly believes. He claims that he would be bankrupt, maybe in jail or begging in the streets, if not for the intercession of Satan into his business affairs." Martin grinned faintly. "Of course, he's in jail now, for accessory to murder."

Casey leaned forward. "Did he tell you who the Master is?"

The lieutenant shook his head. "I'm afraid not. Swears he doesn't know, has never seen the Master without his robe and mask. Furthermore, he said he wouldn't tell us even if he did know."

"How about the other members of the Council, does he know the identity of any of them?"

"Either doesn't know, or wouldn't say."

"Damnit!" Casey pounded her knee with her fist. "Another dead end! Even if you have Turner nailed, even if we get all the Council members, we have nothing without the Master. And who's to say Turner is telling the truth! He could be the Master, himself. After all, one person in a cape, hood and mask looks just like another!"

"I know, Casey; I thought of that too. Well, what did you find out in California?"

Again, Casey outlined what had happened in Beverly Hills. In conclusion she said, "The call Tate received at three in the morning from Sedona had to be from the Master, telling him about me. So when I showed up at Tate's office with a Beverly Hills officer, he must have assumed we were there to arrest him."

"So our only hope is to trace the money, find out to whom it was sent."

She nodded. "Although I'm sure it wasn't sent directly to our guy. He's too smart for that."

"Well, we'll give it a shot. Give me Tate's address, both home and business. Federal Express offices are located in Flag. It's too late today to check with the post office here, but I doubt he would have sent fifty thousand via US mail."

Casey gave him the information, and sat back, waiting while he called Federal Express in Flagstaff. After talking for several minutes he hung up with a shake of his head. "Nothing. But I'll call UPS."

After spending another few minutes on the phone, he slammed down the receiver. "Nothing there, either. But I think our best chance is a courier service that serves Sedona, called Fast Delivery. They'll be open, they offer seven-day service."

Fast Delivery was located in a mini-mall on Highway 89. Most of the premises was taken up with a loading dock and a sorting room; there was a small reception room with a counter, manned by one guy. Martin leaned on the counter, with Casey flanking him.

The lieutenant said, "I'm Lieutenant Martin, Sedona police. We have a problem I hope you can help me with."

The attendant was young, not much beyond twenty, with a face still marred by pimples. His watery blue eyes peered at the lieutenant warily. "Glad to help if I can."

"I need to know if you people delivered a package to someone in town." Martin gave Tate's name, both home and business address, and the date the package would have been delivered.

The attendant backed up a step. "I can't give out that information, the boss told me to never do that. The law protects us on that. Many people don't want it known when we deliver to them."

"Then I'll have a word with your boss."

"He ain't here. It's Saturday, he took the day off. Never comes in less it's an emergency."

Martin slapped a hand on the counter. "This is an emergency. This is a homicide investigation. I suggest you get him on the horn. Like right now!"

The young man picked up a phone from under the counter and punched out a number, half-turned away while he talked. After a moment he turned back. "The boss, Mr Baker, says no way."

"Let me talk to him." Martin practically tore the phone away from the youth, and snapped into the phone, "Mr Baker? This is Lieutenant Martin. I'm investigating a homicide here, and if a certain package was delivered by your company, it's vital information . . . No, I don't have a warrant or a court order . . . Yeah, Mr Baker, I know you provide confidentiality for your clients, and that's commendable, but this is a homicide investigation . . . This is Saturday, I doubt I could find an available judge to issue a court order. I might have to wait until Monday, and that would unduly delay our investigation. If I have to wait, you're going to be in deep shit with the local police. Now, I suggest you cooperate . . . Yes, he's right here." The lieutenant held the receiver out to the attendant. "He wants to talk to you."

As the attendant talked into the mouthpiece, Martin winked broadly at Casey.

The attendant hung up. "Mr Baker said to give you the information you want. If you'll just wait, it'll take me a few minutes to track it down."

The attendant went through a door in the back. As they waited, Casey paced nervously.

The young man was back in less than fifteen minutes. "Here it is." He held out a slip of paper.

Martin took it and read it quickly. "It was delivered to Vickie Steele, Casey, at the Steele Magnolia. Let's catch her before she closes the salon for the day."

* * *

When Casey and the lieutenant entered the Steele Magnolia, Vickie was busy with a customer. She glanced up and saw them. Even the length of the shop Casey could see Vickie go pale. She motioned for them to stay where they were. In a couple of minutes she hurried up to them.

She was quite agitated. In a low, furious voice she said, "I can't have cops coming into my shop like this! It'll drive all my customers away!"

Lieutenant Martin said, "You should have thought of that, Miss Steele, before you hooked up with that cult."

"We *do* have a murder investigation to conduct, Vickie," Casey interjected.

Vickie glared at her. "You're a sneak, do you know that? You made out to be Rena Rainier, scouting locations for a movie, and all the time you were a cop. You should be ashamed of yourself, going around fooling people like that!"

Casey said composedly, "Perhaps. But I don't go around murdering people, either."

"Neither do I. I know nothing about any murders."

"I think you do, Vickie. At least I think you suspected what was going on, afraid to speak out."

"What do you want with me? You've already questioned me."

"Something has come up. The day before Barbara Stratton was murdered, a package was delivered by courier here in your shop." Casey held up a hand. "Now don't bother to deny it, Vickie. You signed for it. We've seen the slip."

"Well, yes . . ." Vickie faltered, her glance sliding away. "I do remember receiving a package that day."

"What was in it?"

Vickie kept her gaze averted. "Just some . . . stuff for the salon."

Casey said, "Stuff for the shop? By *courier*?"

Martin said harshly, "You're lying to us, Miss Steele. That

package was sent by one Paul Tate, from Beverly Hills. He had nothing to do with beauty shop supplies."

"You're only making things worse for yourself by lying to us, Vickie," Casey said gently.

Vickie looked around finally, her eyes wild. "All right, all right! I don't know what was in the package, okay?"

"You delivered it to the Master, didn't you?"

"Yes," Vickie said in a dead voice.

"How was the delivery made?" the lieutenant asked.

"He had called me, the day before, told me to expect the package. I was to deliver it to him at the foot of the trail leading up to the mesa that evening at ten o'clock."

"The mesa where you took me that night for the cult meeting?" Casey asked.

"No. The . . ." Vickie's voice dropped to a whisper. "The mesa where that woman, Barbara Stratton, was killed."

"How did he come? On foot?"

"No, on horseback. He rode up after I'd been waiting about ten minutes." All resistance had drained out of Vickie now.

"Was he wearing the robe and mask?"

"Yes."

Lieutenant Martin said, "Did he say anything to you?"

Vickie shook her head. "Not a word. He didn't even get off his horse, just took it and rode off."

"And all these times you've been around him, you have no idea who he might be?"

"No! How many times do I have to tell you? Do you think I'd lie to you, after all I've learned?"

"You tell me, Miss Steele," Martin said dryly. "But I'm warning you again. If I find out you've been lying to us, I'm going to make it hard for you." He turned about. "Casey?"

She sighed heavily. "I don't have any more questions, Lieutenant."

Outside the shop, she said drearily, "It went down about

as I figured it would. We know no more than we did before."

"At least we have confirmation that this cult leader was paid fifty grand."

"Yes, but who the hell is he? It's beginning to look as if we may never find out."

"We'll find out," he said grimly. "We're closing in on him."

"I'm glad you think so. Well . . ." She ran her fingers through her hair. "It's been a long day for me. I'm heading to the hotel, see if I can forget this case over a drink and a good dinner. Not that I'm likely to. See you in the morning, Lieutenant."

"That sounds like a plan, Casey. Wish I could do the same, but I have a couple of hours of paperwork to do."

There were still a couple of hours of daylight left when Casey entered her room at the Enchantment. The first thing she did was to put in a call to Josh in Phoenix. She hadn't called him in two days, and she had stirrings of guilt about that.

There was no answer at his house, and when she called the station he worked out of, she was told that he had the weekend off.

Strange, he hadn't mentioned that to her the last time they had talked. Usually, when he had the weekend off, he worked around his house, or went to a ball game. Basketball season was over and football season had yet to start. Josh wasn't much for camping or fishing. She recalled once that he had taken her and Donnie camping for a weekend, and had grumbled all the time about how he hated roughing it.

With a shrug she dismissed it. She'd call him later in the evening. She discarded the clothes she'd been wearing and got into her running clothes. Maybe a good run would clear her head; it often did clarify her thinking. The threat the Master had made a couple of nights ago entered the mind. But it was still daylight, and she intended to run only in the hotel grounds. If she wasn't safe here, she wouldn't be safe anywhere.

Nonetheless, she was reassured as she ran the road by the golf course and saw the course still teeming with golfers. And the tennis courts on her left also resounded with the plonk of balls and the shuffle of feet.

As she gradually increased her pace, her muscles loosened, the kinks leaving her. Sweat sheathed her body, and she began to feel good. For the first mile or so, she tried to keep her mind free of the maddening case. But inevitably, thoughts intruded, and she gnawed at the puzzling aspects of it again. Who *was* the man all the cult members called the Master?

But it was on the last leg of her run, on her way back to the room, that something Gabe Stinton had told her, and something Vickie had said, clicked into place. And what Vickie had said looped back to the night on the mesa when she, Casey, had almost lost her life.

Was she correct in her thinking? Did she finally know the identity of the Master?

There was only one way to find out.

She ran all out and arrived back at her room out of breath. Inside, she stripped off the running clothes, took a quick shower, and got dressed again. She strapped on the ankle pistol that had saved her life the other night, hoping she wouldn't have to use it again.

Before she left the room, she made a fast telephone call.

Chapter Twenty-Four

The sun had gone down by the time Casey drove out of the hotel grounds, but it was still quite light. Before she got to Highway 89A she turned off on the road leading to the Haydon Ranch.

She saw no sign of activity, as she drew up and parked before the house. A lean woman with a faded beauty answered the doorbell; Casey had never met Alex Haydon's wife but she assumed this was her.

She said, "I'm Casey Farrel. I'd like to see Mr Haydon, please."

"Oh, Alex is out at the stable, grooming some of the horses. We're short of help this week." She pointed. "It's out back."

"Thank you."

Casey went around the house. The stable was a long, low building about fifty yards behind the main house. The wide, double doors were open. She took a deep breath and went in. It was dim inside, and she stopped for a few moments for her eyesight to adjust. Then she heard sounds toward the back, and she walked in that direction.

One of the stable doors stood open, and Alex Haydon, his back to her, was washing down a huge bay horse, using a large bucket of water at his feet. He was wearing a yellow rain slicker. Apparently he wasn't yet aware of her presence. The horse rolled its eyes and tossed its head at the sight of Casey, but gave no other indication of alarm.

Casey watched for a moment or two in silence as Haydon

splashed water liberally on the back of the horse. Then she said quietly, "Is that the horse you used to get to the mesa the other night, Mr Haydon? When you tried to kill me?"

Haydon went perfectly still for a few moments, hand holding the dripping sponge in midair. Then he dropped it with a splash into the bucket.

Without turning he said, "Casey Farrel, I gather?"

"Correct, Mr Haydon. How did you know my name?"

Haydon laughed harshly. "Why, it's common knowledge in Sedona now that Rena Rainier is really Casey Farrel, cop." He turned then, slowly, a slight smile on his weathered face. "I had a feeling that you'd be coming around soon."

He seemed to be completely unbothered by her presence. Casey frowned. "You don't seem very upset by the fact that I'm here."

"Why should I be?" he said calmly. "I have nothing to be afraid of."

"I should think that a man who has killed four people, that we know of, has a great deal to be afraid of."

"I suppose you have a tape recorder in that purse you're toting? But then it doesn't really matter."

Casey went tense at the chilling threat in his voice. She thought of the ankle gun, but before she could act on the thought, Haydon pushed back the slicker on his right side, and whipped out a gun. A huge .45, worn in a holster belted around his waist, old West style.

"Like I said, I've been expecting you, Ms Farrel." He motioned with the .45. "And don't even think of reaching down for that ankle piece you wore the other night. I made a mistake that night, in not searching you myself. And I promise you I don't make many mistakes."

The calmness with which he was taking her accusation, even openly admitting his guilt, was unnerving. Why was he so confident?

"You know why I'm not worried about your tape recorder?"

"I gather you intend to kill me," she said in as steady a voice as she could muster.

"Right! Give the lady a silver dollar."

"That cannon pointed at me can be heard a long way."

"Not to worry. Nobody around but my wife, and Betty does just what I say."

"I called the Sedona police before coming here, told them where I was going."

"Come on, Casey, give me credit! You've been seeing too many TV mysteries. The lady detective confronting a killer always says that. A cliché. Never turns out to be true." His smile was arrogant. "Now I suppose we're going through the obligatory questions and answers before I kill you. Okay, I'll oblige. I'm curious myself. How did you get onto me?"

"A couple of small things, but when they all came together, it made the picture whole. First, I recalled hearing a horse galloping away after I got down off the mesa the other night. Then Vickie Steele told me that she delivered the money from Paul Tate to a robed and masked figure on horseback. True, other people involved probably have horses, but you're in the business of horses."

Haydon grunted. "So the Steele woman talked, did she? Can't trust anybody these days."

"But another thing really tied it all together. Up until these killings started you were barely hanging onto your ranch by your fingernails. Then, all at once, you were in the black. Of course, you told everybody it was because you turned a working ranch into a dude ranch. But that won't hold water."

Haydon was nodded. "I knew that was a weak spot. It always arouses a cop instinct when someone in bad financial shape is suddenly flush. But I had to save my ranch, so I had to use the money. I was intending to get out before things heated up, but the money was too tempting. That was my big mistake."

"I must say you thought up an original scheme, hiring out

to kill executives, so the executive who hired you could get a promotion."

"I think so." His smile held more than a hint of pride. "I called it 'eliminating the competition'."

"Wasn't it hard to get clients? You couldn't very well advertise."

"Didn't have to. Word of mouth. The first one more or less fell into my lap. After that it was easy. Always some ambitious VP out there who'll do anything to get ahead."

"And you dreamed up this whole charade, cult, masks and robes, to hide your real motive. If push came to shove, you could just slip away, and the homicides would be considered sacrifices to Satan."

"Right again, little lady."

"But Leo Thornesburg, you weren't hired to kill him, were you?"

"Nope, he was for free. Somehow he got suspicious. The only way I've been able to figure it, the Stratton woman must have phoned him, early the night we, uh, 'sacrificed' her and mentioned that she was attending our cult meeting. That was when I should have resigned as cult Master, called it quits. I guess you could say I was too greedy, wanting to do one more."

"Tell me, Mr Haydon, do you, did you ever, believe any of that stuff? The cult, the rites, the blessings of Satan? *Are* you a Satanist?"

"Of course not. Do you?" He laughed scornfully. "I don't believe in Satan, or God, or any of the above, or below. I believe only in myself. Whatever I accomplish, I accomplish without the aid of God *or* Satan."

"Do any of the Council members know who you are, or any of the cult members? And do you know the identities of the Council members?"

"Of course I know who they are. I selected them. And nobody knows who the Master is." He frowned darkly. "Until now."

"I suppose you realize that the members of the Council are equally guilty of murder, even though you wielded the knife?"

"I realize that, yes," he said with a careless shrug. "But then at the moment you're the only person who knows aside from me. And you're not going to tattle, are you, Casey?" His grin was mocking. He raised the .45, aligning it with her heart. "I think this has been going on long enough. I'm getting bored. Goodbye, Casey Farrel . . ."

A harsh voice behind Casey said, "Put the gun down, Haydon!"

Alex Haydon froze, his startled gaze going past Casey.

"Put the gun down. Now!"

Haydon's gaze drifted back to Casey, and she saw his finger begin to tighten on the trigger. He was going to shoot her! She tensed in preparation to throw her body to one side.

But a shot rang out before she could move.

She experienced a flash of amazement that she was unharmed. Then she saw the .45 fly from Haydon's hand, and he was staring in shock at his wrist which was oozing blood.

The bay, startled by the gunshot, reared, forequarters striking Haydon on the shoulders, knocking him down against the wall of the stall. Hoofs pawed the air. As they came down, they struck dangerously close to the cowering Haydon. The horse neighed piercingly, then bolted past Casey, who got out of the way just in time. The horse thundered up the lane between the stalls, and outside the stable.

Lieutenant Martin, holding his weapon in both hands, ranged alongside Casey, his gaze never leaving the man on the ground. Concern in his voice, he said, "You okay, Casey?"

"I'm okay, Lieutenant. A little shaken, is all." She laughed shakily. "Did you hear everything?"

"I heard enough, enough to know he's our perp."

Casey's glance went to Haydon, who was staring up at them dazedly. She said, "You evidently should watch more TV, Mr Haydon. *Sometimes* the lady detective has sense enough to bring along backup when confronting a killer."

"Casey," Martin said, "why don't you go out to my unit and call for the medics? Haydon needs medical attention. We don't want him to die on us at this stage. I managed to get a warrant to search the house. We may not find very much, but maybe we can find something to help us identify the Council members. I called the sheriff's department on my way here. They should be arriving about now, as well as some of my own people."

A half-hour later Casey sat in her rented car, the driver's side door open, too emotionally drained and physically exhausted to summon up the energy to even start the car and drive away. The adrenaline high was gone, and as always after a difficult case had been successfully concluded, she felt at loose ends, difficult to decide what to do, where to go, next.

Her car was surrounded by police vehicles, both city and county, some with their coloured top lights still revolving, flashing bars of colour against the darkness that had finally fallen. A subdued Alex Haydon had been taken away in an ambulance, and Lieutenant Martin and other officers were engaged in a search of the Haydon house for whatever they could find. Mrs Haydon had accompanied her husband in the ambulance.

Approaching car lights flashed behind Casey's car. Disinterested, assuming it was another police vehicle, Casey didn't bother to look around.

Car doors slammed, running footsteps sounded, and a familiar, piping voice said, "Casey!"

With a start Casey looked around. Donnie stood by the

open car door, beaming at her. "Donnie! How on earth did you get here, kiddo?"

A deeper voice said, "I brought him, babe."

Casey slid out of car the car, sweeping Donnie into her arms. She looked over his head at Josh Whitney. "What're you doing here, Detective?"

The big man smiled at her amiably. "I took the weekend off and drove up to Prescott to have a visit with the kid. He wanted to drive up here to see his mom. So, here we are."

Casey stood, and Donnie stepped back, looking eagerly up into her face. "Did you nail the bad guy, Casey?"

She smiled down affectionately, scrubbing a hand through his hair. "Yeah, kiddo. I nailed him. Finally. I thought it was never going to happen."

Josh said, "Congratulations, babe, for another down."

"How did you know where I was?"

"I drove to your hotel. You weren't there, and no one knew where you were. So I played a hunch and called the local cop shop, asking for Rena Rainier. They said she no longer existed. How did that happen?"

"My cover was blown. Long story. I'll tell you about it."

Josh nodded. "Anyway, I was told that one Casey Farrel was out here. So here we are."

He spread his arms wide, and she stepped into them, snuggling close as he embraced her, relishing the warmth and patient strength of this man. She turned her face up and he kissed her lightly.

A cough sounded behind her. "Casey?"

She broke free of Josh's arms, and faced around. "Oh . . . Lieutenant. Finished?" At his nod she said, "Josh, I want you to meet Lieutenant Martin, Sedona police. Lieutenant, this is a friend of mine, Josh Whitney, of Phoenix Homicide."

As the two men exchanged wary greetings and shook hands, Martin said, "Not up here on business, I hope? We've had enough of homicide to do us for a while."

Josh laughed. "Nope, that's Casey's bailiwick. I have enough on my plate in Phoenix."

"Lieutenant," Casey said, "what did your people find in there?"

"A few things of interest. A robe and mask, and a knife that would *seem* to fit the murder weapon. It was pretty well hidden, but we found it. It's clean, but the lab may be able to find traces of blood from one or more of the victims. It's damned near impossible to remove all traces of blood from a weapon like that."

"But with both of us overhearing Haydon confess, plus the mask, robe, and knife, I'd say we have a strong case here."

"I also found something in his desk, a list of twelve names, addresses and phone numbers, all men. There's nothing that identifies them as the Council members, but Turner's name is on the list, so that points it in the right direction. I'm fairly confident that a couple of them will crack under stiff interrogation and identify the the others."

"Are you going to prosecute all twelve?"

"That'll be up to the prosecutor's office," Martin said with a shrug. "I know one thing. The threat of prosecution, or even just exposure, will effectively destroy the Children of the Enlightenment . . ." He broke off as a voice hailed him from the house. He flipped a hand to say he was coming. "I'm being paged, Casey. Nice to meet you, Detective Whitney. You going back to Phoenix now, Casey?"

"Yes, but don't hesitate to call me, Lieutenant, if you need me for anything, and of course I'll testify as to what Haydon said in the stable when the trial happens."

With a nod Lieutenant Martin turned away and strode briskly back toward the house. Casey said absently, "Nice man, the Lieutenant."

"Not *too* nice, I hope," Josh growled.

Casey grinned at him. "You're going to have to get over that, Detective."

"Get over what?"

"Being jealous of every cop I team up with."

"I don't do that!"

"Oh, yes, you do." Her hand crept into his. "But on the other hand, keep at it. I sorta like it."

"Hey, Casey!"

She looked down at Donnie's upturned face. "Yes, kiddo?"

"You didn't introduce *me* to that detective!" He got a wounded look. "Just because you think I'm a little kid."

"I'm sorry, kiddo. I didn't, did I? That was remiss of me." She leaned down to kiss his cheek. "It won't happen again, I promise."

Josh placed a hand on the boy's head. "We're going to have to watch that, forgetting that you're grown up. Almost." He looked at Casey. "What's on the agenda, babe?"

"Like I told the lieutenant, I'm getting out of here. Maybe we can all spend a few more days at Uncle Dan's ranch. Donnie?"

Donnie clapped his hands. "That would be neat!"

"Can you get a few more days off, Josh?"

"Probably. I have some time coming, and there's no pressing cases at the moment. Yeah, I can manage a week."

"That's what we'll do then. You guys come back to the Enchantment with me to pack. Maybe we can have dinner there.

"They have great food. Then you can drive with me to the airport, I'll return the rental, and then we're off."

Josh nodded. "Sounds like a plan to me."

Outside her room at the Enchantment, Casey opened the door, then glanced at Donnie. "Why don't you wander around and explore, Donnie? But don't stray too far. I'll give you a holler when I'm ready."

Donnie nodded and wandered away down the paved path.

Inside, Casey sighed faintly. "Good to have this one wrapped up. You know, I was thinking. I could write a movie script. While I was Rena Rainier I was constantly having to make up movie scenes, imaginary characters, and plot. Which means I became an accomplished liar, Josh."

Josh shrugged. "All a part of working undercover, babe."

"Well, undercover ain't all it's cracked up to be . . ."

She broke off as she saw that intense look on his face. She well knew what that look meant, and as he reached for her, she thought of resisting, but instead she flowed into his embrace, welcoming his arms around her. His lips were hot and seeking, and as his knowing hands roamed over his body, she felt a heated arousal. She relished the languor stealing over her.

She broke away, and said breathlessly, "No, this isn't the time, Josh, much as I want to. Donnie's just outside. He might come knocking on the door any minute."

Disappointment flooded his face.

She reached to trail her fingers gently across his mouth. "I'm truly sorry, Josh, but I wouldn't feel comfortable."

As she turned away toward the chest of drawers, he said in a grumbling voice, "If you'd marry me, like I've been asking and asking, and both of you come to live with me, we wouldn't have to worry about the boy. Depend on it."

The decision that Casey had been mulling over for so long suddenly became firm in her mind. In an off-hand manner, a throw-away line, she said, "All right."

There was a few moments of stunned silence. "What? What did you say?"

"Your hearing gone bad, Detective? I said, all right, I'll marry you." She faced him.

His face lit up, and he took two swift steps toward her. She held up her hands, palms out. "Not now, Josh."

He skidded to a stop. "When? When do we do it?"

"Soon."

"How about this coming week, in Prescott?"

"Don't rush it, Detective." She laughed. "But I'll give it some thought."

"Hot damn, I don't believe this! I'd about given up."

"What is it you've always told me about a hard case to crack? Never give up. You should heed your own advice."

"I've got to tell the kid about this," Josh said jubilantly. He whirled away, jerked open the door, and bellowed, "Donnie! Get in here! We have some good news for you."

Loud enough to rouse the dead, she thought fondly; the people in the adjoining room would probably think a madman was among them.

Smiling softly to herself, she turned and started packing.